STONE COLD

STONE COLD

By Valerie Davisson

Published by Vaughn House Publishing, Depoe Bay, OR
First Edition
Print ISBN - 979-8-9864774-8-0
Ebook ISBN - 979-8-9864774-7-3
Cover and Interior Design by Kimberly Peticolas, www.kimpeticolas.com
Library of Congress Control Number: 2025913523

10   9   8   7   6   5   4   3   2   1

STONE COLD

A LOGAN MCKENNA NOVEL

VALERIE DAVISSON

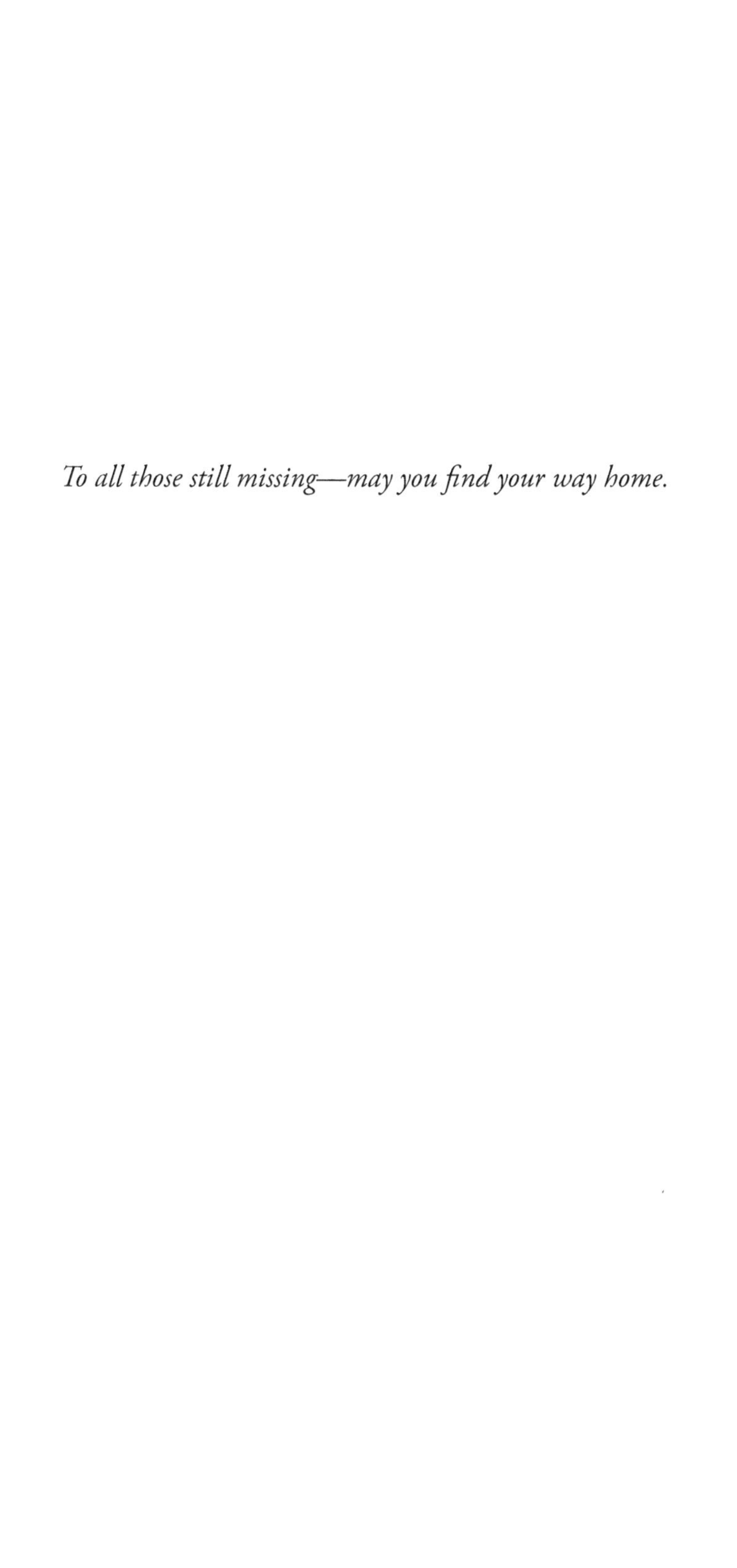

To all those still missing—may you find your way home.

PROLOGUE

Parking his truck and trailer around back, Jim Bremmer crunched his way across the gravel parking area and pulled open the front door of the busy cafe. Warm air infused with the comforting aromas of bacon, cinnamon, and fried everything made him glad he'd made time for breakfast. Nodding to people he knew, he slid into his favorite booth by the window and ordered his usual. Chicken fried steak, sausage gravy, hash browns—cremated—black coffee, eggs sunny-side up but whites fully cooked, Tabasco sauce—green—and keep the coffee coming.

His server, Tina, pushing seventy and not more than a hundred pounds soaking wet, scribbled his order quickly on her pad before moving on to the next customer. Tina was new, but to her credit, a few minutes later she slid a large, steaming platter of hot food in front of him. The eggs looked good, the hash browns were charcoal, and she got the right color Tabasco sauce. Mentally, he upped her tip.

By 7:15 a.m. he was on the road, both he and his truck fully fueled. His plan was to be at the job site and unloaded by eight. The lot was already cleared, but digging the foundation would take most of the day. With another job lined up for tomorrow, Jim wanted to wrap this one up before dark.

A few minutes later, skillfully merging onto Highway 229, Jim slowed his pace. The Siletz Highway was well maintained but had its share of tight turns after Kernville and there was reduced visibility in some places due to overhanging branches. And then there were the deer. October was mating season. You never knew when one of the excitable animals would dash across the road. No sense winding up in a ditch before he even got to the site.

But Jim was an experienced operator. He'd worked for several other excavation companies out of high school before opening his own small business eleven years ago. He knew the ins and outs of almost every road and highway in Lincoln County. That's why his Yelp reviews were as good as Otis Café's. Well, the Café had almost a thousand reviews, while his business only had thirty-two, but still, they both averaged above 4.5 stars.

He turned on the radio, but all he could get out here was a country station, NPR, and a talk radio guy who was outraged about something. Finally, he switched it off and cracked a window. Listening to the wind was better than that.

Before he tried again, he saw the entrance to Riverview Luxury Homes. The signage was large and new, with looping, gold script and an artist's vision of what the development would look like once the houses were built. He had to admit it was an attractive area. Conveniently located between Lincoln City to the north and Newport to the south. Right by the Siletz River. Quiet. Lots of trees—although most of those would be cut down.

STONE COLD

He followed the newly surfaced streets to lot 72. When he arrived, he saw that the owner, a rich Portland guy he had only met once, had the lot cleared and the foundation area blocked out with stakes and string, so it was ready to go.

Rolling slowly from the street onto the dirt, Jim pulled his trailer to the right of the delineated area and parked. Leaving his coffee inside the truck for now, he walked to the back of the trailer to unload Minnie, his mini-excavator. He'd gambled on buying the best he could afford when he opened his own shop, and Minnie had never let him down.

Removing and storing the chains that secured the machine en route, he lowered the ramps and walked around the trailer, giving everything a once-over. Making sure the wheels were aligned, he climbed in, started her up, rotated the arm one-eighty so it now led the way, and rolled it off the trailer onto the dirt, keeping the bucket partially extended, just skimming the ground. Being a solo operator he'd learned to not take any shortcuts. There was no one to rescue him if he tipped over.

Retrieving his coffee from his truck, Jim hoisted himself into the operator's seat, placing his insulated mug into the cup holder and checked his controls. When he was satisfied everything was good to go, he let off the safety lever and got to work.

Building codes required anything near the river to go with an elevated foundation, keeping the house above ground moisture and mitigating flood risk, so today he would be trenching for concrete footings, which would later hold everything up. This consisted of digging a narrow trench about three-feet deep, just inside the string-marked perimeter. Lowering the boom arm, lining up the scoop just inside the string, he let Minnie take her first bite.

Even though he'd been doing this for many years, Jim still enjoyed the rumbling of the engine and the soothing rhythm of the work. On mornings like this, time fell away, the levers and pedals becoming mere extensions of his body, the boom and bucket gracefully and efficiently slicing into the soil, lifting, swinging, dumping, then going back for more.

At the end of each day, he could see what he had accomplished for himself. Straight lines, crisp corners, clean edges, and everything level. That's how he measured success.

Grabbing a granola bar he had in his truck, Jim washed it down with the last of his coffee and worked through lunch. The trench now reached more than three-quarters of the way around the foundation footprint. With any luck, he'd be out of here before dark.

Swinging himself back up into his seat, he fired Minnie up and lowered the arm to take the next scoop. He was only halfway in when the bucket stalled. Must have hit something, but this wasn't a rocky area. He tried again, repositioning the bucket to take another bite. It didn't stall this time, but something definitely didn't feel right. Tree root, maybe.

Irritated at the potential delay, he climbed down and peered into the pit to see what he'd hit and if he could pull it out by hand.

"What the hell . . ."

Next to the metal teeth that had unearthed it lay a thick, long bone with a distinctive knobby end. A flatter bone stuck halfway out of the side of the trench nearby. Both were stained various shades of dark brown.

Realizing what he was probably looking at, Jim scrabbled back from the edge of the trench to the safety of his machine. With shaky hands, he reached up and powered off the excavator, then pulled out his phone and dialed 911.

He would not be going home early today.

Chapter One

Logan loaded the last of her and Ben's laundry from their trip into the washer, added soap, made sure the setting was on cold, and hit start. One load would do. Next, she rolled her bag out to the garage and tucked it next to Ben's on one of the open shelves of the metal storage racks he had installed along one wall.

She smiled. Someday they would probably be schlepping CPAP machines, shoeboxes full of medicines, and orthopedic shoes for these trips, but for now they could still get away with one carry-on bag each.

Besides, all they needed in Jasper, California, Logan and Ben's hometown, were bathing suits, shorts, t-shirts, and flip-flops. Logan wore little to no makeup, so besides a toothbrush and a scrunchie to keep her hair out of her face, she was ready to hit the road with just a few minutes' notice. Having endured a very high-maintenance fiancée at one time, Ben was grateful.

Coming back into the house, Logan shut the door to the mud room behind her so she didn't have to listen to the washing machine and walked into the sunny kitchen where Ben was making sourdough bread. Lifting one corner of the damp towel that covered the glass bowl on the counter, he poked at the ball of dough inside with one finger and watched the indentation it made. Logan had no idea what this action was supposed to accomplish.

"Needs a little more time." he said, replacing the towel over the bowl and scooting it closer to the warm stove. He started rummaging through the fridge.

"Any requests?" he asked. "The bread won't be ready until later, but we've got eggs, bacon . . . some bell peppers . . . onions. Or I can make oatmeal. What are you in the mood for?"

Since she couldn't remember ever being in the mood for oatmeal, Logan opted for the omelet.

"With cheese, please," she added, giving Ben a peck on the cheek. "And thank you!"

As Ben pulled out a carton of eggs, both dogs came racing into the house from the back deck, neatly bypassing the new doggie door Ben had installed. Other than both canines refusing to use it, Ben's latest labor of love worked like a charm.

It joined the new doghouse Ben had built out back that neither dog had ever used either. True Northwesty dogs to their core, both preferred laying outside on the open deck, no matter the temperature.

Max, Ben's one-year-old English Cream Golden Retriever, was living up to his name. He was already seventy-seven pounds, and the vet said he'd be at least a hundred before he was done. Logan swore most of it was hair. Max's copious shedding clogged up the vacuum cleaner on a regular basis.

By comparison, Logan's three-year-old rescue dog, Dixon, was a lean, forty-five-pound labraheeler whose rough, short coat of gray, black, and white splotches barely shed at all.

Nose down, Max galloped into the kitchen, searching for any scraps of food he may have missed earlier. Food was Max's love language.

Dixon's was speed. He shot past the kitchen in a blur, coming to a screeching halt and a perfect sit at the front door, looking back at Logan eagerly, one ear pointed straight up, the tip of the other ear flopped over.

Logan laughed. "Trying to tell me something, Dix?" she said, leaning down to hook him up to his halter. He didn't really need a leash for their morning runs, as he never left her side, but that was the law and Logan obeyed the law . . . most of the time.

Promising Ben they'd be back by eight, she slipped on a lightweight jacket and laced up her running shoes, but didn't bother with gloves. Even a year ago, this morning's temp of forty-two degrees would have felt very cold to her Southern California self, but now it seemed downright balmy.

After a loose jog down their steep gravel drive, Logan looked back up at the house. 354 Baird had been a real fixer-upper when they bought it, but it had good bones and with the help of a local handyman and a lot of elbow grease, she and Ben had turned it into the warm, solid, family home it was always meant to be.

She loved that it was nestled against a mixed conifer forest in back and overlooked the Pacific in front. If you didn't count Highway 101, the five-block strip of tourist shops that constituted downtown Depoe Bay, they had oceanfront property.

Thinking of the fluffy cheese omelet and thick slabs of pepper bacon waiting for her at home, Logan made her and Dixon's morning run to Fogarty beach in record time. On the return trip, when they reached the sea wall in Depoe Bay, she took a minute to enjoy the breathtaking view, the rising sun warming her back. Pure white clouds stood out against an azure sky. Diagonal waves of various shades of blue and green rippled smoothly across the glossy surface of the ocean.

Logan ruffled Dixon's fur and proclaimed it "Absolutely spectacular!"

Dixon didn't comment, but she was sure he agreed.

People thought Oregon was always gray and overcast, but brilliant sunbreaks like these were the best-kept secret on the coast. Giving Dixon one last scratch behind the ears, Logan turned around and waited for a break in traffic, before sprinting across the highway to head up the hill.

Chapter Two

Spending Labor Day weekend with friends and family had been great, but it was good to be home. Over breakfast, which was worth every calorie, she and Ben got out their computers to coordinate calendars for the upcoming week. With the windfall from her music videos and Ben's investments, she and Ben were semi-retired but their schedules seemed to fill up quicker than ever.

"I've got Beachcrest this Saturday," Logan said, "that Celtic duo from Portland is coming down." In addition to writing and recording her own music, Logan performed at local venues several times a month. She specialized in instrumental Scottish laments but liked to mix up her musical genres with bluegrass, folk, and jazz. "This Thursday you've got your radio thing, right?" Logan said.

Their handyman and good friend, Clay Nilsen, had talked Ben into getting his radio technician's license as part of Ben's interest in emergency preparedness. Now that Ben had his entry-level license, he and Clay both volunteered with the Depoe Bay emergency communications team, which met the first Thursday of every month.

Logan still couldn't keep all the terminology straight. When the two men got to talking radios, Logan's eyes glazed over. GMRS this and TXP that. It's like they were both Navy SEALs speaking in code.

"Yep," Ben verified. "Thursday, seven-thirty, but don't forget he and Belinda are coming over tomorrow night for dinner."

"Got it," Logan entered it in her computer calendar. "I'll do a Freddies run. Make me a list."

They were halfway through the week when Ben's phone rang.

"Hey, Cal," he said, "what's up?"

Ben's nephew, Calvin, rarely called anymore since the landscape business he took over from Ben was running smoothly. They had just had a good visit with him, so Logan's curiosity was piqued.

Ben listened, then sat up straight and asked, "Are you okay?"

"What happened?" Logan asked.

Ben held up his hand in the universal wait signal and listened intently while Cal explained.

"Good, yes . . . I'm sure it could have been worse," Ben said, nodding his head in agreement even though Cal couldn't see him. "I'll head out Thursday, but I can come down earlier if you . . . Let me know if anything changes."

Ben put the phone down and shook his head.

"Idiot," he muttered.

Logan raised her eyebrows but waited for the whole story.

Yesterday, while helping a friend clean the gutters on his house, Cal had taken a shortcut to save time. Instead of moving the ladder over a few feet first to reach the far corner of the roof, he decided he could reach it from where he was. He couldn't. The ladder tipped, and Cal came down hard on his left leg. It wasn't broken, but his knee had swollen to twice its size.

Logan was relieved it wasn't more serious than that but still felt sorry for the kid. Cal had been so proud of how he had kept Ben's business going.

"Bart can finish up the last couple of small jobs this week," Ben said, "but Cal's going to need some help for a new job he just got. I'm going to have to go down there and see about hiring and possibly overseeing a crew until he's back on his feet."

"How bad is it? Does he need a knee replacement?" Logan asked. She knew those took weeks to months to heal.

"The doctor doesn't think so," Ben said, "but won't know until the swelling goes down and they can get a good x-ray. Not a quick fix, but hopefully not too bad. He has an appointment with his doctor on Friday. His wife is taking care of him now, but she has to be back at work Monday morning."

Ben sat down at the table across from Logan, keeping his phone in his hand.

"Hopefully, I won't have to be down there long, just long enough to help him hire a crew and get them started on that new job. I know some good guys. It will just depend on if they're free or not. I'll make some calls."

Logan offered to make plane reservations while he was doing that, but Ben said he planned on driving so he could take Max with him. His old dog, Purgatory, had been a permanent fixture on the passenger seat of his truck back in California. He'd taken Purgatory on every job. He saw no reason why Max shouldn't do the same. Besides, Max was still a handful, and Ben didn't want to burden Logan with walking and caring for both dogs while he was gone.

"Hopefully I'll only be a couple of weeks," Ben said, already scrolling through his contact list on his phone, "Will you be okay?"

Logan hoped he wouldn't be gone long, either, but wholeheartedly supported him helping his nephew out of a jam. It was what family did. She resisted the urge to roll her eyes and assured him she'd be fine. He always seemed to forget she had taken care of herself and Amy for many years before he came on the scene. But it was sweet that he cared.

With that crisis being dealt with, Logan went to switch the clothes in the washer to the dryer and returned to the kitchen.

Having left messages with some of his old crew members he thought might be available to help Cal, Ben was working on his shopping list for tomorrow's dinner.

Logan said she was okay if he wanted to cancel, but Ben said there was nothing more he could do until Thursday, anyway. Besides, Clay was bringing fresh Coho salmon to grill, and his wife was making one of her oversized, freshly baked blackberry pies. Corn on the cob, coleslaw, and Ben's sourdough bread would complete their late summer meal. Oh, and vanilla bean ice cream for the pie.

Logan wrote that item on her list . . . in capital letters.

Chapter Three

Wednesday was another glorious sunny day. After her morning run, Logan left Ben to his upcoming trip preparations, then drove the few blocks to Pirate Coffee to meet her two good friends, Sam and Jean, for breakfast.

On the ocean side of the highway, Pirate's was a local institution, laying claim to the best coffee on the coast and Logan couldn't disagree. The only seating inside or out was picnic tables, and they didn't offer a full menu, but their breakfast burritos and pastries were fresh, filling, and ferociously delicious, so they were always busy.

Normally Logan walked, but she needed her car to do her Freddies shopping in Newport, so took the Hyundai Tucson. She pulled into the gravel parking area, next to a light green Toyota truck. Sam was already there.

Sam, byline Samantha Badger, was a local reporter for the Lincoln County Leader. She and Logan had met several years ago after Logan was held hostage by a gambling addict indebted to the wrong people and had barely escaped with her life. In the process of Sam interviewing Logan for the story, they discovered they were both rabid Pink Martini and Allison Kraus fans and loved junk food. Sam was the one who introduced her to Jean

Pullman, Sam's sister-in-law, and the third member of their Wednesday breakfast club.

The inimitable Dr. Jean Pullman, a family doctor with a thriving practice in Lincoln City, just ten miles north of Depoe Bay, was also the part-time medical examiner for Lincoln County. Jean's culinary tastes ran more to pasture-raised chicken, fresh vegetables, and an occasional croissant with Earl Grey tea vs greasy cheeseburgers, so Logan and Sam never had to worry about her stealing any of their fries when they went to lunch together.

Dubbed the 'Cormorant Coffee Crew' by Sam's commercial fisherman husband, Tim—cormorants being lucky seabirds— the three friends met most Wednesday mornings when Jean drove through Depoe Bay on her way to her ME office in Newport.

Office was a generous description. Logan had seen it, and it was more like a walk-in closet. Lincoln County didn't even have a morgue. All suspicious deaths needing an autopsy were shipped to the ME in Portland, Cyndi Birdwell. Luckily, Cyndi was very competent, and she and Jean had a good working relationship. Cyndi often moved Jean's cases up to the front of the line without her having to ask.

Out of habit, Logan looked at the horizon before she went inside. The weather was still holding, but there was a squall blowing in. The brilliant sunbreak was about to be over.

Sam waved her over to a table near the windows—as if there was any way she'd miss her. Sam's sleek, black bob and rhine-stone-encrusted hot pink cat-eye glasses made her easy to spot. As usual, she had her phone faceup next to her and her laptop open, scanning several open websites. With newsprint in her veins, Sam was never disconnected from her technology.

Before Logan had a chance to sit down, Sam pointed to the pastry case. "They're almost out of cinnamon rolls, better get one quick."

STONE COLD

Logan did as she advised, ordering a bacon breakfast burrito—extra cheese—to go with it, and a sausage one for Ben to be made just before she left. Kathy, their favorite barista, knew the drill. Kathy would bring out the rest of Logan's order when it was ready.

"Jean coming?" Logan asked between bites.

"Maybe—she said she would try to stop by, but the commissioner called a rush meeting for later this morning," Sam said. "She is not a happy camper. Says he just calls meetings to talk about when to schedule more meetings."

Logan understood that. Bureaucracies weren't her thing either. Her short stint as a public schoolteacher taught her that she was much happier self-employed.

Next, they caught up on each other's lives. Sam's eighteen-month-old daughter, Miss Magnolia, was healthy and happy and getting into everything. Good thing Sam and Tim had a good daycare situation with a neighbor, a wonderful woman who had successfully raised four children of her own and was flexible enough to deal with Sam and Tim's erratic work schedules.

"How's Tim? What's he fishing for now?" Logan asked. Logan was slowly learning that there were certain seasons for certain fisheries. Crab fishing being the most lucrative, but also the most dangerous. That season didn't start until December.

"Rockfish is reliable, but he's also going out for tuna," Sam said. "He just texted me. They're bringing in a pretty good haul today. Good thing, baby needs new shoes!"

A noise made Logan look up. The squall that threatened had delivered on its promise. Wind-whipped branches of a lone pine were scraping against the window and solid sheets of silvery gray slid down the glass. She spotted Jean walking through the parking lot from her car. When she opened the door, a gust of cold wind blew her and some of the rain in with her, but Jean remained unscathed. Nonchalantly hanging her Burberry raincoat on a hook inside the door, she patted her French twist with the distinctive white skunk stripe, placed her order at the counter, and slid onto the picnic bench next to Logan. Slim black slacks, cashmere sweater. Today's flats were peacock blue.

Logan gave her an exasperated look.

"What?" Jean asked.

"Not a hair out of place and your shoes aren't even wet, Jean," Logan said. "How do you do that?"

Dismissing Logan's observation with a wave of her French-manicured nails, Jean regally accepted her pot of Earl Grey tea from Kathy.

"No meeting?" Sam asked.

"It's been rescheduled for this afternoon," Jean said, pouring her tea and adding a lemon slice.

As the morning sun broke out of the clouds and splashed bright yellow light across the picnic table, the three friends shared updates on their personal lives and gossip about people they knew in common.

By the time Kathy came over to hand Logan Ben's breakfast burrito, wrapped in two layers of foil to keep it piping hot until she got it home, they were pretty much up to date on each other's lives.

"Enjoy your day, ladies!" Kathy said as she hustled back to her place behind the counter to take the next customer's order.

After extracting a promise from Jean to fill her in if anything newsworthy was discussed in the commissioner's meeting and asking Logan to keep her posted about Ben's nephew's surgery, Sam got back to work. As a reporter, she was never off work.

Logan followed Jean out the door, Freddie's grocery list in hand.

Chapter Four

Ben and Max got on the road early Thursday morning, hoping to arrive in Jasper by Friday night. By himself Ben could make the trip in one day, napping at rest stops along the way, but he said there was no sense pushing it until he saw how well Max did on a long drive.

Max had behaved himself at the dog-friendly motel in Redding last night and loved riding shotgun in the truck as long as he could stick his nose out of the window and let his ears flap in the wind. When they got to Stockton, Ben pulled over for lunch and a stretch break.

Logan had no big news to report, so Ben said he'd call her tonight when he got to Cal's place. She made a silent note-to-self to keep her phone nearby and the volume up. She was infamous for putting her phone on silent while playing Bella, then forgetting to turn the ringer back on. She'd only seen Ben's call because the phone was face up on the table next to her laptop. She'd been working on a new composition when he called.

Placing Bella back in her case, Logan went into the kitchen. Might as well have some lunch herself. Ben left her several meals to microwave plus some leftover bacon, turkey lunchmeat, a few hard-boiled eggs, and a bowl of freshly cleaned and dried romaine lettuce. The man was a gem.

After throwing together a hefty chef salad, Logan smothered it in blue cheese dressing and chowed down. Dixon, sensing food in the vicinity, trotted in from outside and sat at her side, eyeing her bacon. The well-behaved dog didn't try to snatch food when she wasn't looking but wasn't above begging. He politely waited for her to toss some bacon his way, which she did.

After rinsing off her dishes, she stood in the middle of the kitchen with her hands on her hips and looked around. With Ben and Max gone, it was way too quiet in here.

Snatching her car keys off the counter, Logan grinned at her dog and headed for the front door.

"Hey Dix, wanna play?"

Dixon knew exactly what those words meant! He let out an excited bark and sprinted for the front door. Within minutes they were headed south to one of Dixon's favorite places, the dog park in Newport.

A block off the highway in a modest residential neighborhood, sixtieth street dog park was nothing fancy—just a large, scruffy, often muddy rectangle of grass enclosed by a chain link fence with a water bowl at the entrance and a couple of benches for pet parents scattered around. There was some grass, but not much. Not exactly a thing of beauty, unless you were a dog. And then, it was nirvana!

Logan and Ben tried to take the dogs here once a week. She loved seeing Dixon and Max run and play off leash with other dogs. Pure joy! Today there were about half a dozen dogs and their owners already there.

As she followed Dixon through the double-gated entrance, Logan recognized a few regulars. Vern, a very tall man with a bristly salt and pepper mustache leaned against the fence at the water station with his dog, Rocket, a mixed breed about Max's age, that looked like a small, black-and-tan German shepherd with a little beagle thrown in. She thought Vern was in law enforcement but wasn't sure exactly what he did.

Lois, a retired school administrator, was on the far side of the park, throwing a tennis ball for her two shelties, who never tired of the game. Over and over they streaked after the ball, bringing it back two seconds later, dropping it at her feet, and waiting expectantly. That woman was going to need shoulder surgery someday.

Once inside the gate, Dixon made a beeline for Lily, a cute, mostly white pit bull mix with a pink and black nose. Her owner, a young night nurse named Misty, waved in greeting. Logan waved back, then went over to fill Dixon's collapsible water bowl from the hose at the fence and said hi to Vern and Rocket. Several dogs followed in her wake. All the dogs knew Logan kept liver treats in her jacket pocket, so she was a very popular visitor.

Lily and Dixon started a playful game of chase, the two winding in and around the legs of one of the park benches someone had dragged out to the center of the park. Vern's dog, Rocket, soon joined the fun.

But Rocket and Dixon weren't Lily's only playmates. A very tall Great Pyrenees who had just come in the other gate seemingly objected to Rocket's attention to what he must have considered his girl, because before his owner could stop him, the huge dog lunged forward, yanking his leash out of her hands, and headed straight for Rocket, growling and snarling.

Chapter Five

Logan instantly sized up the situation. This was going to be bad. Before the monster could reach Rocket, who didn't see him coming, Logan grabbed the water hose hanging on the fence, turned it up full volume, and squirted the big dog in the face, sending him running back to his owner. Vern went to help the dog's owner who had fallen flat on her face. The elderly woman looked dazed and confused but managed to get the Pyrenees hooked back up to his leash. Shouting apologies back over her shoulder, she dragged the growling beast to her car and drove away.

Lois stomped over, pointing at the woman. "That dog should not be allowed in here! Thor's a menace and one of these days he's going to kill one of our dogs!"

"I agree! People shouldn't have dogs they can't control!" someone else chimed in.

Crisis averted, Logan returned the hose to the fence and sat down on the bench until her adrenaline stopped pumping. The dogs were already back to playing again as if nothing had happened. Vern checked on Rocket to be sure he was okay, then came back over to join her.

"He okay?" Logan asked.

"He's fine," Vern said, folding himself down onto the bench. "Rocket's not the brightest bulb in the box. I don't think he ever knew he was in danger."

Logan smiled. Rocket was a sweet dog.

"But thanks are in order, just the same," Vern said. "You've got good reflexes. Do you have some kind of EMT or law enforcement background?"

Logan laughed. "Not unless you count my violin as a lethal weapon," she said. "My brother's a K9 cop in California, but I do music."

They talked about their dogs for a while, Vern sprinkling in more questions about her background. She found herself telling him about Fractals, the math/music program she designed for kids, and they discovered they both knew Detective Monson in Newport and of course, Jean, in her role as medical examiner.

Vern, it turned out, was a retired homicide detective, currently in charge of investigating cold cases in Lincoln County. Like a lot of Oregonians, he and Logan were both from somewhere else. He, originally from Colorado, she from California. Both agreed they were lucky to have landed here and had no plans of ever leaving.

Eventually, Dixon and Rocket came running over to Logan for another treat and some water. Most of the other dogs were already gone, so Logan grabbed Dixon's leash and stood up to leave, too.

Vern did the same and they started walking the dogs to the exit gate.

Adjusting his ball cap, Vern hesitated for a minute and asked, "I don't know if you're interested, but we're short-handed in our cold case unit right now—my assistant up and quit on me—and I could use some help. Before you answer, it's nothing glamorous. Just scanning documents at first, that kind of thing. I can't pay you anything, it would be all volunteer."

Logan started to say something, but he asked her to hear him out.

"I know you have your music and all, but it would only be part-time, and we can work around your schedule. And I'd train you if you want. It's pretty interesting work. If you're up for it, we can get your clearance started. All you need is fingerprinting and a simple background check. You don't have any felonies in your closet, do you?"

He smiled and waited for her to answer.

"No, no felonies," Logan laughed. "But don't you have a lot of people wanting to get in on digging into cold cases? There are so many movies and TV shows about it now."

"Yes, there are," Vern said, "and that's exactly why I want to pick someone who isn't trying to worm their way in. I don't need any crime junkies mucking up the works."

Logan stopped at the gate and let her brain run through the offer quickly. She wasn't volunteering at the Raptor Center in Eugene anymore—they had plenty of volunteers from the college, so that freed up some time.

Before she could change her mind, she told Vern yes. Not wanting to come across like a crime junkie, herself, she kept her tone of voice casual, but inside, she was pretty excited. She'd watched some of those TV shows and was fascinated by all the technological advances being made that helped cold case units identify victims as well as bring their killers to justice. She was in!

They shook on it and Vern seemed relieved. He told her she could even come down later today if she didn't have anything else going on. She could get her fingerprints done and he'd get the background check started. He said if there were no snags, she would probably get clearance to start her training in a couple of weeks.

Cool! That worked for her. She waved goodbye and loaded Dixon into the car. She couldn't wait to share the news with Ben when he called later tonight. Ben was a bit overprotective and would probably not like the idea of her being anywhere near criminal activity, even very far removed. Given the number of times she'd landed herself in hot water by getting mixed up in homicide investigations, she had to admit he had good reason to object.

But it's not like she was going to be a real cop. She wouldn't be anywhere near active cases. Scanning cold cases in an office in the bowels of the police department? What could possibly be dangerous about that?

Chapter Six

WEDNESDAY, OCTOBER 2

After giving Dixon his breakfast, Logan hopped in the shower before heading over to Pirates to meet Sam and Jean. Ben had been gone less than a week. She sure missed his cooking.

That's not the only thing she missed . . .

Ben wasn't back yet because Cal's knee had required surgery, so his doctor wouldn't release him to return to work for two more weeks. And only to supervise, he wasn't to do any of the actual labor himself.

Luckily, Ben had been able to find a good two-man crew to help Cal fulfill his contract for the important landscaping job, but they couldn't start for another week, so Ben had been filling in in the meantime.

Other than needing an Epsom salt bath now and then to ease his aching, middle-aged muscles, Ben was enjoying the work. When she asked how Max was doing, he said other than wanting to join Ben digging in the dirt, he was learning to wait for him in the truck. Cal and his wife—like everyone else in

SoCal—had a goldendoodle, which adored Max. Of course, everybody, canine or human, loved Max.

Ben was accepting if not thrilled with Logan's news about volunteering with the cold case unit. Her background check came through and Vern said she could start that day. He'd said to give him a call when she got there so he could walk her in and get her started. She was going down right after meeting Sam and Jean for breakfast.

Leaving Dixon to his morning nap, Logan zipped up her hoodie, shut the front door behind her, and got into her car. Fall had officially arrived last week, but the Oregon weather gods hadn't gotten the message. Temps were in the sixties, which was practically shorts weather on the coast. Even so, Logan had learned to keep a jacket in the car just in case.

In a hurry to get to Pirates and not yet fully caffeinated, Logan almost backed into Clay's work truck, which was pulling in right behind her. Luckily, Clay was able to come up on her left, neatly avoiding the collision.

Logan rolled down her window and apologized profusely. Clay said not to worry. To keep Logan from apologizing again, he said he just stopped by to pick up his cooler. He'd left it the other night and was going out fishing again today if the weather held.

"Sure," Logan said. After getting his cooler for him out of the garage, she asked, "More salmon?"

"You can never have enough salmon," Clay said, hefting the cooler into the back of his truck. "Where are you off to today?"

Logan told him about the cold case volunteering, adding, "I'll only be scanning old files at first, but I'm hoping someday to be able to help out on real cases—even unsolved local homicides—Vern says he's working on one where they think a guy was killed and buried right here in someone's backyard just two years ago. He said there a ton of cases like that, where families never know what happened to their loved ones."

Clay froze for a second, then got into his truck, but not before Logan caught the hesitation and the glimpse of sadness that crossed her friend's face.

Before she could stop herself, Logan asked, "What?" She hoped she hadn't stepped in it and Clay didn't have a murdered relative she didn't know about.

Seeing her look of concern, Clay rolled down his window and said, "It's nothing, Logan. Just brought back some memories from a long time ago. Ancient history. While I was in Vietnam, my sister, Maggie, ran away from home. By the time I got back, she'd been gone over a year. We never heard from her again."

"Oh my god, Clay," Logan said. "That's terrible! Did your parents file a missing person's report?"

"I'm sure they did, but there wasn't much the police could do back then. That was '67, the 'Summer of Love,'" he added quotation marks in the air. "Maggie joined a river of young hippie girls heading for Haight-Ashbury in San Francisco."

"And you never heard anything more from the police?" Logan asked.

"No, Maggie was a headstrong girl. She wanted to go, and she did. Probably made a new life for herself in California. We hired a private investigator, but he didn't find anything. Said if anything bad had happened to her we would have heard. We were always close. I kept thinking I'd get a letter or a phone call from her eventually, but I never did."

Shrugging one shoulder, Clay closed that topic and said he'd better get going or he'd miss the boat.

Logan stepped back so he could get by, wished him good fishing, and got back in her car.

Clay was right, if his sister was injured or in a hospital or if she had died, someone would have notified the family. No news was good news, but still, Logan felt sorry for him. How awful to have your sister run away while you're off in a war zone unable to do anything about it, and when you come home, and she's gone, and you never see her again.

It's like their old neighbor back in Jasper, an ER nurse, always said, "You never know what pain other people are going through."

A sobering thought.

As Logan backed down the steep driveway—carefully this time—she resolved to be kinder to everyone she met.

Chapter Seven

Over breakfast at Pirates, Logan peppered Sam and Jean with questions on how to navigate the labyrinth of law enforcement entities down at the Lincoln County Courthouse where she would be volunteering. There was a lot Logan had to learn about her new digs. She wanted to be as prepared as possible going in.

Peering over her cat-eye glasses, Sam was happy to dish. As the crime reporter for the Lincoln County Leader, Sam spent a lot of time at the courthouse. She was full of helpful tidbits like who was having an affair with whom, who left early on Fridays, and who could be trusted should the need arise.

Jean's advice was much shorter. "Keep your mouth shut, your head down, do good work, and you won't have any problems."

Okay then. You could always count on Jean to be concise.

***

An hour later, driving south toward Newport, Logan sipped scalding hot coffee carefully from her to-go cup and mentally reviewed everything Sam had shared, but knew not much of it would make sense until she could put names to faces and see the actual layout of the place in person.

A few lights past Freddies and Walmart, she made a right on West Olive Street, toward the ocean. A couple of blocks later, she turned left onto SW Nye and took the second entrance to the red brick courthouse's rear parking lot.

One of Sam's factoids was that the courthouse had been built in 1954, while the blocky, white and gray structure on the other side, the jail, had been added more recently in 1992. Jail and courthouse were connected by a skyway.

After she parked, Logan got out of her car, pulled out her phone and gave Vern a quick call. He said he'd meet her at the entrance and walk her back.

Pulling open one of the heavy doors, Logan looked around and got her bearings. It was just as Sam had described—commissioner's offices on this side, but you had to get through a security station to access the rest of the building.

A short, stocky security guard, hand on his holstered weapon, neither smiled or scowled as she gave him her name and who she was here to meet. After she assured him she had no knives or other implements of destruction on or about her person, he let her pass through the metal detector. When no alarm bells went off, he did take his hand off his gun but still stood there looking scary and doubtful she could be trusted.

Vern's friendly face coming around the corner was a welcome sight. Clad in khaki pants and a polo shirt, he greeted the security guard, whose head only came up to Vern's chest.

"Hey, Joe," he said. "Thanks! This is Logan McKenna. You'll see her around. She's going to be helping us out for a while—doing some scanning. We've got an ID badge coming, but in the meantime, just wanted you to know who she is—she'll be coming in a few days a week."

Joe nodded as the next person approached. Not a big talker, Joe.

A right turn past security landed them in front of what Logan assumed must be the cold case office. The entrance was obscured by a partition. Logan was grateful it wasn't down some labyrinth of narrow hallways. At least she wouldn't get lost tomorrow when she came in by herself.

Before they went in, Vern pointed to the room next door and two offices across the hall, "Commissioners' hearing room on your right, victim's assistance and detectives there and there."

Vern introduced Logan to a couple more people as they walked by, none of whom were particularly welcoming, particularly the ones in uniform. Maybe they were just too busy to stop and chat. What did she expect? A welcome wagon with warm brownies in a basket?

Logan squared her shoulders. She wasn't there to win a popularity contest. Might as well get to work.

Before she could turn to go inside the office, an older, serious-looking dark-haired man in a rumpled suit—the only person wearing a suit she'd seen so far today—exited the detectives' office on the left, a manila file folder under his arm. The man was taller than Logan, but Vern had at least four inches on him. Logan recognized him right away. Detective Monson. Her heart dropped.

Logan had a history with Detective Monson. She met him several years ago and had been inadvertently showing up at his crime scenes ever since. She knew from experience that he was a calm, intelligent interrogator. Once, he'd even suspected her of murder, a case she later sort of helped him solve. Last year he'd made some crack about her always showing up at his crime scenes. What would his reaction be to her working with the cold case unit, hanging out on his turf, right across the hall?

Logan's body tensed, waiting for his reaction, but instead of the scowl she expected, the venerable detective smoothly tucked the manila file folder under his left arm and reached out his right to shake her hand.

"I see you passed your background check, Ms. McKenna," he said with what looked almost like a smile. She could swear his eyes were twinkling. "Welcome aboard. Vern's a good man."

With that, he continued down the hall to wherever he was going and Vern ushered her into her new digs.

Logan wasn't sure what to expect of her new workplace, but upon first glance, she could see why Vern called it the "dungeon." A hodgepodge of scrounged, mismatched furniture including two desks and a rectangular folding table had been crammed into a small, windowless room with flimsy, hollow doors, low, acoustic-tile ceilings, and inexpensive faux-wood flooring. It reminded her of a seventies-era basement conversion, which is essentially what it was.

Metal filing cabinets and bookshelves filled with black and green binders lined the room. Banker's boxes were tucked under and stacked on almost everything.

On one wall she noticed a white board with a grid of what she assumed were the cold cases they were working on now. There were about ten last names in the first column.

The only lighting came from overhead fluorescent squares in the ceiling and a table lamp with a pleated shade someone must have brought from home. In one corner stood a skeleton with an ID badge hung around its neck. Reminded Logan of the plastic one in her high school biology class.

"That's Murdoch," Vern said. Logan hoped it wasn't the remains of one of the homicide victims.

Vern tossed his ball cap on one of the desks—the cluttered one. Logan had never seen Vern without his hat. The man's smooth, pale scalp made his bushy eyebrows and full mustache stand out. In this cramped space, he looked like a misplaced Norwegian troll. One of the nice ones, she hoped. Other than brief interactions at the dog park, she really didn't know the man all that well.

The table next to Vern's desk was empty, but the second desk, opposite his, had a monitor, a laptop, and what looked like a scanner, on it. Front and center someone had placed a fresh legal pad, some yellow Post-It notes, and a chipped mug with some pens and pencils in it. A generic trash can was tucked underneath.

Listing to one side, the chair looked doubtful. Maybe she could bring one from home if this desk turned out to be hers.

It was.

"Home Sweet Home!" Vern said. "I picked out a few supplies for you—stapler, paper clips . . . if you need anything, just ask." He pointed to a stack of printer paper behind her desk on the open bookshelf. "You'll go through those pretty quickly, let me know when you need more. Cell phone and ID badge are coming."

"There is a landline," he said, indicating one on the table, "but it rarely rings. We use our cells."

Walking over to a mini coffee station perched on top of a black four-drawer filing cabinet, Vern held up the pot and nodded at the large to-go cup she had in her hand. "Refill?"

Since she'd polished off most of her Pirates coffee on the way here, Logan took him up on the offer. Not seeing any cream, she added extra sugar. She took a tentative sip. Not bad; nothing like the toxic sludge she expected from watching cop shows on TV. She noted a small coffee bean grinder next to the pot. She'd have to make sure she brought in some good whole beans when it was her turn to replenish supplies.

After making sure she knew how to use the standard Microsoft Office programs on her laptop, Vern gave her the Wi-Fi password and went to grab his chair. While she logged on and got ready, he rolled over to her desk, grabbing one of the black binders on the way.

Chapter Eight

"**O**kay," Vern said, jumping in without preamble, flipping open the binder so it lay flat in front of her on the desk. "This is a murder book. Well, actually the first binder of one you'll be scanning. Each complete murder book can contain ten or more binders, depending on the complexity of the case."

He leaned back in his chair. "I know you've heard of a murder book, but you will be learning how they're put together and later, when you're ready, what to look for: what's missing, where the holes are in some of these cases, or what physical evidence we might want to resubmit—or submit for the first time—for DNA testing."

Vern leaned back in his chair, "Now, I can tell you that you will not be popular with most LEOs—law enforcement officers—nobody wants to be second-guessed, especially by you. I have a little more leeway—partially because I'm a retired homicide detective, and you didn't hear this from me, but also because I'm a guy. It's not fair but just know going in that some of these guys are troglodytes."

He smiled and went on, "But to be fair, think how you'd feel if you worked a case hard—sometimes for years—never could solve it, then someone comes along and questions your every move."

Logan got it. The gender thing was something she had not had to deal with in her music career, but it had cropped up occasionally in the computer training business she and Jack had run together. Even though she had most of the expertise, some clients insisted on dealing only with Jack, assuming he was the head of the company, being male. They eventually caught on.

Vern gestured to the whiteboard on the wall behind his desk, "Those are the cases we're actively working now."

"How many cold cases are there in Lincoln County?" Logan asked.

"I have no idea," Vern said, "but it's more than we'll ever solve, so we pick the ones we think we can crack and when we're lucky enough to solve one, we slot in the next one."

Logan wanted to know how many had been solved but was afraid to ask in case the number was too discouraging.

Vern went through the list on the board, "Brett Hardinger, homicide victim, 2012, age thirty-six at time of death . . . Brooke Louise Crawford, reported missing 2008, age sixteen . . . Vincent Connelly, elderly man, eighty-two, suspicious death—died at home, possible elder abuse—daughter who was living with him and supposedly caring for him was the main suspect. She inherited everything and the man was dead for two days before she reported it . . ."

Vern continued giving a brief summary of each case on the whiteboard before returning to the binder in front of Logan.

"This one's not up there. Blake Atwater, homicide, 1999. One we closed last year—but it's a good murder book for you to learn from and needs to be scanned. It's one of the most complete murder books. Your predecessor, Makena Cook, was very organized. Her system's a little different—she lists the witnesses alphabetically versus chronologically like the police do, so all of the interviews for each witness are together in one place. But in general, all murder books contain the same components, no matter how they're put together."

He'd been talking for a while, so Vern got up and refilled their coffees, then returned to his chair, which squeaked when he leaned back. Logan made a mental note to bring in some WD-40 tomorrow.

"Now, a little history," Vern said.

Logan opened a Word document and took notes.

"In the early 1980s, someone in the Los Angeles Police Department decided it would be a good idea to create a case file structure for their homicide investigations. It helped homicide detectives manage their heavy caseloads and standardized the compilation of the reports, photos, and other materials in a way that made it easier for detectives, supervisors, and prosecutors to review and locate what they needed."

Logan had never thought about that.

"This has now become standard practice," Vern said. "Everything in this murder book is discoverable, which means its contents have to be turned over to the defense council during pre-trial proceedings."

"Which also means," he gave Logan a meaningful look, "every i must be dotted and every t crossed before handing it over."

"It's also why we try to keep as many of these cold cases active as we can, meaning we make at least one contact or report each year—minimum—otherwise later the judge can throw it out, saying it's too old and nobody was working it . . ."

Logan looked confused.

"Never mind," Vern said. "I'm getting ahead of myself. For now, just focus on scanning the Atwater murder book."

Vern pointed to the divider tabs on the inside of the binder. The top one said "chronological record."

"These tabs keep the material organized into sections—more or less correlating with the original twenty-eight that LA uses."

He proceeded to explain the various sections, starting with the first tab, which contained a summary form of the chronological record of the investigation, recording the date and time of each entry, as well as the name of the detective who authorized that entry.

This was followed by the crime scene log, death report, property and evidence, crime lab reports (including DNA analysis if they had it), arrest report, search warrants, etc. There was one whole section for the victim's information, along with tabs for suspect(s), photos, and witnesses.

Logan's brain was swirling, but she hoped when she got into scanning, more of this information would sink in.

Vern assured her it would, showing her how to work the desktop scanner, load it with paper and where she could get more when she ran out. He then left her to it and rolled back over to his own desk.

Logan glanced over to see if he was watching to make sure she didn't screw anything up, but within seconds, Vern was working on his computer, completely ignoring her.

Chapter Nine

Stuffing her jacket behind her to support her lower back in the wobbly chair—she was definitely bringing in a better one tomorrow—Logan shifted until it more or less filled up the space and scooted it forward. Making sure her coffee was positioned far away from her laptop, she popped open the rings of the binder, placed it on her left, and lifted out the first section. She planned on scanning each page, placing them into an empty binder Vern said she could have, recreating the murder book as she worked through it so none of the pages would be out of order. She'd transfer the label from the original binder when she was finished and start work on the next one.

She was halfway through when it was time to break for lunch. Logan hadn't thought to bring anything and there was no cafeteria, so Vern said he knew of a good place nearby. It was cold, but not raining, so they bundled up and walked the few blocks to the Nye Beach Cafe. Vern had the prawn quesadilla and Logan got a generously stacked Reuben on rye with kettle chips and a steaming bowl of clam chowder on the side. Girl's gotta eat. They walked a little slower on the return trip but were still back in the office by 1:30 p.m.

Logan started on the second binder of the Atwood murder book. This binder contained the primary suspect's information, along with less detailed information on the other suspects that had been eliminated. Being a fast reader, Logan skimmed it as she worked. The killer had been the man's girlfriend whose DNA was all over the murder weapon. Not bothering to plead innocent, she said he hadn't left his wife soon enough to suit her.

Today's job was to finish scanning this binder. Once she had all of them scanned in—hopefully in a few days—Vern said he wanted her to go back and read the whole murder book thoroughly, to familiarize herself with the case, then they'd talk about how it got solved. She couldn't wait! This stuff was fascinating.

She forced herself to get back to it, methodically working left to right. Lift, scan, place, lift, scan, place.

The DNA report made her wonder if Clay had ever thought about sending off his DNA to one of those websites that traced family trees. Maybe he could find his sister that way. It was a long shot, but she'd have to suggest it to him if he hadn't already done it.

Logan's shoulder was getting sore. She had just finished and was reassembling the last binder when Vern's cell phone rang. He glanced at the caller and put it on speaker.

"Hey Baxter," Vern said. "What's up?"

"Looks like we've got one of yours, Vern," Baxter said. "You know that new housing development, River View, out here in Siletz? Excavation guy prepping a lot for a build this morning dug up what looks like human remains. Better put on your dancing shoes and get yourself down here.

"I'm setting up a perimeter, but I don't know when media will get wind of this. I'll text you the address. I already called it in, but thought you'd want to know sooner rather than later."

"Thanks, Baxter," Vern said, already out of his chair and reaching for his jacket. He grinned at Logan and said, "Saddle up! This will be a good training opportunity. Hope you're not squeamish."

By the time Logan grabbed her purse out of her bottom desk drawer and her jacket off the back of her desk chair, Vern was already out the door. Jogging to keep up with her mentor's long, loping gait, Logan caught up with him in the parking lot and climbed in on the passenger side of his truck. As he drove, Logan thought about what lay ahead. She'd had the unfortunate experience of having seen a dead body before.

On the drive over Vern gave her a short course on the Lincoln County Major Crimes team, some of which she knew, most of which she had forgotten.

"Major crimes is activated whenever there is a homicide or like this, human remains discovered, cause of death unknown. The team is made up of representatives from the FBI, Lincoln County Sheriff's Office, DA, OSP (Oregon State Police), all three police departments, Lincoln City, Toledo, Newport . . . In this case, since it's out in Siletz, the sheriff's office will probably take lead."

Twenty minutes later, after turning off Highway 20 onto Highway 229, they turned left again onto a narrow access road and followed the signs to River View Luxury Homes. Only there were no homes yet, just neatly paved streets named Morning Cloud, Salmon Court, and Cedar Way. Pale green utility boxes dotted the lots, but no homes had yet been built. Few trees remained, although the surrounding landscape indicated the land had been fairly densely forested before being developed.

As they coasted down one of the steeper hills, Logan rolled down her window. Her twelve-year-old self yearned for a bike or skateboard. She could feel the wind on her face and the surge of joy only a child can experience from freedom and speed.

When they turned the corner at the bottom of the hill, Vern headed for the only lot with any activity on it. In addition to a patrol car Logan assumed belonged to the officer who had called

Vern, what looked like a small bulldozer sat next to a rectangle marked off by string with a partially dug trench running around the inside. An OSP SUV, a small, dented, blue Toyota truck, and another unmarked vehicle were parked on the right, beside a large truck and trailer.

Vern pulled his truck in behind the SUV. As promised, Baxter had marked off the lot with crime scene tape, using the few remaining trees and some stakes he had put in the ground. The lot had been cleared of brush.

Luckily, it hadn't rained last night, so the ground wasn't muddy.

Before they got out, Vern gave Logan last-minute instructions. She was to observe and take notes—only. If she had any questions, he'd answer them later. She could take pictures with her personal cell phone, but none could be shared. She could send them to him, deleting them later.

"Of course," Logan said.

Phone in hand, she left her bag in the truck and followed Vern over to where a man wearing heavy work boots, Carhartts, and a battered hard hat tucked under his arm was pointing into the end of a narrow trench he had apparently been digging, showing something to a young, uniformed OSP officer and a short, plain-clothes brunette with sunglasses. The heavy equipment had been turned off, so without any houses or a highway nearby, it was eerily quiet. Logan could hear their conversation clearly.

"Looks human to me," Work Boots said. "I called the owner—he's on his way down here from Portland, but what do you want me to do? How long will this keep us shut down? He's got his guy scheduled for next week if the weather holds. I need to get this dug before then."

"We won't know that officially until the ME gets here and tells us what we've got," the woman said. Looking up at him, she added, "But I can tell you it's not going to be today. We'll have to find the rest of whoever this is, and we can't use your equipment or even regular shovels to see who else is down there. Could be more than one. And if it turns out to be the bones of an indigenous person . . . it could be a long while."

"Well, you can tell him that, not me," Work Boots said. "He is not gonna be happy about this." Setting his jaw, he clomped back to his truck to wait for his boss.

Chapter Ten

The woman with the dark-brown ponytail crouched down, balancing on the balls of her feet, peering into the trench. Vern and Logan looked over her shoulder and did the same. The trench was only a few feet deep. A hill of loose dirt that had been removed was on the other side.

Expecting to see white bones starkly contrasted against the dirt, at first Logan couldn't see anything, but eventually she made out one long bone stained the color of tobacco and another one, slightly lighter in color, partially buried. Wider than the other one, this bone showed both flat and curved surfaces. A few smaller bones or fragments of something lay scattered nearby.

"Hey, Barb," Vern said.

"Hi, Vern," Barb said, standing up, wiping her hands on her pants. "Baxter call you?"

"Yeah," Vern said. "Thought it might be one of ours. Any idea how long they've been in there?" he asked, nodding toward the pit.

"Nope," Barb said. "Not my area of expertise. Jean should be here soon."

As if summoned, Jean's ME van rolled up and parked next to Vern's truck. While Jean pulled on gloves, boots, and white coveralls before coming over, Vern made introductions.

"Logan, Barbara Bianchi, our FBI rep on the major crimes team. Barb, this is Logan McKenna, our new volunteer cold case trainee."

That was a mouthful.

"Welcome aboard, Logan," Barb said, giving Logan a firm handshake.

Vern didn't know the OSP guy; he was new on the team, so Barb did the honors. "Logan, Curtis, Curtis, Logan."

Curtis nodded and mumbled "nice to meet you," but kept his arms folded. He didn't say it out loud, but his look clearly said, "What are you doing here?"

Another LEO not enamored of volunteers. Fine with Logan, she was just here to observe.

When Jean walked up, trailed by her assistant, she didn't acknowledge Logan. Logan didn't take offense. Jean was on the job.

After greetings, everyone stepped aside so Jean could get down into the trench with the bones. Logan assumed the outer gear was to keep the area from being contaminated should this turn out to be a crime scene but also knew Jean's fastidiousness with her clothes. She'd never seen a speck of dirt on them. Jean would probably suit up to take the dogs for a walk—if she had dogs . . . which she didn't.

First, Jean took dozens of photographs from every angle of the bones as they were found. After handing her camera back up to her assistant, who was similarly attired, she proceeded to carefully examine the exposed bones.

Using what looked like a small paintbrush she had in her pocket, Jean was able to gently remove the dirt from around the bone until it was fully revealed, and she could safely remove it.

She turned it over in her gloved hands a few times, held it up, and squinted down its length.

Logan wondered what the bone told her.

In the meantime, Jean's assistant, a young, thin man with a mop of black hair spread a white, plastic sheet onto the floor of the pit next to where his boss was working. After carefully examining each bone, Jean handed it to Todd, who labeled it, then placed it on the sheet, and recorded it in his notebook. Jean also recorded her observations orally on her phone.

Once all the visible bones and fragments were collected, Jean carefully staked out a square with some blue string she produced from her pocket before proceeding to meticulously and methodically dig deeper, searching for more. It was well past dinnertime and almost sunset before Jean finally climbed out of the shallow pit and said, "That's about all I can do today. We'll take these to Blake's."

Logan knew she was referring to Blake's Funeral Home in Newport. The pile looked pitifully small. Sad that that was all that was left of a human being.

"Well?" Vern said.

"Just my initial observations," Jean said. "but so far you've got one individual, female, young."

"How young?" Barb asked.

"Hard to tell without more bones, but density is good, the distal femur—the lower end of that thigh bone—is fused, so older than fifteen, younger than seventy."

Vern and Barb looked disappointed Jean couldn't narrow it down more.

Jean sent her assistant back to the van for a box and they carefully placed each bone inside and replaced the lid.

Watching Jean work, Logan was fascinated with the process. Science had always interested Logan, but being a double math/music major, she hadn't had a lot of room in her schedule to fit in science courses. Oregon Coast Community College was nearby, and they had an online catalog. Maybe she could take an anatomy class.

"How long do you think she's been in there?" Vern asked.

"Not archaic, less than I'd say fifty years, depending on soil conditions. This is sandy soil, but we get a lot of rain. I can send her up to Birdwell or even Vance for more precise dating if we can't ID her."

"I'd love to get some teeth or even part of a skull," she mused. "But for now, I'd start looking at any females who went missing between fifteen to fifty years ago."

Vern turned to Curtis. "We need the cadaver dogs," he said. "If there are any more bones out here we need to find them."

Curtis shook his head, "Both our dogs are out on a search in Bend—lost hiking group. We only have the two."

"Damn," Vern said. They usually used OSP's dogs. Even without soft tissue, the two dogs, one a lab mix, the other a Doberman, could usually detect any human remains.

"Anybody else?"

"Betty's dog got cancer. He's out of commission," Barb said, referring to a woman's German shepherd up in Salem. Not as good as the OSP dogs, but still.

Logan tentatively raised her hand like she was in school, asking permission to speak.

Vern looked at her with raised eyebrows but waited.

"I know someone out in Eddyville who does search and rescue," Logan said. "I don't know if her dogs are trained for cadavers, but if anyone knows of any in the area that are, it's Oletta."

"Can you get her on the phone?" Barb said.

Logan could and did. Neither Hawk nor Kraken were cadaver dogs, Oletta said, but she knew of a man who had one. She'd see if he was available.

Five minutes later, Chuck LeBlanc called and said he and his dog, Roux, a seven-year-old chocolate lab, could be there at first light, which at this time of year was about seven thirty. A retired chef from New Orleans, Chuck said he named his dog Roux because she was the exact color of the browned butter and flour base he lovingly made for so many of his favorite Creole and Cajun dishes.

They gave him directions and made preparations to secure the scene until morning. Vern got a sheriff's deputy to do night guard duty while Jean and Todd walked back to the van with the box.

All members of the Lincoln County Major Crimes team had been notified and would convene in the morning. The sheriff was out of town until next week, so he put Vern in charge until then.

Vern sent the heavy equipment operator, whose name was Jim, home. He was reluctant at first since his boss still hadn't shown up, but with a police officer on guard, Vern reassured him the site would be safer than usual. In addition, he gave Jim his card with his cell phone number on it. Said if his boss gave him any trouble to have him call. Finally, Jim allowed himself to be talked into leaving.

"Guy's a prick anyway," Jim said as he locked up his equipment and got into his truck to go home.

Barb's blinking taillights were just cresting the hill exiting River View's empty housing development when a luxury sedan came barreling down the middle of the street, almost crashing into Barb head on. A red-faced man launched himself out of the car.

"What the hell do you think you're doing on my property? And where the hell's Jim?" he shouted.

As predicted, the owner was apoplectic when Vern told him his site would be shut down for the foreseeable future. "Nothing more anyone can do tonight. Tomorrow, after the cadaver dog does her job, we'll talk. Until then, there are several decent motels in town—in fact, several, depending on what you are looking for," Vern told him.

Since the owner couldn't pierce Vern's authoritative nonchalance, he eventually left, but said he'd be back in the morning. If anything came up between now and then, he would be at the Salishan Resort.

Of course you will, thought Logan. Salishan was the most expensive place to stay on the coast.

Chapter Eleven

In order to meet Vern at the excavation site at dawn as she had promised, Logan had to forego her morning run with Dixon. Letting her dog out for a short potty break, she promised him a nice long run when she got back. That promise, along with a large, cold-smoked beef bone she'd been saving for him, seemed to satisfy. When she left, he was happily gnawing away.

By the time Logan arrived at River View Luxury Homes, Vern and several other major crimes team members were already there. Bless his heart, Vern had picked up coffee and donuts on his way in and there were several good ones left. Logan chose an old-fashioned glazed and topped off her travel mug.

Chuck was already at work with his dog, Roux. The morning sun glinted off the chocolate lab's shiny coat as she worked, nose to the ground, tail straight out behind her.

Vern gave Logan a play-by-play as they watched. "He's got a grid pattern laid out, working one section at a time. We're starting with this lot first, expanding into the surrounding lots one area at a time until we're pretty sure there aren't any more remains out there."

Logan nodded. Chuck had Roux on a long lead, and they were walking slowly through the first grid. Vern continued his tutorial.

"The handler understands that the scent of human remains disperses in a cone shape, with the strongest concentration at the source. So Roux's job is to detect and follow this scent cone to pinpoint the location—if anything's out there, she should find it, as long as it's not too far down."

It wasn't until the second grid that Roux sat down and gave one sharp bark. Chuck stuck a flag in the ground, praised his dog, then put her back to work. By lunchtime, there were seven more flags in the ground.

Jean and her assistant excavated each area carefully. On the third flag, Jean let out a whoop, "We've got teeth!" she said. "And most of a skull!" The other bones recovered were not as critical to identifying the deceased, but all were carefully collected and stored in the van.

"Teeth not worn down and wisdom teeth not fully erupted," she said. "If I were you, I'd pull murder books on missing females between the ages of sixteen and thirty.

"And," she said, turning the skull fragment in her hand, pointing to an area where the side of the skull was depressed and cracked. "You've got a probable cause of death. Blunt force trauma. Of course, she could have been poisoned or died of the flu, but that bash to the head didn't help."

Logan's spine tingled. She couldn't wait to get back to the dungeon and start figuring out who this young woman was and who'd killed her—if she had been killed—Logan knew she should keep an open mind.

So she was disappointed when Vern told her to go home and write up her notes. He had a mandatory meeting with the DA this afternoon regarding his testimony on another cold case. They'd pick up where they left off back at the office tomorrow.

STONE COLD

Vern must have come in early, because when Logan arrived he already had three stacks of binders on the table next to his desk. He waited while she took off her jacket and dropped her purse into the bottom drawer of her desk.

"Pull up a chair," Vern said. "Before we crack these open, I want to give you the overview, so even though you'll know some of this already, bear with me."

Logan was fine with that. She was here to learn.

"Our first job when human remains are found is identifying them. These," he said, jerking his thumb back at the binders, "are the three cold cases that fit within the parameters Jean gave us: female between the ages of sixteen and thirty, reported missing within the last fifty years."

"Of course, the young woman may have been killed three counties away and dumped here, or been hidden away in a basement, escaped and not ever reported missing, or abducted by aliens and then returned . . ."

Logan smiled and nodded. Barring the alien abduction, she hadn't thought about the number of plausible explanations for a young woman being killed and buried in what used to be forest land in rural Lincoln County.

"But we have to start somewhere," Vern said. "These cases haven't been scanned yet, so we'll have to go through them old school. The two most viable are Rosemary Swanson, age sixteen when she ran away from home in 1969. Father, George Swanson, mother, Adeline, one brother, four years older. Mother not in the picture, kids raised by the father. Says he has no idea where his wife went."

"Is the father still alive? Can we interview him?" Logan asked.

"Don't know if he's still around," he said, "we'll have to check that out."

"There's only one binder for Rosemary. Not much to go on there," he said, tapping the binder with the knuckle of his index finger. "Not many people knew the family. They lived in a small rural area between Newport and Toledo."

Lifting Rosemary's binder off the top of the stack, he set it aside.

"Next up we have sixteen-year-old Brooke Louise Crawford. Disappeared without a trace in 2008. We have a lot more on her. Three binders and I started a fourth. Last seen on Highway 20, driving home with a friend from a Scottish fair in McMinnville. Both girls were Highland dancers—you know, bagpipes and high stepping," he said, bobbing in his chair with one hand curved over his head, the other in a fist on his hip, miming a dancer, but not making fun of one. "Brooke had competed at the fair that day and she went missing on the way home. Brooke came from a middle-class, respected Newport family."

Being of Scotch-Irish descent, Logan was familiar with the popular Highland festivals, although she had never learned the dances.

Vern stopped to take a sip of his coffee.

"Did they have any suspects for either of these cases?" Logan asked. "Any evidence of foul play?" The minute she said "foul play" Logan regretted it. Sounded like a line from a *Murder She Wrote* episode.

"Some," Vern said. "In the Swanson case, the father was interviewed but without a body or any sign of 'foul play,' they didn't have any leads to follow."

Logan, ignoring his pointed dig at her naive gaffe, said, "What about friends? Did she have a part-time job? A boyfriend?"

"Some of that's in there, but nobody stood out—at least not to the detectives who caught the case at the time."

Hmmmm . . . Logan couldn't wait to dig into that binder and see what stones may have been left unturned.

"As for Brooke Crawford, they looked at the parents, but the main suspect was the boyfriend, twenty-year-old Dylan Scarth. But he had an alibi, and her parents defended him."

Logan wondered about that. Not many parents would be happy about their sixteen-year-old daughter going out with a twenty-year-old man. Vern answered that question before she could ask it.

"Parents thought he was a solid guy. He planned on marrying Brooke as soon as she graduated from high school."

He reached around behind him to the last binder. "Which brings me to the third possible match to our remains, Eleanor Riley. She's an outlier but might fit. Age thirty-two. Reported missing in 1984. Originally from Tillamook, but moved here with her husband, Nathan Riley, in 1979. Main suspect, her husband—Eleanor had been in and out of the hospital numerous times, but a body was never found."

"Friends? Anyone ever hear from her?" Logan asked.

"No," Vern said. "Didn't have many friends."

Not much there," Logan pointed to the binder, slimmer than the others.

Vern set his jaw. "Husband was a cop. Not much investigating was done."

Wow.

Logan was surprised that Vern, a former member of law enforcement would be so candid about the reluctance of the rank-and-file to question fellow officers in cases of domestic violence. She'd heard that happened way too often.

"But it will be now," he added.

Good for Vern. That moved him up a notch in Logan's esteem.

Chapter Twelve

Since the cadaver dog found a partial jawbone with teeth, their first job was to track down the dental records of all three women to see if they could get a match. That was the quickest way to get a definitive ID. Once they knew who the victim was, they could set the other cases aside and focus on their official homicide investigation. That is, if any of the dental records were a match. This could still be a victim killed somewhere else and dumped here.

But first, they needed the names of the missing women's dentists. Since Eleanor was the oldest case, Vern decided to start there. Witnesses and suspects moved or died, he explained, so you wanted to work on the oldest cases first. Nathan Riley, Eleanor's husband, would be about seventy-five now. Hopefully, he was still alive.

They lucked out. He was not only still alive, but still around. Retired from the Newport Police Department for sixteen years, he lived on a half-acre property twenty minutes south in Waldport.

Vern said face-to-face was always better than on the phone, so they drove down.

"Shouldn't we call first? Make sure he's home?" Logan asked.

"We could," Vern said, "but it's better to catch him off guard. See the look on his face when we tell him we've possibly found his missing wife's remains."

Nathan Riley's place was about a mile off the highway. A newish black truck sat in the driveway, but there were no other signs of anyone home. Vern pulled in next to the truck.

A narrow walk led to the front door of a manufactured home, yellow with white trim. They weren't halfway to the front door when a huge dog, all slavering jaws and rippling muscles, came barreling around the back corner, snarling and snapping, stopped only by the six-foot-tall chain link fence that surrounded the yard. That fence didn't look nearly high enough.

Vern didn't seem concerned at all. Seeing Logan's look, he opened his jacket and tapped a small can of what she assumed was pepper spray.

"Air horn," Vern said, "We'll get you one. Never leave home without it. Stops dogs dead in their tracks and you don't have to worry about spraying yourself."

Logan nodded, trying to look calm, and they continued up the path.

Before Vern could knock, a ruddy-faced man came out and opened a gate next to the front door, "Beastie! Here!"

Instantly, the dog trotted over and sat at the man's feet.

Impressive.

"Sorry, I wasn't expecting company," he said. "Is there something I can help you with?"

If Logan had been expecting an unshaven, potbellied caveman in a wife-beater with a beer in his hand, she was sorely disappointed. The man before her was well-groomed and neatly dressed, with a blue plaid shirt that matched his eyes tucked into jeans with a braided belt. He wore Ugg slippers and held a paint brush, not a beer, in his left hand.

"Nathan Riley?" Vern asked.

"That's me," he said, "but please, call me Nate." His eyes were friendly but curious. "How can I help you?"

Logan wondered how Vern was going to approach this.

Vern identified himself as a retired homicide detective—good move there, bonding with a fellow LEO—and current cold case lead for the DA's office. He introduced Logan vaguely as his assistant, then got right to the point.

"Two days ago, human remains were discovered at a construction site out in Siletz. We've been tasked with identifying those remains. As I'm sure you know, it's standard procedure to pull all the missing person's cold cases to see if we can get a match. I'm sorry to have to bring up unpleasant memories, but your wife, Eleanor Riley, is one of the cases that fits within the parameters identified. We need to ask you a few questions that will help us either identify those remains as Mrs. Riley's or eliminate her from consideration."

The man hesitated for a second before he stood back, opening the door wider. "Of course, please come in. You'll have to forgive me, but I haven't heard that name in quite a while."

Logan looked around the dim interior. Two leather recliners sat angled in front of a fireplace with a matching love seat at right angles. On a card table by the window was a tray of watercolors, a jelly jar of water, more brushes and a half-finished painting of a black and orange bird with white splotches on its wings. From what she could tell from where she stood, it was pretty good.

Seeing Logan looking at the painting, Nate pointed to a busy birdfeeder outside the window. "Beth got me that when I retired. I'm not very good, but it keeps me off the streets. That one's a spotted towhee."

A slim blonde woman came out of the kitchen, wiping her hands on a towel. Introductions were made. This was Beth, Nate's current wife.

Logan couldn't help but look for bruises or signs of subservience, but there weren't any. Maybe they got it wrong, and his first wife was just accident prone. Or maybe Nathan Riley had reformed over the years. Then again, a savvy abuser made sure the bruises he gave his wife wouldn't show.

"What can I get you?" Beth asked. "We've got Diet Coke, Coke, or coffee. And I think I have some tea around here somewhere."

Vern took coffee, Logan went with a Coke. Diet anything tasted like cat piss in her opinion, and she'd already had plenty of coffee. Pointing at the loveseat for Logan, Nate gave Vern one of the recliners and sat in the other. Beastie scampered around like a puppy before settling at Nate's feet, drooling on his shoe. Beth delivered the drinks, then went back into the kitchen.

Nate turned to Vern and said, "I don't know what I can tell you—I haven't heard from or about my first wife in years, but I'll help if I can."

"Well, we were lucky to recover some teeth, so in order to identify the remains as Eleanor's or someone else's, we need dental records. We looked for dental records in the file, but there weren't any. If you could just give us the name of her dentist, we can take it from there."

Logan could see the gears whirling in the man's brain. This was critical. If he refused to cooperate, he would appear guilty, but if he gave them the name of the dentist and the records matched the recovered teeth, the case would be reopened and Nathan Riley would become the prime suspect in what was now a homicide, not a missing persons' case. Vern had conveniently left out the detail about the blunt-force-trauma crack on the skull.

Logan was almost disappointed when Nate said, "Of course, that would be Dr. Zale, we both used to go to him until he retired. I see Dr. Samson now. He bought the practice from Zale a few years ago. Do you want me to get his number?"

Chapter Thirteen

Dr. Samson's office was not open weekends, so Vern left a message for him to return his call on Monday.

Rosemary Swanson's missing person case was the next oldest, so they pulled her binder next.

"You sure you're okay with working on a Saturday?" Vern asked.

Logan reassured him she was fine as long as she got home in time to feed and walk Dixon. She'd left the doggie door unlocked so he could get out to the back deck and relieve himself if needed. She hoped he'd use it in an emergency. She'd find out when she got home.

Logan picked up the binder. The name Rosemary Swanson had been neatly printed with a black, fine-point Sharpie on a white, adhesive file label on the three-inch spine. Inside were tabbed sections similar to the ones Logan had seen in the murder book she scanned.

Someone had cared what happened to this girl.

Vern began flipping pages, reciting the basics of the case as he went.

"Rosemary Adeline Swanson, born 1969, Salem, OR to George and Adeline Swanson. Doesn't give the exact year, but sometime after she was born the family moved to the coast—at least the dad and kids did—the mother doesn't seem to have been in the picture. Neighbors don't remember seeing a woman around. George was an auto mechanic. He had his own shop.

"In 1986, at age seventeen, Rosie is reported missing. The school said she had been absent for at least a week, but phone calls home went unreturned."

"So the school reported her missing, not her father?" Logan asked.

"More or less," Vern flipped the witnesses tab and continued, "Police went out to the house to see why Rosie was truant. Their next-door neighbor, a Mrs. Alma Wilcox, reported father and daughter often argued and had had a big fight in the front yard that Sunday night.

"When they talked with George, he claimed that's why he didn't report her missing right away. Assumed his wayward daughter would come home in a few days. He finally went down to the police station and filed a report."

Vern got up to get some coffee. There was only enough left for one mug. He offered to make a new pot, but it was mid-afternoon, and Logan shook her head. She wanted one, but knew if she indulged, she'd be up all night.

"Did the neighbor know what the fight was about?" Logan asked.

"Neighbor said she couldn't hear all of it. Something about what Rosie was wearing," Vern said.

"And the father—George—did he ever say where the mom was?" Logan asked.

Logan asked because her own mother had chosen to leave their family when she was thirteen and Rick was nine. She had showed up on Logan's doorstep a few years ago giving a semi-reasonable explanation for her absence and they had reached a tentative detente, but the hurt was still there.

Logan understood the kind of pain young Rosemary must have experienced growing up without a mom, particularly since she never bothered to come back for her children. Children understood divorce—a woman leaving her husband—but not leaving them. For years, Logan had wondered what she had done wrong to drive her mother away.

Vern turned to the suspects section and skimmed until he found what he was looking for. Logan brought her mind back in time to hear most of what Vern was saying.

"... According to the interview with the dad, the mom left not long after Rosie was born. 'Deserted' was the word he used. Here," he turned the binder toward her. "Why don't you read up on ole Georgie while I see if he's still alive and living around here, try to get his current address? According to that, he was born in 1945, which would make him . . ."

"Seventy-nine," Logan said, before Vern could even find some paper to scribble on. She couldn't help it; Logan was naturally competitive and had always been good at mental math. Vern didn't seem to mind.

Logan began to read. She had to hand it to the detectives who investigated the teenager's disappearance. There were multiple interviews with the dad, teachers, and neighbors over a period of several years, but no leads had been generated.

"What's NamUs?" Logan asked, seeing it mentioned in the most recent report.

"National Missing and Unidentified Persons System," Vern said, "It's an integrated set of two internet databases, combines profiles of missing persons with unknown persons whose remains are found in the United States. Didn't really get going until 2008."

He looked at the page in the binder. "Looks like they submitted her data again a few years back, but nada. No matches to human remains found anywhere. If we don't get a match with one of these three cases, we'll add our Siletz victim to NamUs.

Maybe get a hit that way. Like I said, those remains could have come from anywhere and been dumped out here. Not necessarily a Lincoln County homicide."

Logan nodded and continued reading.

From what she'd read, George certainly looked guilty of something—bad parenting at least. Neighbors and teachers reported him as being very strict with his daughter, not allowing her to join clubs, attend school dances, date, or even spend the night at a friend's house. His attitudes didn't seem to stem from religious beliefs, as they didn't attend church, but he did seem determined to keep his daughter as cloistered as a nun. No wonder she rebelled.

Logan next read the interviews with Rosemary's school principal and teachers at Newport High. They reported her as being a good student, but unremarkable in any way until her junior year. She began the year as usual, keeping her head down, good grades, regular attendance. Her yearbook pictures from freshman and sophomore years show a shy girl in conservative clothing, with pale blonde, straight hair held back with a headband, Alice-in-Wonderland style.

But something must have happened sometime during her junior year; she looked like a totally different girl. Scowling out of heavily kohl-lined eyes, her blonde hair was still long but permed and gathered up in a scrunchy on the top of her head. Instead of a modest, pastel blouse or sweater seen in her other school portraits, in this one she sported a black, ripped off-the shoulder t-shirt and skull and crossbones earrings. The school report showed two incompletes, and they said if she didn't take summer school and carry a full load her senior year, she wasn't going to be able to graduate with her class.

Logan looked into the smoldering eyes of the seventeen-year-old Madonna-wanna-be and wondered what had changed.

What happened, Rosie? What made you leave? Logan thought. Or worse, who stopped you before you could?

Chapter Fourteen

Logan rubbed her eyes and sat back in her chair, scrunching her shoulders up to her ears to relieve the stiffness in her neck. Her mind ran through everything she'd read.

"If she ran away, how did she do it? She didn't have a car," Logan said, "and none of her few friends say they gave her a ride anywhere. . . ." She flipped the binder back to the first section in preparation for reading it through one more time. "Of course, they wouldn't admit to helping her if they did. At least not to the cops or her dad. Maybe she bought a bus ticket."

Vern scribbled something onto a Post-it Note next to his computer, lifted off the bright yellow square and waved it in the air. "Found him! Don't know what kind of shape he's in, but old Georgie is in an assisted living place down in Waldport."

He reached for his cell phone to dial the number he'd just written down. While he waited for someone to answer, he said, "Could have had a friend drop her off out of town and hitchhiked from there. There was a serial killer operating in the area during those years. If he picked her up that would explain a lot. Most of his victims were found farther north, which was where his major hunting grounds were, but one was found off Highway 20 this side of Toledo."

Logan sighed. No wonder this case had gone cold. There just weren't any good leads. Until now. Now they had human remains. She knew they couldn't solve all of the homicides and missing persons cases in the binders, but hopefully they could solve one, bring one victim home and deliver justice to whoever was responsible for killing her and stuffing her body in the ground.

After Vern identified himself, Paradise Falls of Waldport verified that yes, Mr. George Swanson was a resident at their assisted living facility. There were graduated levels of care and Mr. Swanson was currently receiving mid-level services such as medications delivery and help with personal hygiene such as bathing and nail trimming. If and when he was in hospice or needed a memory care unit, he would have to be transferred to a facility that could provide those services.

Logan reminded herself never to get old.

Since it was nearing four o'clock and the residents were being taken down to the dining room for dinner, Vern made an appointment for the next morning at ten. The receptionist said that although he could visit anytime between 8:00 a.m. and 8:00 p.m., mid-morning was when their residents were at their sharpest. Most napped in the afternoons and went to bed early, or more often, fell asleep in their recliners watching TV.

Vern and Logan agreed to meet back in the office at nine o'clock tomorrow morning. A drive out to Paradise Falls to see what Rosie's father could or would remember about his daughter's disappearance thirty-nine years ago was a long shot, but the box needed to be checked.

STONE COLD

A brown and white, blocky two-story building with rows of narrow windows faced a gravel parking area. If this was Paradise Falls, it had an overly optimistic moniker, but a small sign with flowing, gold script announced they were in the right place, so they got out and walked up to the entrance. Logan counted the small windows on the second story as they approached. Eight. Even if there were eight on the other side, that still meant only sixteen residents.

An automatic door swished them into the lobby area, where they followed a threadbare gold and rust-colored carpet to check in with the receptionist. Logan could see through to the dining area on the left, a short hallway to offices in the back, and there was a small elevator door to the right.

At least the receptionist, Mary, was friendly and efficient, directing them to take the elevator to the second floor and turn right to room 217. "I'm sure he'll be happy to see you. Mr. Swanson doesn't get very many visitors."

After reading his file, Logan could imagine why.

When they arrived, the door to room 217 was open. An aide was helping lower a thin, frail-looking man into his recliner. Sunlight coming in the window highlighted parchment-thin skin mottled with cancers in various stages of progression. Tucking a lap blanket around her charge's legs, the aide patted him on the arm, handed him the TV remote, and asked if he wanted some water before she left. He didn't answer, but she got him a bottle from a mini fridge anyway.

When she saw Vern and Logan at the door, she smiled widely, "Oh, Mr. Swanson, looks like you have visitors!"

George didn't look overly enthused that he had guests, but didn't object when she waved them in. Two more waters were delivered before she made her exit.

Vern explained his strategy in the car on the way over. After introductions, he would ask a few softball questions, mainly to see if Swanson was of sound mind. George gave short answers but seemed to understand where and who he was. However, he became suspicious quickly.

"What do you want?" he asked. "Why are the police here?"

"We are here to let you know that human remains of a female were found recently. They have been in the ground for quite a while. Naturally we hope to identify those remains for the family if possible, so we are looking at any unsolved missing person's cases that might match the remains. Rosemary's file is one of the ones we are looking into."

It looked like George was going to say something, but Vern continued, "A partial jawbone was found with some teeth. This is great news, because dental records can help us identify these remains. That is why we are here, Mr. Swanson. If you could give us the name of your daughter's dentist, we will research it from there. And if for any reason she never saw a dentist, we can do a simple cheek swab from you to collect your DNA. We will of course, notify you if there is a match . . ."

Logan had been watching George's eyes grow darker and darker, his hands gripping the armrests of his chair. He didn't look frail now.

With surprising speed and strength, he pushed himself up out of his recliner and shouted, "Get out!"

Dizzy from the sudden movement, he immediately dropped back into his chair but continued yelling at them as they exited his room.

"Get out!" he yelled, "and don't come back!"

This last utterance was punctuated by what sounded like the TV remote control splintering as it hit the door.

Chapter Fifteen

When they got back in the car, Logan asked, "Now how are we going to get Rosie's dental records?"

"Don't worry, we should still be able to find them. It will just take a little longer," Vern said.

Logan wondered how they were going to do that. Even if they called every dentist in town, the one they were looking for would not still be practicing, and probably not even alive. Or they could have moved away.

Vern didn't leave her hanging.

"Ideally, law enforcement would have obtained dental records of a missing person at the time they went missing, and they'd be in the file, so you wouldn't have to go hunting for them now. But, for whatever reason, they're not in the file, so we're going to have to track them down.

"This is the not so glamorous part of police work. First place I'll try is the historical society in Newport and look at phone books for dentists practicing during that time. We call the dentist if they're still around. Sometimes they have their records, sometimes they've passed them on when they retired or sold their practice."

"Isn't there some master data base with all the records?" Logan asked.

"I've heard the state is working on one, but it's not up and running yet," Vern said as he drove across the bridge into Newport.

Since she and Vern wouldn't be able to get in touch with anyone until tomorrow, Vern dropped Logan off in the courthouse parking lot by her car. They agreed to pick up where they left off at 9:00 a.m. The historical society wasn't open on Mondays, so he said they'd dig into the third missing person's file, Brooke Louise Crawford.

Realizing it was almost one o'clock, Logan stopped off at The Horn for some lunch. The Horn was a popular place, so she was surprised when she walked in and had her pick of tables. She opted for a small one near the back on the harbor side and ordered fish and chips with extra tartar sauce, double fries, and a King Tide IPA.

While she waited, Logan closed her eyes and reveled in the late summer sun streaming through the windows, warming her face and arms. A stiff breeze rippled the surface of the placid water in the harbor, but here in the restaurant, she was warm and dry.

As she listened to an Americana soundtrack on loop in the background and dishes clattering in the kitchen through the swinging doors, she let her mind wander. Looking out at the boats neatly tied up at the docks, a flash of movement almost directly beneath her window caught her eye. Two harbor seals dove a few times, then hung suspended in the water, faces turned up toward the sun. Logan didn't know if it was true, but she'd heard that although 99 percent of a seal's body was insulated with thick layers of fat, when the water was cold, they would expose their non-fatty body parts, like faces, toward the sun to keep warm.

STONE COLD

Tilting her own face up a few degrees toward the sun, Logan felt a kinship with the funny looking creatures. *We all do what we gotta do.*

Sipping her beer and waiting for her meal, Logan slowed her mind down and sorted through all she had heard, seen, and read in the last few days. Learning how murder and missing persons' books were put together, accompanying Vern when the human remains were found, learning how age, sex, and burial time had been narrowed down, and methodically going through the three missing persons cases that fit the facts they had. It was fascinating and overwhelming at the same time.

She made herself focus on what they knew so far.

Sometime in the fairly recent past, a woman—or girl, they weren't sure of her age yet—was killed by a blow to the head and buried out in what were then the boonies, near the Siletz River. There she had lain, undiscovered for years. This was a real person. One with a family, friends . . . Someone had loved this woman and someone—possibly the same someone—had killed her.

Their job was to identify her.

Eleanor Riley, Rosemary Swanson, and Brook Louise Crawford. As Logan learned more about each woman, they were becoming important to her, more real.

She wanted to know who had loved and cared for them. Who, if anyone, had been devastated when they went missing? Hopefully, one set of dental records would match the teeth they had, giving their victim a name.

But what about the other two? Were they still alive? Why hadn't they ever come home, and where were they now?

Chapter Sixteen

After a long, hot soak in the slipper tub Ben installed for her last year, Logan got in her PJs, curled up in front of the fireplace with a hot toddy, and gave her husband a ring. They tried to talk every night, if only for a few minutes. Even when she didn't have much to share, Logan liked to hear his voice. They caught up on the latest.

Calvin was healing well but slowly. Since Ben wouldn't allow Cal to pay him for helping him out, Cal's wife tried to compensate by feeding her uncle-in-law huge, carb-heavy, "man meals" like beef stroganoff, mac and cheese, and pork chops with mashed potatoes and gravy and chocolate lava cake for dessert.

"So much for my paleo diet," Ben groused, but he didn't sound like he minded the delicious dinners very much.

The landscaping project was going well, but the new crew could use his help, and he was enjoying the work. He estimated he'd be home in a couple of weeks, if that was okay with her.

Logan was fine with that—if not actually a teensy bit relieved. There was a snag in a new composition she'd been working on and a few uninterrupted hours in the evenings would be welcome.

After Ben finished catching her up on his week, she filled him in on her first few days with the cold case unit, focusing on the boring but safe scanning of documents task, and not on the recently discovered homicide victim and tagging along with Vern to interview possible killers.

After they disconnected, she picked up Bella and played for a while. Lovingly made for Logan's Appalachian great-grandmother by a talented Italian violin-maker, the instrument's rich, warm sound rivaled that of the finest violins of Europe. Hours later, letting the fire die down, she tucked Bella back in her case and herself into bed. She must have slept well, because Logan woke refreshed and anxious to get to work. She was up, showered, dressed, and on the road by 7:30 a.m.

She fit in a good run with Dixon before breakfast, during the twenty-to-thirty magical minutes when the day dawned and the sky began to gradually lighten. She remembered one of her teachers in college telling her this time was called 'civil twilight.' Dixon, unaware and unconcerned with this scientifically correct term, simply reveled in the cold morning air, promptly curled up on the living room rug when they got home, and went to sleep. Life was simple for a dog.

MONDAY, OCTOBER 7

After a pit stop for fresh donuts at the Chalet Bakery, Logan pulled into the parking lot of the courthouse just after eight. In hopes of getting the security guard to smile, she got one for him, too. The right side of his mouth may have gone up a few millimeters, she wasn't sure. Not quite a full smile, but he didn't say no to the maple bar.

Logan had the coffee brewing—dark roast she brought from home—when Vern walked in. Grabbing his mug, he made a beeline for the coffee. After taking a minute to breathe in the aroma, he took a drink and gave it a thumbs up.

"Excellent," he said. He was even happier when he noticed what she'd left on his desk. She'd already eaten hers.

"You're hired," he said. Polishing off his bear claw in three bites, he wiped his hands on the napkin and tossed it in the trash.

"I called Dr. Samson from the car," Vern said. "His receptionist said he already started seeing patients so wouldn't be available until probably noon. Hopefully he'll call us back then. If not, we play telephone tag until he does."

Logan was learning that working cold cases required patience, which wasn't her strong suit. She'd have to work on that.

"Okay," Vern said, rolling his chair over to Logan's desk. "Brooke Louise Crawford. Most recent, and has the most data."

Logan had just started looking through the first binder, so she flipped back to the beginning and Vern proceeded to give her an overview of Brooke's case.

"Born 1992 in Newport, Brooke lived with her family until she went missing in 2008 at age sixteen. Five-seven, bright red hair, hundred-and-twenty pounds."

Vern lifted out a full eight-by-ten color yearbook portrait from the left side pocket of the binder.

Wow.

The photograph had so much life and energy it practically jumped off the page. A mass of fire-engine red curls framed an oval face. Bright blue eyes crinkled at the corners. A wide smile with perfectly straight, white teeth beamed out at them.

If she had a dentist, he must have been a good one. Unfortunately, there were no dental records in this file, either. At least none that Logan had found so far. She asked about that.

Vern didn't waste time second-guessing why her dental records weren't included in the file. "Don't know. There's a tab for them, but they're not here. I have a call into the mom, but haven't heard back," he said. "She has a real estate office in

Depoe Bay. If we don't hear from her this morning, we'll drive over there and see if we can catch her in person."

Vern turned to the next section in the binder. "Interviews with the family, friends, and boyfriend. The day she went missing, she had been at a Scottish Festival in McMinnville competing in a Highland dance competition. She won her event that day," he said.

"When was she last seen?" Logan asked. "I only got to skim through these binders. Did anyone ever hear from her after she disappeared? Did the family file a missing person's report right away?"

"Tell you what," Vern said, "I'll give you some time with the binders and then you tell me what you find. Look for what's missing as well as what's there."

For the next hour, Logan did just that.

Unlike the other two missing women, Brooke Crawford—on paper anyway—came from a happy, stable, two-parent home. At the time of the interviews, her father, Will Crawford, fifty-three, was a commercial fisherman. His two sons, Jason, twenty-eight, and Charlie, twenty-five, crewed for him on the family boat, the *Northern Star*. Her mother, Victoria Crawford, fifty-one, was a stay-at-home mom. Brooke's older sister, Mary, thirty, single, had an apartment in town. An OSU business school graduate, she did the books for the fishing business.

Brooke's boyfriend, Dylan Cameron Scarth, age twenty, owned a sheep ranch in Siletz."

"Isn't that a little young to own a sheep ranch?" Logan asked.

"According to the file, it was left to him by his grandmother. He was raised on the ranch. Ran the place when she got sick. Inherited it when she died," Vern said.

He continued, "Dylan also bred and trained border collies. Gave demonstrations at Scottish festivals in the area. That's where he and Brooke met. They were planning on marrying as soon as Brooke turned eighteen and graduated from high school."

The age difference wasn't huge, but Logan was again surprised that the parents were okay with their daughter dating a man already out of school. She wondered why they hadn't encouraged her to go to college or at least to work for a while, discover who she was, and see other people before settling down. But, to each their own.

In one of her interviews, the mother said Brooke was a whirlwind of impulsive energy—headstrong at times. She felt Dylan's calm nature was good for her daughter. "They're the perfect match. Brooke needs physical activity to keep her settled down, burn off all that excess energy she always has. That's why we got her into Highland dancing. And she loves animals—dogs, sheep, horses—Dylan has all that. Acres of open space, fresh air, lots of work to do. And Dylan is solid as a rock. He's a good man. He is just devastated . . ."

Logan looked up from the file.

How headstrong was Brooke? Even the best teenagers make mistakes. Kids get into drugs, get pregnant, mix with the wrong crowd. Had Brooke been in trouble? Too many questions and not enough answers. Logan dismissed her wild guesses. For now, she'd stick with the facts she had.

Chapter Seventeen

Logan continued reading. Finally, she got through all of the interviews, taking notes and creating a timeline in Excel of all that happened from the time Brooke left the festival in McMinnville until she disappeared.

According to the missing person's report her parents had filed, Brooke competed in the McMinnville Scottish festival with her friend, Shelly Brown that day. Dylan was there, too, giving sheepdog demonstrations with his prize border collie, Blitz.

Around lunchtime, Dylan had to leave early to take care of an emergency back at his ranch. He got a call from an angry neighbor that a few of his sheep had gotten out and made themselves at home on the neighbor's property, getting into his garden. One had gotten itself tangled in some barbed wire. Rather than have the neighbor shoot the animal, which he threatened to do, Dylan told Brooke he would call her parents to come get her since he couldn't take her home as he had planned.

But Brooke told him she would get a ride with Shelly after all the events were over, which she did. In his interview, Dylan said he didn't like leaving her, but Shelly did have her driver's license and her parent's car, a three-year-old Ford Explorer. He made Brooke promise to call him when she got home safely. The two girls left the festival around five o'clock.

Logan skimmed Shelly's interview again. About an hour and a half after leaving McMinnville, the Ford ran out of gas a few miles east of Toledo. Wanting to avoid a lecture from her parents on remembering to fill up the tank, they decided to handle it themselves. It was only one or two miles down the road to the Pac Pride, a small gas station on Highway 20. Shelly stayed with her mom's car, while Brooke volunteered to grab the gas can from the trunk and walk down the highway to get it filled.

The last time Shelly saw her, Brook Louise Crawford was walking west along Highway 20, and it was getting dark.

***

Shelly texted and called Brooke's cell phone several times to see what was taking her so long, but did not receive an answer. She left several messages, but her friend didn't call back, either.

When asked why she waited so long to call for help, Shelly said she didn't want her parents to know she hadn't checked the gas tank before driving home. But two hours later, when Brooke still had not returned, Shelly knew she needed to ask for help. First she tried Dylan, but the call didn't go through, so she finally gave up and called her dad.

Mr. Brown drove his truck out to get her, stopping briefly at the gas station to see if Brooke ever made it that far. She hadn't. The attendant said he hadn't seen anyone in the last hour and no walk-ins all night. The dad described Brooke, but the attendant said he would have remembered an attractive young woman with bright red hair.

Not wanting to alarm Brooke's parents, after rescuing his tearful daughter, Mr. Brown said he drove slowly back to Newport, he and Shelly checking both sides of the highway as best they could in the dark. No Brooke.

An all-out search was eventually mounted, but not until almost nine-thirty that night.

Logan pulled a piece of blank paper out of the scanner and drew a rough map of Highway 20 from Shelly's approximate location to the gas station, noting all the salient points and times—when and where Shelly's car broke down up to and including the area the search party covered.

Logan checked the physical evidence tab, but it was empty. No items were listed because there was no crime scene, no trace left by her killer, and no body, so DNA testing was not an option, either.

Only one name was behind the suspects tab. Dylan Cameron Scarth. The boyfriend. Born in 1988 in Siletz—that would make him thirty-six now. Twenty at the time of Brooke's disappearance. There were several interviews, all thorough and in one case, blatantly bigoted. In most of the reports, Dylan was listed as 'Indian' but in the last one the detective asked if he always dated white girls. Dylan had declined to answer.

Logan was surprised that question wasn't edited out.

Logan looked at the small photo stapled to the top, right corner of the first interview. Fair-skinned with short, straight black hair, Dylan stood in front of a sheep pen, with a black and white border collie at his side. No beard, tattoos or other identifying features. The snapshot must have been taken at his ranch. The day the picture was taken must have been warm because the sun was bright, his jacket was open, he wore no hat, and a pair of work gloves stuck out of one pocket. He was not smiling, but neither was he scowling. Just staring straight at the camera.

In all of the interviews, Dylan stuck to his story, and it always checked out. He and the neighbor had ongoing issues, but the neighbor verified the time of the incident and Dylan's arrival to collect his sheep. He managed to free the tangled ewe by cutting the barbed wire. The neighbor had even watched him patch up the injured animal before allowing his dog to herd it home.

No one had seen Dylan after that, but neither had he been spotted anywhere on Highway 20. By the time the police got to his house to question him, it was almost ten o'clock. They rousted him out of bed but had no reason to arrest him. One officer noted that the engine on his truck was cool, so if he had been out earlier, he'd been home for at least thirty minutes. That still left a gap of time when Dylan could not account for his whereabouts.

Logan opened Google maps. Drivetime from Dylan's ranch to the stretch of Highway 20 near the Pac Pride was only fifteen to twenty minutes. That didn't prove anything. A lot could happen between six-thirty and nine-thirty. And the human remains they found had been buried in Siletz, not far from Dylan's ranch.

Homicide detectives kept the case open and active for several years, but with no new leads, the trail grew cold and there were only occasional entries where law enforcement checked with the family and friends to see if anyone had heard from her.

Until possibly now. Logan sat back in her chair.

She wondered which would be worse. Knowing or not knowing—if knowing meant for sure your daughter was dead, and worse, had been murdered.

Chapter Eighteen

While going through the binders, Logan appreciated the last cold case investigator's filing system. Instead of placing each new document into the binders in absolute chronological order, all of the interviews were organized chronologically by person. She could see how this would help anyone new to the file see if a witness's story changed over time or a family member or friend remembered or discovered additional information or physical evidence. It was a way to catch someone in a lie, but also to decide how best to allocate an investigator's time—who they may want to talk with again or ask questions that hadn't been asked the first time.

She also made a note to herself to see what physical evidence there might be in storage, even if it wasn't recorded in the binder. They may be able to submit or resubmit something for DNA testing in case dental records could not be found.

Vern said DNA could be extracted from remains even after being buried for many years. With the rapid advancement of DNA analysis methods, resubmitting physical evidence for testing was becoming standard practice with cold case units.

He said several homicides had been solved this way, and a few wrongly convicted people had been freed.

Logan shuddered. How horrible to be accused of murder and put in prison for life—or worse yet, on death row—when you were innocent.

Logan was deep into the third binder when Vern's cell phone rang, jolting her out of her concentration. She glanced at the clock. Eleven forty-five.

It was Dr. Sampson. Vern thanked him for returning his call, explained what he needed, and put his phone on speaker.

"Yes," Sampson said, "happy to help. Unfortunately, Dr. Zale passed away shortly after I bought the practice, but I think his widow still lives in town."

"Do you have access to his old files? We're looking for the dental records of one of his patients, a Mrs. Eleanor Riley."

"When was she a patient?"

Vern gave him an approximate range of dates.

"I kept the records of patients who stayed with this office even after Dr. Zale retired. But if she wasn't an active patient of mine, I won't have her records. After a couple of years, I sent all those older files to his home. I'm not sure what happened to them after that. I do have his old landline number. If his widow hasn't moved, it might work. She should know where they are."

Vern jotted down the number, thanked him, disconnected the call, and dialed. An older woman picked up the call. He put it on speaker. Her voice wavered slightly, sounding thin and far away.

"Hello, Mrs. Zale?" Vern asked.

"Yes, this is Mrs. Zale," the woman said. Vern gave Logan a thumbs up. So far so good.

"But if you're selling anything . . . ," she said.

Before she could hang up on him, Vern identified himself as law enforcement and told her generally what they needed.

She said her husband had stored his patients' records in the large crawl space under the house. They didn't have an official basement, but it was large enough to almost stand up straight in.

"He intended to build shelves to get the boxes off the ground—they're just paper banker's boxes—but he became ill before he could and passed away soon after, so that didn't happen, I'm afraid. Due to my own mobility issues, I can't go down there, so I don't know what shape the boxes are in, but you are welcome to come over and go through them. I hope they have what you're looking for. How awful that someone is missing, and her family doesn't know what happened to her . . . what did you say her name was again?"

"Eleanor. Mrs. Eleanor Riley," Vern said. "Why? Did you know her?"

For a few seconds, there was silence. When the widow spoke again, her voice was stronger and clearer. "Not directly, but for several years I worked in Lloyd's office as his receptionist. Eleanor was one of his patients."

They waited, but Mrs. Zale didn't elaborate, so Vern made an appointment for the next morning.

"What was that about?" Logan asked. "It sounded like she had more to say about Eleanor Riley."

Vern nodded. "I think so, too. We'll follow up on that tomorrow in person, but in the meantime, let's go see Brooke's mom."

Chapter Nineteen

Logan quickly reviewed Brooke's file before they left. In 2010, someone had added a note in the family section that her father and older brother had died when their fishing boat had capsized in rough, winter seas.

Logan had suffered losses in her life, but not this many. Victoria Crawford must have been a strong woman, because she somehow survived the triple whammy of losing three family members in as many years.

But two years later, the woman had obtained her Realtor's license. Brooke's sister, Mary, followed suit and in 2015, mother and daughter opened a real estate office together in Depoe Bay. Logan recognized the name. She ran past it every morning—it was almost next door to Pirate Coffee—but she had never been inside.

Twenty minutes later, Vern parallel parked in front of an attractive, one-story building with the name Coastal Crest Realty carved into a large, wooden sign out front. Building and sign were painted Pacific Ocean blue with bright white trim. Current property listings with images, stats, and prices were taped inside of the window on the left side of the entrance.

Vern had to duck so as to not hit his head when they walked in. A small brass ship's bell attached to the top of the door announced their entrance.

On the left was a small waiting area consisting of three chairs, a square coffee table, and a kitschy lighthouse lamp. Along the back wall of the airy space, a good sized conference table with several chairs had been placed under a large picture window with a spectacular view of the rocky bay. To the right of the entryway, the rest of the office had been partitioned into three separate work areas, each with their own desk. Two of them were occupied. One by a slender woman with stylishly cut white hair talking to someone on the phone. The other a bit heavier brunette, bent over some paperwork. Both looked Vern and Logan's way when the bell announced their arrival.

At right angles to the entrance, a cheerful young woman—too young to be either Victoria Crawford or her daughter—sat behind a smaller desk. A brass nameplate said Jocelyn.

Without mentioning the cold case unit specifically, Vern introduced himself as law enforcement and asked if Mrs. Crawford was available.

From the back of the office the older woman finished her call before rising smoothly from a leather executive chair. Logan admired her unhurried stride and comfortable, yet professional attire. A crisp white blouse topped a long, moss-green, wool skirt and low-heeled, leather boots. A wool blazer hung on the back of the chair she'd just vacated.

"I'm Mrs. Crawford," she said, extending her hand, "but please, call me Victoria."

Vern put away his badge and returned her firm shake.

Looking back and forth between Vern and Logan, she said, "How can I help you, today, officers?"

Vern didn't correct her, but looked around the office, "Is there somewhere private we can talk, Mrs. Crawford? We just need a few moments of your time. It won't take long."

"Of course," she said. "Anything to help our local police. And please, just Victoria is fine."

She led them back to the conference table. Victoria sat at one end, giving her guests the better, ocean view that extended down the coast. "This is about as private as we can get, I'm afraid. Can I have Jocelyn bring you anything? I have water, soda, coffee . . ."

Both Vern and Logan declined.

"Okay, so what can I do for you this morning?"

Vern explained. He kept it short, letting her know human remains had been found and they needed Brooke's dental records to see if they were hers.

Victoria froze and for a minute, Logan thought she was going to throw them out like Rosie's father had. But her large, brown eyes brimmed with tears. Logan could see the mom more than the businesswoman now. Only a few fine lines etched her face, but the woman's eyes were full of pain. Logan's own heart hurt for her.

"I'm sorry . . . please excuse me," she said, reaching for a tissue, "but it's just that no one has asked about Brooke in so long." She dabbed her eyes. "Of course, we want to know if those remains are hers, but I've always hoped . . . ," she folded her hands tightly and looked out at the jade-green ocean crashing silently on the rocks below the window.

Logan noticed she no longer wore her wedding ring. She wondered if she had remarried.

Blinking back tears, Victoria rose and got her phone from her desk. The other Realtor in the office started to get up and come over, a questioning look of concern on her face.

"That's okay, Mary. I've got this," Victoria said, waving her daughter to stay where she was. Mary returned to her paperwork, but Logan thought she must still be listening.

If it weren't for Victoria's white hair, mother may have been mistaken for daughter. Not only was she bulkier than her mother, but even from this distance, Mary looked rougher around the edges. Harder in some way Logan could not define.

The family resemblance was there. She had Brooke's broad mouth and blue eyes, but if her hair had ever been a mass of shiny red curls like her sister's, it was now a dull, brown, cut in an ill-defined chin-length style, with only a hint of copper where the sun hit it. Hair and skin looked dull and rough—wind and sun damaged, or maybe she was a heavy drinker. Hard to tell.

Scrolling through her phone's contact list on the way back, Victoria gave Vern the number. "Dr. Lemon has been our family dentist for years. He's in Lincoln City, but worth the drive. He'll have Brooke's records." She remained standing.

Vern and Logan took the hint, and Victoria walked them to the front door.

"You will let me know as soon as you hear anything, right?" she said, almost in a whisper.

Vern promised and Logan nodded. Spontaneously, Logan leaned forward and gave Brooke's mother a short, fierce hug. She didn't trust herself to speak, but she didn't need to. Moms understood.

Amy was about the same age Brooke would be now if she were alive. Even if the dental records were a match, the best this mother could hope for would be to know what happened to her daughter. The worst would be when they told her she'd been murdered. If they didn't get a match, Brooke's mom would be back at square one, wondering where in the world her daughter was and if she was ever coming home. Over and over, hoping for the best, but imagining the worst.

Vern called the dentist from the car. A cheerful recording told them that Dr. Lemon's new office hours were Tuesday through Friday, eight to six, by appointment only. If this was an emergency, please hang up and dial 911. If not, please leave a message at the beep, which he did.

STONE COLD

Logan offered to buy lunch this time, but Vern said he wasn't hungry and had some errands to run, so they parted ways in the parking lot.

Chapter Twenty

The next morning, after she had seen to her and Dixon's breakfast, Logan drove to the courthouse and was in the office by eight. She put the coffee on as usual and placed this morning's sugary carb offering, a gigantic freshly-baked cinnamon roll, on Vern's desk. She had already eaten hers in the car on the way in.

While she waited for the boss, she went through Brooke's file again. She was in the middle of going through Dylan's interviews, when her phone rang. It was Vern.

He sounded awful. With a temperature of 103, he wasn't coming in. Probably just the twenty-four-hour flu, he said, but he didn't want to give Logan whatever he had. He didn't go into his symptoms in graphic detail, but Logan got the drift. She appreciated his staying home. Losing the contents of her digestive system from both ends was not her idea of a good time.

Before he disconnected, Vern told her he had called Dr. Lemon, who verified he still had Brooke's dental records. Since he was out of commission, Vern asked Logan to pick them up and hand-deliver them to the medical examiner's office.

Logan hadn't had the chance to tell Vern she knew Jean, but didn't go into that now, just reassured him she would make sure the records arrived safely and would send him a text as soon as she had accomplished that task.

She didn't know how long it would take Jean to make a determination of whether or not the human remains were a match, but she planned on camping out at her office until she did.

As Logan slipped her jacket back on and grabbed her keys, she asked Vern if he needed anything like medicine or a ride to the doctor's. He thanked her but declined the offer, saying he'd likely be fine soon.

She made a mental note to make a trip to the grocery store anyway for her standard stomach bug care package: chicken broth, Pepto Bismol, ginger ale, and soda crackers. She would strong-arm his address out of him later and drop off his get-well supplies on his porch.

Once a mother, always a mother.

Jean normally only wore her ME hat on Wednesdays, but when Logan called her office in Lincoln City to let her know she'd scored dental records, Jean had her office manager reschedule her last few appointments and said she'd meet Logan in Newport within the hour. Logan was waiting at the door of her office, file in hand, when Jean arrived.

A shiver of excitement ran down Logan's spine. Finally! Something was happening.

Jean barely got the door unlocked before Logan shoved the letter-sized mailing envelope with the dental records inside into her friend's hands.

The look Jean gave her over her shoulder slowed Logan down—a little.

Still excited, Logan sat in the only other chair in Jean's small office and waited while Jean sat at her desk and extracted the manila file folder with color-coded tabs. Without even removing her coat, Jean began going through the file.

Logan took a minute to look around. Desk, chair, filing cabinets. There was nothing about this small room that differentiated it as a medical examiner's office. Jean did her technical work elsewhere.

After what seemed like forever, but was only a few minutes, Jean looked over her readers at Logan and said, "These are good. I should be able to work with these."

"Great!" Logan said. "Can I wait? I mean, the remains are still at the funeral home, right? I can drive you over there now," she volunteered. "Vern's home with the flu and I have all day. I promise to stay out of your way while you compare them."

Jean smiled.

"Whoa there, Sherlock," she said. "Slow down."

She slid the records back inside the mailing envelope, stood and walked around her desk and held the door open for Logan. "Tell Vern I'll call him as soon as I can, but don't hold your breath. I'm just doing a preliminary. I have some training in forensic dentistry, but the bones and these records need to go up to Portland. Birdwell will do an exam and probably call in an expert. It can take a few hours up to six weeks to get an official ID."

Logan's face fell and Jean smiled. "I'm guessing it will be on the shorter end of that estimate, but don't worry, I'll call you right after I call Vern."

Grudgingly, Logan accepted Jean's timeline. It's not like she had a lot of choice.

All the spring had gone out of her step by the time she was back at the courthouse, but when she opened the door to the dungeon to force herself to do some more boring scanning, she spotted something on Vern's desk that made her smile: the thickly-frosted cinnamon roll she brought him this morning.

The thought of biting into that sugary goodness improved her mood immeasurably.

Chapter Twenty-One

Making an executive decision to leave the scanning until later, Logan drove over to Mrs. Zale's house to see if she could make herself useful and find Eleanor Riley's dental records in the boxes stored in the crawl space. It would be nice to have something tangible to show for her work when Vern got back.

When she got to the modest, two-story home, Mrs. Zale invited her in, offering tea or coffee before she got started.

Lifting her thermos up to show her she already had some, Logan thanked the widow, but said she wanted to get started. Remembering Mrs. Zale's hesitation when Vern asked if she knew Eleanor Riley, Logan made a mental note to take the widow up on her offer once she had the dental records in hand. This woman knew something, and Logan wanted to know what.

Mrs. Zale—she did not ask Logan to call her by her first name—led her guest through a simply furnished living room to the back deck, which had stairs leading down to a small, fenced backyard. Pointing to a hand-cut door at the bottom of the stairs to her right, she apologized again for the temporary storage area and said, "That just lifts off. You can lean it against the house while you're in there. Just be sure and put it back when you're done. There's a light switch on your right as you go in. I haven't been down there in ages, so if it doesn't work, I can give you a battery-powered lantern or flashlight, or both."

With that, she went back inside, leaving Logan to it.

With only a little tugging, Logan was able to remove the door and sidestep into the crawl space. Dark and dank, it was pretty much as described. The light switch did work, but only illuminated a few feet beyond the door, so Logan used the small flashlight Ben made her carry in every jacket pocket. Carefully, she stepped across the uneven ground to the haphazardly stacked pile of banker's boxes.

Looking around she saw several large, empty plastic bins. She wondered why the medical records hadn't been stored in those but then remembered Dr. Zale passed away before he could do so. Pulling one of the sturdy containers over to sit on first, she decided to transfer the records from paper to plastic as she went through them. Better late than never. Her father always told her and Rick to leave things better than when they found them if they could.

Using her flashlight to move the files around to check for any living creatures who might have taken up residence in the box before she put her hands in there, Logan gingerly pulled one file at a time, checking the name before placing it in the plastic bin next to her.

Two hours later, Logan had three plastic bins full, and she still hadn't seen any file labeled Eleanor Riley or Mrs. Riley.

Hmmm . . .

Turning off the light and replacing the ersatz door behind her, Logan brushed off her pants and went back upstairs. Mrs. Zale was seated in an upholstered side chair to the right of the fireplace. She looked up when Logan knocked on the sliding glass door and reached over to turn off an old-fashioned tape player, and came over to let Logan in.

"Sorry about that," she said. "I was listening to the latest Louise Penny book. My eyesight isn't what it used to be. I listen to mostly audio books now. Hope you weren't waiting long."

Logan reassured her she had just arrived, and this time took her up on her offer of something hot to drink. The something hot turned out to be chamomile tea, which Logan thought tasted like dirty dishwater, but it was drinkable after she doctored it with a spoon of sugar, followed by a chaser of ginger snap cookies the widow brought with it. They settled on two chairs facing the fireplace.

Mrs. Zale nodded at Logan's empty hands, "So no luck?"

"No, and I looked through every box," Logan said. "And Eleanor Riley's dental records are not in her missing person's file either." She ate another cookie before adding, "Do you have any idea where else I can look?"

Mrs. Zale took a sip of her tea, then placed her cup carefully back onto its saucer.

"As I mentioned before, I handled the front office for a few years—some of them the years Eleanor was my husband's patient."

The older woman stared into the fire as if deciding whether to go on.

"Most of my husband's practice was routine. Fillings, exams, root canals. I'll never forget the first day Mrs. Riley came in. That visit was anything but routine."

"Her husband brought her," she added, with obvious distaste. Staring into the fire, she continued.

"Eleanor was a petite, little thing. She came in pressing a baggie of ice wrapped in a hand towel, covering most of her lower face. Her left eye was swollen shut and turning color. I have a little nursing training, and I knew that meant she'd had that shiner for at least a day already.

"Her husband, resplendent in his police officer's uniform, lowered her lovingly into a seat in the waiting room—said she'd taken a fall down the stairs in their home and cracked a tooth. Could the dentist take a look?

"I took her back right away, of course. When we removed the towel, the full extent of the damage became evident. Half of her mouth was caved in, several teeth were cracked, one missing completely, and a couple of others were loose. In addition, her nose was also swollen with some dried blood and several more bruises were blooming. One on her collarbone and several smaller ones that looked like fingerprints on her neck. She wouldn't let us check the rest of her body, but we should have insisted."

This revelation ignited Logan's fury at the relaxed, confident man they had interviewed a few days ago, with his watercolor paintings of birds and his fake cooperation. He hadn't hesitated for a second when they asked him for his wife's dentist's name. He must have known they wouldn't find her dental records, but how?

"Did your husband report her injuries?" Logan asked, halfway knowing the answer before she asked.

"Yes," she said. "Albert was a good man. He did the right thing, but as far as we know, no one ever followed up. At least no one ever contacted us about it." Here her voice lowered to almost a whisper. "Mrs. Riley came in several times after that, each time brought in by her husband . . . Eleanor Riley had a lot of falls."

Logan thanked Mrs. Zale for her time, and silently, for her candor. At the door, the older woman turned to her and said, "I hope you find her records. That man deserves to go to prison for what he did to that lovely woman."

Chapter Twenty-Two

When Logan got back to the office, she pulled out her laptop to write a report for Vern on what Mrs. Zale had shared with her about Eleanor Riley's injuries. Just the thought of Riley's phony 'Mr. Nice Guy' persona made her furious. He sat right there and pretended to cooperate with them, knowing damn well evidence of the beatings he'd given his wife would never be found. Whether he somehow managed to bury them or had a cop buddy on the inside remove Eleanor's incriminating dental records from her missing person's file, they were gone.

She wondered if the new Mrs. Riley was also being abused by her husband. If she was, he had gotten a lot better at it, which is what most successful criminals do—get better at what they do and at not getting caught.

Logan set her jaw, more determined than ever to wipe the confident smirk off this slimeball's face.

Stabbing the keys on her keyboard, she almost didn't hear her cell phone buzz. It had been on vibrate while she was visiting with Mrs. Zale.

It was Jean. She called to let Logan know she was sending the human remains up to the ME in Portland, Cyndi Birdwell, along with the dental records for verification of her preliminary findings. Knowing Vern was out sick, she notified him by email, then called Logan to give her a heads-up.

Logan was disappointed. She wanted to nail this bastard yesterday. Officer Riley had killed his wife, and Logan couldn't wait to prove it.

If they could not locate the dental records, maybe they could try DNA. Logan didn't know exactly how that worked, but she knew it had to do with finding living relatives whose DNA might match what was recovered from the bones.

"I know you and Vern wanted results ASAP and this will take a little longer," Jean said, interrupting Logan's thoughts. "but we want to get it right; 80 percent confidence won't cut it in court if you get that far. Once Cyndi verifies my preliminary findings, she'll pull in Nici."

"Nici?" Logan asked.

"Oregon State Forensic Anthropologist, Nici Vance," Jean said. "She has the equipment and expertise to analyze the skull fracture. Her testimony will bump it up to 95 percent and give our guys the ammunition they need to pursue this as a probable homicide."

Feeling cautiously optimistic, Logan said she'd keep her phone charged. As she tapped the screen to disconnect, she saw a text from Vern, thanking her for the care package she'd left on his porch. He was feeling a bit better and hoped to be able to come in tomorrow. She texted back a thumbs up and said she'd leave her report on his desk as soon as she finished it.

***

The next day, Jean called and said she needed to catch up with patients today, so wouldn't make it to Pirate's this morning. The Cormorant Coffee Crew may have been down a member, but Sam and Logan managed to eat enough for all three of them before going their separate ways.

STONE COLD

Today was a relatively slow news day, so Sam was taking the morning off to spend some time with her daughter, whose new passion was art.

"I can hold my own in fingerpainting," Sam said. "It's when she gets old enough to figure out that my green blobs look nothing like trees that I'm in trouble."

Logan laughed. She had several of Sam and Magnolia's abstract art pieces on her refrigerator at home.

Sam was covering the story of the human remains found out in Siletz, so when they got to the parking lot, Sam reminded Logan to keep her in the loop as soon as there was any news she could print. "You know Jean, sister-in-law or not, she won't tell me anything."

Logan promised. Now that she was working cold cases, she knew this would become a more frequent request, but she didn't think it would be a problem. Sam always pushed hard for the story but knew where the line was. And in spite of the fact that Sam had honed her skills in the crucible of state politics in Olympia, she wasn't about to burn a source—or a friendship—just to get the story. Logan respected that.

Chapter Twenty-Three

Vern was already at his desk when Logan got to the office. He'd made the coffee this time and was reading the report she'd left on his desk. Logan handed him his morning sustenance, a small ginger scone, apologizing for the meager offering as she did. "Kathy said this was your best option given your recent gastrointestinal adventures."

He thanked her anyway. While nibbling on his scone, he had her tell him all about her afternoon with Mrs. Zale, even though he'd just read her report.

They spent the next hour deciding next steps while they were waiting to hear from Jean or Birdwell, the Portland ME. There wasn't much more they could do on any of the missing person's files until the remains were identified, so Vern put Logan back on scanning.

A few minutes later, he stood up and refilled his coffee. Instead of going back to his desk, he started toward the door, "I hate sitting on my hands. I'm going to go talk to Monson, see if he remembers anything about Riley from back in the day."

Logan nodded. She was glad Vern wasn't afraid to cross the blue line if it was required. He wanted to nail Riley, too.

Interrupted only by a short lunch, Logan was still at her desk later that afternoon when the phone rang. This time it was the landline, which Logan had never heard ring before. She could hear Vern down the hall, shooting the bull with somebody. She wasn't sure she should answer it, so she let it go to voicemail. After three rings, the recording started.

"Vern, this is Cyndi. Jean sent me your Jane Doe along with some dental records. Said you were waiting on it, so I came in early and took a look."

Vern came in and when he heard Cyndi's voice he was across the room in two long strides, snatching the phone out of its cradle.

"Cyndi, hi," he said, putting it on speaker so Logan could hear. "Thanks for getting back to me so quickly. What have you got?"

"Got a match, Vern," she said.

A spike of excitement ran up Logan's spine, but she forced herself to keep her butt in her chair and listen. She did take notes.

Birdwell's voice took on a professional tone as she briskly listed her findings.

"Ante and post-mortem x-rays are identical—same alignment, spacing, root structure. Wisdom teeth—at least the one I've got here on this jaw—haven't erupted yet. Unless you have another young missing girl between sixteen and twenty who had the exact same dental work done, I'm looking at Brooke Louise Crawford."

"Thanks, Cyndi," Vern said.

"I hope to have even better news for you soon," she added. "Nici's in town testifying on another case. Said she'd take a look at the skull fracture, see if she can make any definitive conclusions about cause of death. I have an idea from the indented nature of the fracture, but I'd like her to take a closer look before I put my two cents in."

"Thanks again, Cyndi, and thank Nici for me, too." Vern said. "I owe her one—and you. Maybe dinner next time I'm in town."

"I'm in, but only if it's Jake's," Cyndi said. "They make the best Kettle One martini in town."

Vern agreed and said he'd be in touch.

Sounded like a date, Logan thought and wondered about her new boss's social life. He hadn't mentioned being married or divorced and she didn't think he was living with anyone. Her match-making antennae went up. But maybe he liked living alone. He did have Rocket for company.

She didn't have much time to contemplate Vern's love life because after he hung up with Cyndi, he spun his chair around to the whiteboard and erased it. With a black marker he got from the metal tray, he wrote Brooke's name at the top of the board.

Next, he scooped up his cell phone from his desk and dialed.

"Now for the hard part," he said, in a more somber tone, pulling on his jacket, making sure his keys were in the pocket.

Maybe it was the fluorescent lighting in the dungeon, but Vern's face looked drawn, like he had aged a few years in the past few seconds.

Logan glanced at her own phone. It was almost two-thirty. She shifted her weight, impatient to go and get this over with.

One more ring and someone picked up. Logan recognized the voice.

"Coastal Crest Realty!" the cheerful young woman said, "How can we help you find your dream home today?"

Logan wished that was what they were calling for.

Vern identified himself and asked if Mrs. Crawford was in. The receptionist, whose name Logan remembered was Jocelyn, said both Mrs. Crawford and her daughter, Mary, were out of the office. Mary was showing houses to a couple who had just moved to the area—a beautiful property overlooking Depoe

Bay had come on the market recently—and Mrs. Crawford had an errand to run, but she believed she was going home after that. Did they want her to try to reach her on her cell or leave a message for her?

Vern thanked her but said no, he would try back tomorrow.

Flipping open Brooke's binder, he jotted the home address down on a sticky note and handed it to Logan to plug into her GPS.

"Might as well get this over with," he said.

Logan nodded grimly and followed him out to the parking lot. They still had to meet with the major crimes team later this afternoon. This was going to be a very long day.

Chapter Twenty-Four

Thankfully, Vern wasn't in a talkative mood as they drove the twenty minutes north to Depoe Bay. Logan occupied her time looking out of the windshield, searching for glimpses of the ocean above the houses and trees. At Beverly Beach, the view broke wide open. Brilliant sunlight danced across the Pacific, bejeweling the surface of the dark blue water before it turned into smooth jade waves rolling onto the empty stretch of beach.

As they grew closer to their destination, Vern gave her some background information on the Crawford family. Some of it Logan already knew, some of it was new.

Two years after Brooke went missing, her father, Will Crawford, and her two brothers, Jason and Charlie, died when their fishing vessel capsized not far from shore. That left just Brooke's mother and sister as the sole survivors.

"Not sure of the exact order of events, but she sold the old house, built this one for her and her daughter and opened Coastal Crest Realty," Vern said.

He put on his blinker to turn left onto a narrow, paved side street. "Here we are."

Logan was not looking forward to this. Playing the violin, teaching public school, running a computer software training company—none of her previous occupations prepared her for notifying a family that their loved one was dead.

Descending down and around a steep, curving street, Vern slowed to check the addresses located on the side of garage doors and on mailboxes until he came to 729 Seagull Drive, which looked at first glance, with its matching driveways and garage doors, like a high-end duplex.

Which it kind of was. The only difference was this half-acre lot contained one large house, albeit with two separate entrances.

The house was designed for dual occupancy with side-by-side connected units—bedrooms, bathroom, and garage downstairs, kitchen, living area and half baths upstairs. Both mother and daughter had ocean views.

Very egalitarian. If it was just her and Amy left standing, Logan could envision building something like this for the two of them. They had always gotten along, and she could help raise Ian. Maybe when they were old and gray and their men had kicked the bucket. Men did tend to die before their wives, and Logan was all for breaking tradition if it met everyone's needs. Why not? Who said every family was husband, wife, dog, and 2.5 children?

Logan didn't know what the resale value of this property would be, but Victoria, being a savvy Realtor, probably had it designed so it could be sold separately if desired.

Vern and Logan parked in the driveway and walked up the steps to the main entrance on the left. Logan did the honors. The doorbell chime was something vaguely Gregorian or maybe Westminster Abbey, Big Ben, or something with sonorous and stately bells.

A perfectly groomed and attired Victoria Crawford answered the door. Gray slacks and a pale pink blouse tucked in, black leather belt and shoes.

"Please, come in," she said, standing aside. Vern did not have to duck to get through this vaulted doorway.

The living room was tastefully decorated in creams, taupes, and a few touches of Pacific Ocean blues. A large cast—or replica—of some kind of prehistoric fossil reigned over the large, stone fireplace and on the glossy cedar mantle were chunks of baseball size agates, smooth, black river rocks with white stripes, and a lifelike carved wooden pelican, a fish in its beak. Low, gas flames flickered in the fireplace. A thick, Persian rug—or again, it could have been a replica—in faded ivory, beige, and blue anchored a saddle-leather couch, leaving acres of gleaming hardwood floors all around.

Wow. If this woman hadn't won the lottery, she sure knew how to pull together a luxurious room on a budget.

Victoria offered them a seat on the buttery soft leather sofa and took a seat opposite them in a graceful rocking chair that fit her perfectly. Mary, Logan noticed, was already there, seated in a matching chair. End tables with Tiffany-style lamps bookended the sofa and several books lay on the gleaming glass surface in front of them: coffee table books—whale watching, owls, logging.

Logan wondered if anyone had read them or if they were just for decoration.

This time, Victoria did not ask if they wanted anything.

Vern cleared his throat but got right to it.

"Mrs. Crawford," he said, then turned and included Mary with a nod. "Mary. We obtained Brooke's dental records from Dr. Lemon, and we have received positive identification that the human remains found last week in Siletz are those of your daughter—and sister—Brooke."

Logan watched the two women's reactions to this news.

The mother looked both relieved and stricken at the same time. Her arm shot out automatically to reach for the comfort of her daughter's hand.

"Are you sure?" she asked weakly. "There's no doubt?"

While Vern answered Victoria, Logan was free to observe Mary. Mary took her mother's hand but did not otherwise get up to comfort her. Her face remained stoic, as if the information had not yet penetrated. Or was it because she was not surprised? That's what struck Logan. It was almost as if Mary had been expecting this news.

Straightening her spine, Victoria Crawford gave Mary's hand one last squeeze. She clasped her hands together tightly in her lap.

"What are the next steps?" she asked. "When can I get my daughter back?"

Logan was surprised she didn't ask what happened—if they knew how her daughter died.

"As soon as the final forensics are completed," Vern said.

"What do you mean completed?" Victoria asked. "This is my daughter and we will want to have her properly buried . . . or cremated . . . we've never talked about the details."

Mary seemed to come to life at this point. "Don't worry, Mom, we can work all that out. You don't have to decide right this minute." She turned to Vern and said, "How long will it take to bring my sister home?"

Vern shook his head. Logan could tell whatever he said next would destroy what little peace this devastated family had left. But they needed to know.

"I can't give you exact details at this time, but during the forensic examination of Brooke's remains, it was determined that her death was not an accident. We will get your daughter back to you as soon as possible, but this is now a homicide investigation, and we'll need to examine her remains thoroughly to find and hold whomever was responsible for her death accountable." He waited for this news to sink in. "I'm sure you want that, right?"

"Homicide?" Victoria asked, her voice rising in volume as the realization took hold. "What? Are you saying Brooke was murdered?!"

"I am saying that the forensic evidence points to that. This is an active homicide investigation, now, so I can't give you the details, but I promise to give you the full report as soon as I can."

Chapter Twenty-Five

With the notification done, Logan and Vern headed back to the office. As they were passing Walmart on the way into town, Vern got a call from Monson. The sheriff's deputy detective's deep voice boomed out through the car's speakers. Vern quickly turned the volume down to below deafening.

Now that they had a positive ID on the remains, Monson said he wanted Vern to take the lead, as he and Logan were the most familiar with the cold case file. He also said he'd order lunch in and would meet them in the conference room in an hour—give the rest of the team time to get there.

Logan already respected Monson, but she liked him the better, now, for two reasons. One, he wasn't pawning the lunch order off on an assistant, and two, he wasn't being territorial over jurisdiction or who would take lead.

As they parked and walked into the courthouse, Logan could feel the change of energy in the air. She quickened her pace to keep up with Vern's long strides.

When they got into the office, working smoothly together, they added Cyndi Birdwell's full report, which she had faxed over this morning, to what was now Brooke Louise Crawford's active murder book. After copying and assembling six more binders, they joined the others who were already seated around the table. Logan recognized a couple of the faces, but most were new to her. She distributed the binders.

"If you want something besides pineapple or anchovies on your pizza, you'd better grab a slice now," a heavy-set uniformed officer advised, lifting a hot slice of pizza out of one of the boxes. He gestured with it to a small table against the wall. "Sodas are over there—or there's coffee."

From here, Logan couldn't tell which department the officer was from. Her mouth watered as she watched him catch a long string of mozzarella and place it back onto his pizza before taking a big bite. Logan was fine with both pineapple and anchovies, so she reached for the nearest box and slid three slices onto a paper plate. They seem to have ordered plenty, so she wasn't worried about being shy.

While they were eating, Vern introduced Logan as the newest member of the cold case unit, not specifying her background. He did say she was a volunteer, but that in itself would not prejudice any law enforcement against her as the last person to fill her shoes was a retired homicide detective. For all they knew, she was Harry Bosch.

FBI rep, Barbara Bianchi, recognized her from the other morning where they'd met at the site where the remains were recovered and waved hello. Curtis, the OSP officer nodded, and Monson welcomed her to the team. Detective Grant, Monson's partner—younger, buffer, and more neatly dressed— having finished his pizza—was over at the other side of the room hooking up the technology. He gave a quick salute in greeting and got back to work. Gary Smythe was the Lincoln PD detective with the pizza eating skills. He said the Newport PD representative, Detective Rex Williams, was out on a call, but would join them as soon as he could.

Someone had thought to bring a large, lined trash can into the room, so clean up was quick and easy. After everyone refilled coffee mugs or grabbed another soda, they assembled at the long rectangular table in front of a large white board next to the wall monitor and waited for Vern. Logan sat at the end of the table. She was glad to be a member of the team but knew when to keep quiet. Time to listen and learn.

The room came supplied with dry-erase markers and erasers. The two Newport detectives entered, apologized for being late, and took seats.

Taking one of the markers, Vern wrote Brooke's name at the top of the whiteboard, saying her whole name out loud as he did so, bringing them up to speed, telling them who this victim was. Good kid. Good grades. Good friend. Nice family. Highland dancer. A girl with a future.

". . . sixteen-year-old Brooke Crawford was murdered and dumped in the boonies," he said, "Sixteen . . ."

He swallowed and his prominent Adam's apple bobbed. "As you know, technically I only have you for five days. Five days to find this girl's killer. Unless we make significant progress, on day six, you all go back to your regular departments, and we may never find him or her. Normally those five days are more of a guideline than a rule, but this time, due to budget constraints, they tell me they're going to hold the line. So we're going to hit this hard—look at every person in Brooke's life—dig out anybody we missed last time. This time we'll know we're looking for her killer. Somebody must know something."

Having everyone open their binders, Vern went over the interviews he and Logan had already conducted and had the group brainstorm on what leads may not have been followed up on last time and what other ground needed to be gone over again.

"Gary, you've got phone records," he said. "Write the paper, we'll get it signed. We want to know who she talked to or messaged the last few weeks of her life. Any unusual patterns, unknown players."

Curtis raised his pen like he was in class and asked, "But since she's dead, there's no expectation of privacy, right? We can just go through her phone."

"True," Vern said. "But we want to dot our i's and cross our t's in case this goes to court. Don't want to give the defense any excuse to throw out whatever we find."

"Ahh, got it," Curtis said.

Vern moved on.

"Barb, it's unlikely to be a stranger, but check your databases for any serial killers operating in the area around that time. Focus on the date she went missing and the weeks after, even. He could have abducted her, kept her, then gotten rid of her body later when he got tired of whatever sick game he was playing."

"On it," Barb said.

Monson knew Nici Vance, the forensic anthropologist, so Vern assigned him to follow up on that end. "Get as much detail as possible. What can she attest to on the witness stand if we ever catch this guy? Any additional detail about what caused the blunt force trauma that cracked the skull. Type of weapon? Any other leads to follow from the human remains."

"Also, somebody—Grant—dig up an old map of the area to see what that lot along the Siletz River looked like back in 2008—roads in and out. Who owned it? Had it been subdivided into lots yet? Any nearby houses—possible witnesses who might be alive still and in the area. Also, since you're our resident techie, can you coordinate putting timelines together, turning all the salient paper into PowerPoint or whatever everyone can see best up there?" He jerked his thumb at the large wall monitor.

"No problem," Grant said.

"Logan and I will keep on the interviews. Meet back here tomorrow at 5:00 p.m. unless you hear from me otherwise."

Chapter Twenty-Six

For the rest of the afternoon, Vern and Logan hunkered down in the office making their plan of attack. Everyone needed to be reinterviewed. It quickly became obvious they would never get through them all if they plodded through the list one at a time, so Vern told Logan she would be conducting some of the interviews on her own.

Logan felt equal parts excited and terrified, but Vern promised he would help her prepare questions before she went out on each interview and debrief in the office before she wrote up her reports to share with the rest of the team. Piece of cake.

Brooke's classmates, of course, would no longer be students at Newport High, but many of her teachers and other staff members might still be around, so Vern called the principal to arrange for two spaces in which to interview anyone who had known Brooke or had been previously interviewed in 2008.

Mr. Dawson, the current principal, turned out to have been the vice principal when Brooke went missing and was anxious to help when he found out the remains that had been discovered out in Siletz were hers. He also agreed to keep that information to himself for now and offered the use of his office for the morning and a small room adjacent to the library that used to be the psychologist's office—back when the school district still had the money to fund that position.

Vern thanked Dawson and said they would be there by nine o'clock.

Next, he tried the last phone number listed for Brooke's friend, Shelly. They weren't surprised when it didn't go through. Vern called Gary Smythe, the Lincoln City detective working on Brooke's phone records and had him add getting Shelly's current phone and address—if she was still in the area—to his to-do list.

"Yeah, that's Michelle, Michelle with two l's," he said. "Okay, thanks, see you tomorrow."

Vern said there was one interview that couldn't wait until tomorrow. He wanted to do Dylan Scarth, the boyfriend, today, before he heard about the identification on the news. This would also give Logan one more opportunity to observe how an interview was done before flying solo tomorrow.

***

It was close to four o'clock when they turned onto Highway 20 heading east, not far from where Brooke was last seen walking west toward the Toledo gas station. The sun was already halfway to the horizon and the afternoon light was soft.

Fifteen minutes later, following the signs to Riverview Luxury Homes, they turned left off of Highway 20 onto the Siletz Highway, also known as Highway 229. Logan couldn't see the lot where Brooke's remains had been found but wondered if the crime scene tape was still up or if the owner had been allowed to resume excavation and construction of his home.

Immediately after passing the last street in the Riverview subdivision, the smooth private road quickly devolved into a narrow, winding, gravel track whose many potholes tested Vern's tires and Logan's back fillings. A few minutes later, they turned in front of a small, metal sign mounted on a fence post indicating the entrance to Scarth Sheep Ranch. In smaller print below someone had added '& Sheep Dog Training' in Sharpie.

There was a simple gate, unlocked, which Logan got out and opened, then closed behind Vern's car after he turned in. She hiked up to meet him after he parked in the large, gravel space in front of a modest two-story farmhouse. Barns and outbuildings were not far away on their right. Open pasture ran along the Siletz River behind the house. It was impossible to tell where Dylan's property ended and his neighbors' began as no other homes were visible on either side of the river.

Vern unfolded himself from his truck and they walked up to the house, but before they could step onto the porch, a man's voice called out from the barn. "Be right with you, just wrapping up here."

They waited for the man to emerge from the dark recesses. He soon did, wiping his hands on a red rag, a black and white border collie trotting by his side.

Dylan Scarth looked very much like the photo of him Logan had seen attached to the report of his original interviews in Brooke's missing person's book—murder book, now, she reminded herself.

Not much taller than she was, maybe 5'9", slightly stoop shouldered, long face, straight black hair, interspersed with only a few streaks of gray. Large ears close to his head. High cheekbones spoke to his Native American heritage, pale skin to the whites on his family tree. Practical ranch clothes, jeans and boots. Hat hair but no hat. She watched as he approached them, a curious but not overly concerned look in his eyes.

He gave his dog a silent signal which sent the intense black-and-white dog immediately up onto the porch, where it turned and lay down, relaxed but alert, head up, watching their every move with sharp eyes that looked like two shiny black marbles.

Chapter Twenty-Seven

"What can I do for you?" the man asked, "If you're here for puppies I don't have any right now, but I've got two I'm bringing along from Scout's last litter," he said, nodding toward the porch. "If you give me your contact information I'll let you know if either of them don't make the cut. I assume you're looking for a pet, not a working dog?"

Logan had to admit she and Vern didn't look like sheep ranchers.

"Not looking for a dog at all," Vern said. "I'm Vern Lambert and this is Logan McKenna. We're from the cold case unit in Newport and we need to speak with you concerning Brooke Crawford. Is there somewhere we can talk?"

Dylan took half a step back as if he'd been punched. He looked back and forth between his two visitors.

"What's this about?" he asked. "Why are you asking about Brooke? She's been gone for sixteen years."

Then it dawned on him.

"You found her," he said.

A series of emotions Logan could not interpret flitted across Dylan's face.

"Yes," Vern said. "You may have heard about the human remains discovered at one of the Riverview excavation sites. Those remains have now been positively identified as those of Brooke Louise Crawford."

He did not say that Brooke had been murdered.

Dylan sank onto the porch steps next to his dog, who whimpered and nuzzled his master's neck, laying her head on his thigh.

Vern gave the man some time, while both he and Logan observed him closely.

Finally, Dylan stood. "You might as well come into the house. We can talk in here."

They followed him inside. The dog stayed on the porch.

Dylan flipped on a light switch, but it still took Logan's eyes a minute to adjust to the darker interior. Immediately to their left, a narrow set of stairs led to what she assumed was the second floor.

They were standing in a comfortably furnished living area. Couch, two chairs all arranged around a coffee table in front of a wood burning fireplace. Straight ahead through an open archway she could see through to a large farm kitchen. To their right, part of the porch, a corner of the barn, and Vern's car were visible out of a small picture window. No TV that Logan could see.

Dylan gave them the couch, poked at the fire to get it going, added a log from a pile in a box behind one of the chairs.

"I've got coffee," he said.

"Coffee would be fine if you've already got some made," Vern said.

"If it's no trouble," Logan said. "Thanks."

"Keurig," Dylan said. "It'll just take a minute." He disappeared into the kitchen and came back a few minutes later with two steaming mugs which he placed on the coffee table in front of Logan and Vern, then went back in to get his own. He returned with a third mug, sugar and canned milk.

"Don't have any cream," he said, sitting in one of the chairs next to the fire.

"Okay," he said, "what can you tell me? When you say remains were found, what does that mean exactly?"

"I'll get to that in a minute," Vern said, "but right now, I need you to tell us about your relationship with Brooke and what you remember about the day she went missing." He pulled out his phone and laid it face up next to his coffee. "You don't mind if we record this, do you? I'm terrible at taking notes."

"You have all that. I gave multiple interviews sixteen years ago. There must be copies of those somewhere. Why do you need for me to go over it all again? The last thing I want to do is dredge up that awful time, those memories," he said. "And yes, I do mind," he said, eyeing the phone, looking less and less friendly.

As if remembering something, he straightened up in his chair and said, "Have you notified her mother? Do you know if they've made arrangements for a funeral or memorial service or . . . I need to call them." He pulled his own phone out of his pocket, but Vern signaled for him to put it down.

"The family has been notified, Mr. Scarth," Vern said. "We are now talking to everyone who knew Brooke, starting with those closest to her, which includes you, her fiancé."

Dylan looked confused and a look of suspicion came into his eyes, "Why? I appreciate you telling me you found her, but you still haven't said how she died or how her remains wound up out here when the last time anyone saw her she was walking on Highway 20 toward Toledo to get gas? What aren't you telling me?"

Logan was glad she didn't have to field this question.

"Mr. Scarth," Vern said, "for reasons I cannot discuss at this time, this is now an active homicide investigation. We need everyone's cooperation to determine what happened to your fiancée that night. We're talking with everyone, not just you."

Dylan blinked, taking that in, and stood, phone in hand.

"You need to leave," he said. "I told the police everything I knew back then. Over and over. So many times. They obviously thought I had something to do with her disappearance then and it looks like you're trying to do it again." He shook his head sadly, looking older and more tired.

"Some things never change," he said to no one in particular..

"So unless you're going to arrest me," he said, "I'd like you to leave. And do your jobs. Find out who killed my Brooke."

"I know this is shocking news," Vern said, taking his time to walk to the door. "We'll see ourselves out, but we will be back. As I said, we're talking with everyone who knew Brooke. We will have this conversation at some point."

Scout gave them a low growl as they passed her on the porch but didn't break her down stay. As they walked to the car, Dylan's voice drifted out the front door, "Mrs. Crawford, it's me, Dylan," he said, "I am so sorry. I just heard . . ."

Chapter Twenty-Eight

On the drive over to Newport High School—Vern drove—Logan checked the bell schedule the principal had sent them. A nine o'clock arrival got them there right at the end of first period, but before students flooded the halls to get to their next class at 9:12 a.m.

As they walked up to the entrance and into the building, Logan smiled. Every high school had similar sights, sounds, and smells. She could have been walking into her own high school back in Jasper, California back in the . . . nineties? Okay, now she felt old.

Rows of large windows marched across the front of the building, topping neat lines of brick. Occasionally, a teacher's voice drifted out of an open door or a student late to class hustled by, footsteps echoing on the hard floor—linoleum or tile—something easily mopped. Just hearing those metal lockers that lined the halls clang open and shut brought back memories.

Bulletin boards with various announcements. Trophy cases. School colors everywhere. A mascot with some fierce name to inflict terror into the hearts of rival schools' sports teams. In this, Newport High differed from the norm. Their mascot was the Cubs. Not exactly fear inducing.

When they reached the principal's office, a petite woman with chin-length, cottony white hair waved them over to her desk. "Logan!" she said, getting up to hug her.

Holding her at arms' length, the woman said, "Let me get a good look at you. You look great! Earl said you were coming. What are you—a cop now?"

Logan returned her hug and laughed, explaining her volunteer status with the cold case unit. "Vern's the only real cop around here, I'm just helping out. Vern, this is Cheryl Meece. We met when I did some math tutoring here a couple of years ago. Cheryl runs this place."

"Earl," Cheryl called back over her shoulder toward the principal's office, "They're here!" Turning back to Logan she said. "Anything we can do to help. Brooke was a great kid. I'm glad they found her so her mother can get some closure, but it's still not the kind of news any mother wants to hear. We always hoped she'd turn up someplace—alive. But Brooke wasn't a runaway type—we knew it would end up like this. Still, the poor family . . ."

Sitting back down as Principal Earl Dawson came out of his office, briefcase in one hand, cane in the other. Almost as tall as Vern, his hair had gone a grizzled gray, but his blue eyes were sharp, and he looked very fit for his age. Logan put him somewhere in his sixties. He limped over to shake their hands.

"Pickleball," he explained, tapping his leg with his cane. I don't know who said seniors should switch to pickleball instead of tennis because it's less prone to injury. We've had three of our team members out with sprained somethings—backs and knees—this year already. Time to take up Scrabble."

He pointed with his cane to another office nearby. "My VP's out today, so I'll be in there if you need me. Just give Cheryl your list and she'll call people back for you. We can pull teachers out of class as you need them—we got a rover to cover." He turned to Cheryl, "Did we get Peterson?"

"Yep," she said. "Full day."

"Good," he said, making his way into the other office. "Peterson's reliable. Don't forget to forward my calls."

Cheryl rolled her eyes and sat back down at her desk.

"Okay, who do you want first?"

Vern handed her the two lists of faculty and staff they wanted to see. She told Vern to go on into Earl's office, pulled up the first name on her computer, and pointed down the hall for Logan.

"I put you in your old tutoring room," she said. "Your coffee maker's still there, so I made you a fresh pot." Making sure Vern was out of earshot, she whispered, "and you might find something sweet for you on your desk, too."

Logan did a silent happy dance and mouthing a thank you, headed toward her home-away-from-home for the next few hours.

***

Logan got off to a halting start, but after the first few interviews, she felt a lot more comfortable; less like an imposter and more like she knew what she was doing. No one had any problem being recorded and all were anxious to help. So far she had ticked off the first four people on her list: a lunch lady, the librarian, and a couple of faculty members. Several had moved away, but she'd talked with Brooke's English and history teachers and after lunch she would have Cheryl send down Mr. Salazar, the biology teacher and the custodian, Mr. Jeffers. Jeffers had been the school custodian for thirty-two years.

Wow. That was impressive. Logan couldn't imagine doing one job for that long.

Lunch choices were still heavily stacked with hamburgers and pizzas, but there was a salad bar and some fresh fruit. The ubiquitous, sad-looking paper cups of celery, baby carrots, and fresh broccoli florets rounded out her options. No one ever ate those, but it made school administrators feel better to check that nutrition box.

Logan remembered real, hot meals made in a full-fledged kitchen by her lunch ladies growing up. Pot roast, lasagna, scalloped potatoes and green beans . . . oh well. She picked up a cheeseburger and fries and joined Vern at his table, where he had started in on a couple of slices of pizza and salad. Drenched as it was with ranch dressing and covered in cheese and croutons, the salad didn't look half bad.

Their lives now ruled by the bell like all of the acne-scarred inmates sharing the cafeteria with them, they were back at it at 12:49 p.m.

Chapter Twenty-Nine

Frank Salazar knocked on the open door jam and Logan waved him in.

She glanced at her notes. Frank taught biology. In his mid-fifties, he'd been teaching that and other science classes at Newport High for the last twenty years, most of them as the head of the department. Squat and solid in stature, his biceps and quads filled out his khakis and navy blue polo shirt. A little extra padding around the middle, but not much. He looked very much like one of the detectives back at the courthouse.

Defying all the gel he used, his straight, black hair was side parted and cut short. He lowered himself into the chair across from Logan, placing his hands on his thighs and said, "Peterson's covering my labs, so you've got me as long as you need me. How can I help?"

Over the next half-hour, Logan established that Brooke had been his student both sophomore and junior years.

"Tell me about Brooke."

"Brooke wasn't super smart, but she was a decent student, and some of my seniors were super dumb."

Logan noted the politically incorrect depiction but ignored it. It wasn't her job to retrain teachers stuck in the fifties. She focused on learning everything she could about Brooke and the social networks at Newport High back in 2008.

"Anyone she was close to? Any friends in your classes?" Logan asked. "Who did she hang with or have lunch with?"

"Brooke got along with everybody but wasn't one of the girls who needed an entourage. She had lunch with her friend, Shelly, and a few times I saw her with her lab partner, Lamar Mangus. They worked on a project together."

"What about extra-curricular activities. Did she belong to any clubs?" Logan asked.

"Not that I know of," he said. "Other than the Scottish dancing, she just attended classes and went home."

"Did Brooke date anyone at the high school that you know of?"

"No," he said. "If you've seen a picture of Brooke, you'll know she could have, but she had a boyfriend already. I assume you know about Dylan."

"Yes, Dylan Scarth. He was somewhat older, wasn't he? Already out of school," Logan said.

She waited, but he didn't volunteer any opinion on their age difference.

"And you're sure she never dated anyone here? No love triangles or jealous boyfriends?"

"That young lady could have had her pick of any of the young men around here," Frank said, "and a lot of them tried to get her attention, but once she hooked up with Dylan, that was it for her."

"What about before that? Any previous boyfriends?"

"Probably," he said, "but I wouldn't know about that—that would have been middle school or something—puppy love crushes, nothing serious."

Logan hadn't anticipated that line of questioning would go anywhere, but she had to turn over every rock.

"Did everyone like Brooke?" she asked. "If she was popular, some girls might have been jealous. Can you think of anyone she ever had trouble with in the time you knew her? Maybe at a school event—a game or a dance?"

"No," he said. "I chaperoned most of the dances back then, along with the vice principal and a few other faculty, and we had the usual testosterone driven fights in boys' bathroom or the parking lot. Our main job was to keep alcohol and drugs out."

"What were the boys' fights about?" she asked. "Any you remember in particular?"

"The usual—girls," he said, "We have our share of cliques—not gangs exactly, but groups that form and reform over the years. Often along racial lines. But teenage boys don't need a reason. We expect them to blow off steam once in a while, but we also don't tolerate it. We usually handled it ourselves with detentions and calls to parents."

Logan paused a split second before asking the next question, "Speaking of crushes, what about faculty? Did Brooke ever have a crush on any of her teachers that you know of? Could she have tried to make her boyfriend jealous by flirting with someone his age?"

"No. I never saw anything like that. And if you're going down that path, it's the wrong path," he said, spearing Logan with a glare, "We all want to help you find out what happened to Brooke, but all it takes is one accusation or even a hint of anything like that and a teacher's life and career are ruined. So don't be throwing around wild questions just to see what you can stir up."

Logan met his gaze calmly. She understood his concern, but she wasn't about to let this guy intimidate her. She stood and shook his hand, "Thank you for your time, Frank, is there anyone else you can think of who would be helpful for us to speak with? Anyone at all, no matter how loosely connected to Brooke?"

Frank Salazar looked at the wall behind Logan's head for a minute. "You'd be best talking with her Scottish dance friends. That's where she spent most of her free time. Her dance teacher sometimes held classes in the gym if it wasn't being used.

"Brooke got along with everyone but didn't hang out much with anyone here at school. I saw her with Shelly at lunch every day and like I said, she worked on a biology project with her lab partner, Lamar, a few afternoons after school when that was due. If she confided anything important, though, it would be to one of her girlfriends, not a shy boy like Lamar."

Logan thanked him again for his time and gave him her contact information. Asked him to call if he thought of anything else to add.

She poured herself another cup of coffee while waiting for her last interview of the day, Mr. Jeffers, the custodian. Her stomach growled and she wished she had something to eat. She'd long since polished off the two old-fashioned donuts Cheryl had left for her this morning. She'd have to wander nonchalantly back into the teachers' lounge and see if there were any left.

Chapter Thirty

Cheryl gave Logan a call to let her know the custodian was coming but would be slightly delayed. Someone had vandalized the boys' bathroom again, and Mr. Jeffers was in the middle of the cleanup job. He would be there as soon as he finished unsticking the toilet paper from the ceiling and successfully unclogged the last toilet.

Fifteen minutes later, looking neat and clean—not a bit like he had just spent the last hour elbows deep into a clogged toilet and mopping up a feces-smeared floor (Cheryl had given her a detailed description of what the monsters did this time), the custodian quietly knocked on the door.

Logan introduced herself and offered him the only other chair in the room. She thanked him for taking time out of his day to help them out.

"Clyde Jeffers," he said, reaching across to shake her hand. "nice to meet you, Ms. McKenna. And we all want to help in any way we can, although I don't know how. We all gave statements back in 2008 when Brooke went missing. Nothing else has happened since then—well, until now."

Mr. Jeffers wore a multi-pocketed canvas shirt neatly tucked into dark work pants held up by a worn, black belt, and thick, rubber-soled shoes. Removing a blue and red Newport Cubs baseball cap, he sat down in the small chair, a large ring of keys attached to his belt loop by a carabiner clip jangling as he did so. His tightly curled black hair was close-cropped and only slightly frosted at the temples. He placed his ball cap on his knee and waited. Large, liquid brown eyes gazed placidly at her out of smooth, almost unlined cocoa skin. Seated, he and Logan were eye to eye. Loose limbed and rangy, his ropy muscles looked like they came from physical work, not working out.

She liked him immediately.

After going over the ground that had been covered before in his 2008 interview, Logan sat back in her chair and sighed. She was tired and she hadn't really gleaned any new information from any of the faculty and staff members she'd spoken with today. The custodian agreed with everyone's assessment that Brooke was a good kid and knew of no trouble she ever got into, love triangles, or rivalries with other girls.

Logan leaned forward in her chair.

"Clyde, I only worked in public education a short time, but I remember my own high school years and my daughter's. I have spoken with other faculty and staff today, but I think you might have a unique perspective. I'll bet you know more of what goes on in this school than anyone, including the principal. Any fights on campus Brooke may have been involved with?"

"We had our share of fights—but no more than other schools. And those were always between the boys. Cops got called once out in the parking lot, but usually we took care of it.

"I don't know if this is helpful, but Brooke did some of her service hours helping me paint the gym that year." He went on to explain, "Every student has to log a certain number of service hours their junior year. Most choose filing in the office or help grading papers, but Brooke wanted something physical. She had a lot of energy," he said. "Couldn't sit still."

Sam's story in the Lincoln Leader with the news that this was now an active homicide case wouldn't be seen by most people in Lincoln County until the physical papers were delivered, but the digital version was already posted. Clyde may or may not have seen it.

She asked and he quietly said yes, he had. Said he read the news online first thing every morning while he had his coffee, before he made his rounds unlocking doors, opening up the school."

"That's a sad thing," he said. "I know you probably can't tell me much, but anything I can do to help you find out who took that young girl's life, I will."

"Thanks, Clyde," Logan said. "What I can tell you is that we're keeping an open mind. A stranger could have abducted her, picked her up on the highway as she was walking to get gas that night. You knew Brooke. In your opinion, would she have accepted a ride from a stranger? Did she ever carry pepper spray?"

He thought for a minute before answering. "Hard to tell what anyone would do, but teenage girls protect each other, and Brooke knew her friend Shelly would be in deep trouble with her folks if she didn't get her mother's car back in time. Shelly was kind of flaky, not as responsible as Brooke. Brooke might take a ride from a stranger if she thought it would get her back to Shelly faster, before her folks realized she'd let the car run out of gas."

"And to answer your other question, I don't know about the pepper spray, but I doubt it. Girls like Brooke know the world's not perfect, but they have no idea how evil it can be."

Logan held his gaze. Jeffers didn't blink. What evil had this man seen? What did he know?

"Brooke was just a kid," he said. "And kids think they can handle whatever little bit of bad might come their way."

He paused.

"So if I were to hazard a guess, I'd say Brooke was a confident young girl who trusted the wrong person, whether it was a stranger who gave her a ride or someone she knew. One thing's for sure, I doubt she had any idea she would die that night."

Chapter Thirty-One

Logan tapped her phone to stop the recording and thanked Mr. Jeffers for his time. She jotted down her contact information for him and asked him to call, message, or email her if he thought of anything else that might be of help. He said he would. If she was going to keep doing this, she really needed some official business cards. She'd have to talk to Vern about getting some or have them made herself.

Emotionally drained from conducting the interviews and looking and listening for any leads they may be able to follow, Logan typed in a few names she wanted to follow up on and powered down her laptop. After emptying and rinsing out the coffee pot in the girls' bathroom across the hall, she gathered up her electronics and walked back to the front.

Vern was still in his borrowed office, finishing up his last interview of the day with Principal Dawson.

Most of the students had exited the building. Fridays were pretty quiet. Cheryl opened the bottom left file drawer in her desk and broke out a Costco-sized bag of M&M's.

"They won't let me keep whiskey, so this will have to do," she said, the bag tilted toward Logan for sharing. Placing her computer on the floor next to her chair, Logan scooped out a handful. "You are my new best friend."

Cheryl reached behind her, retrieving a can of Coke from her mini-cooler, eyebrows raised.

Logan accepted the offering and laughed. "Sugar and caffeine, the two most important food groups."

"The nutrition nazis won't let us have soda or candy in the vending machines anymore so I bring my own."

The two friends sat companionably for a while, munching and sipping their ice cold beverages. Cheryl was the first to speak.

"How'd it go?" Cheryl asked. "Learn anything new?"

Logan swallowed first, then wiped her mouth with a tissue from a box on Cheryl's desk and said, "I need to go home and review it all, but not much. There were a few things I didn't know."

"Like what?"

"Let's see . . . Brooke mainly hung out with Shelly. No extra-curricular activities except her Highland dance competitions. She was friendly with her lab partner, Lamar Mangus, a senior, but she didn't date him or anyone else from here. Everyone knew she was engaged to Dylan Scarth. She was a good student. No love triangles. Oh, and Jeffers mentioned the cops were called out to a parking lot fight once."

"Oh, yeah," Cheryl said. "It's been a while, but I remember that."

"What was the fight about?" Logan asked.

"I don't know if you know anything about Native American culture, but the Siletz tribe has a powwow every August. It's for the tribe but also open to the public. There's food, crafts, vendors. And in the main arena, men and women compete in various traditional dances, make their own costumes, etc. Ever been to a powwow, Logan?"

"Only one," Logan said, "my friends Lisa and Thomas took me to one a few years ago. Lisa was competing. It was amazing. Such a different world."

"Yes, well, one of the shiny, young, new teachers that year decided it would be a good idea to invite some of the members of the Siletz tribe to come out and do an assembly for the students in the gym, share a little local history of the tribe in this area, perform some of the dances. They even had some of the women make fry bread in big soup pots in the kitchen."

Logan's mouth watered. She remembered the plate-sized, bubbled disks of deep-fried dough served with powdered sugar or honey.

Her ears also pricked up at the mention of a Native American cultural event. She wondered if Dylan had been part of that group. Maybe one of the high school boys paid Brooke too much attention and he took her friendly nature as flirting.

"Was Brooke's fiancé there? Dylan Scarth?" she asked.

Cheryl thought for a second. "I don't think so, but he could have been. I never met him, only saw him from a distance when he'd come to pick up Brooke sometimes after school. He always stayed in his truck."

"Okay, sorry to interrupt," Logan said. "Go on."

"They scheduled the event for a Friday afternoon, last period. The assembly was a hit. The local paper even covered it. Lots of good press and intercultural feelings. The trouble didn't start until after the assembly. The dancers had changed and were loading their costumes and drum into their van when some of the senior boys blocked their exit. The women who made the fry bread had already left."

"What happened?"

"Mostly pushing and shoving, but a couple of the boys started swinging baseball bats. Busted up some headlights. Someone called the cops before anyone was seriously hurt."

"Was Lamar part of that group?"

"Yes," Cheryl said. "At least, he and his best friend, Ray Hagerstrom, got suspended, along with everyone else the cops picked up that afternoon."

Cheryl took another sip of her Coke. "You know, it's funny, but back then, I would have pegged Ray as the one to keep an eye on," she said. "Lamar actually had a couple of Native American friends. He might have been trying to break up the fight and got swept up in the arrests because he was there. He was never in any other trouble here at school.

"Anyway, Ray straightened up after graduation. Became a very successful businessman in town. You've probably seen his signs—Hagerstrom Investments & Development. Always helping with a beach cleanup or reading to kids in a classroom. He gives generously to a ton of charities in town. Fishermen's Wives, local shelters, the PAC . . ."

"The PAC?"

"Performing Arts Center," Cheryl said. "He's one of their biggest donors."

"Hmmm . . . ," Logan said. "What about Lamar? How did he turn out?"

"Last I heard, he was crewing on fishing boats down at the docks," Cheryl said, "but I don't know what he's doing now. He and Ray were pretty tight until senior year, but after the holidays, I hardly ever saw them together."

Made sense, Logan thought. High school friendships don't always survive into adulthood.

Cheryl took another swig of her Coke, "Ray was going places. Lamar barely graduated. Someone said he had substance abuse issues, but that must have started later. He wasn't one of the druggie crowd while he was here."

They heard Vern and Dawson's meeting wrapping up, the principal's office door opening. Cheryl tossed her empty contraband soda can into the trash under her desk and added, ". . . and I would have known."

Dawson remained in the doorway but was still talking to Vern as he walked out. The topic had turned to fishing. Vern promised to take Dawson up on his offer to join him on his new boat sometime before chinook season was over at the end of the month.

Catching himself, he said in a more serious tone, "Well, after you catch this guy, of course. That's top priority."

He stood there awkwardly for a few seconds, then melted back into his office.

Cheryl got up to hug Logan goodbye.

Nodding at Vern, she told Logan, "He's already talked with me, but if you think of anyone else you need to talk to or any other way I can help, you call me, okay?"

Chapter Thirty-Two

Vern said he needed to make a pit stop in the men's room before they left, so while Logan was waiting, she went back to Cheryl's desk.

"There is one thing I was curious about—different case—do you remember a Rosemary Swanson? She would have gone to school here in the eighties. She was seventeen when she disappeared in 1986. Lived with her father, George and had an older brother. Don't know if he lived at home still when she went missing. It was a long time ago, so you may not remember her . . ."

"Oh, no, I remember Rosie!" Cheryl said. "Not much in the news about her disappearance as when Brooke went missing, but I remember Rosie. Why? Any progress on her case?"

"No, I'm afraid not," Logan said, "but we're working on it. I can't get it out of my mind. What do you remember about her?"

"She had an older brother, Pete, but he had already gradu-ated. Rosie was the better student, but Pete was the one who went to college. A lot of families did that back then. If they had limited funds, they sent the boy because he was expected to be the one who would need to support a family someday.

"When she went missing she was a different girl than when I first met her, I can tell you that," Cheryl said.

"In what way?"

"Well, I was hired when Rosie was a junior. She came to check her class schedule to make sure she was enrolled in Algebra II. Polite, quiet, good student. I saw her now and then in the lunchroom or walking by my desk leaving for the day with a backpack full of books. She spent a lot of time in the library, too.

"After Christmas break, her grades started slipping, she had some unexcused absences, and she started wearing makeup."

"She must have been what, sixteen or seventeen by then? Didn't she already wear makeup?" Logan asked.

"I don't think so," Cheryl said. "Not this much, anyway. Permed her hair, shorter skirts, dark eyeliner, clumpy, black mascara, big earrings. No major trouble, just minor stuff, but her father wasn't happy about it when we had to call him to come pick her up."

Logan remembered the pictures she had of back in the cold case file. So far, everything Cheryl was saying matched what was in the binder.

"Sometime in April, I'd have to check the dates to see exactly when—Rosie was absent for a few days. I was in charge of attendance. I kept trying to get through to her father in case it was an excused absence. I even tried to reach him at work, but they said he was home sick. I figured maybe the whole family was down with the flu. Finally—it must have been at least a week, the father called in, said his daughter had been missing about a week.

"He didn't seem upset at all! He hadn't even filed a missing person's report. And I don't think he would have if the school hadn't said we were going to do it. I guess he didn't want to go that route, so he finally called it in," said Cheryl. "Can you imagine? Waiting a whole week before even trying to find your daughter?"

She shook her head. "No wonder Rosie ran away," Cheryl said. "I hope she landed someplace safe."

Logan agreed and thanked Cheryl for sharing what she remembered about the former Newport High student. So far, it jived with everything she had read in the reports back in the office. The police had investigated but had gotten nowhere and eventually the case went cold. It had been worth a try, and she would write up her short conversation with Cheryl but there was no new information to add to the poor girl's file.

Chapter Thirty-Three

By the time Logan and Vern got back to the courthouse to compare notes it was almost dinner time. Everyone else seemed to be pouring out of the building as they were walking in. When Vern unlocked the door, the dungeon lived up to its name, looking cold and uninviting. Even Murdoch looked like he could use a coat and gloves.

"Want to grab something to eat?" Vern asked.

"Absolutely," said Logan.

Since they were both driving their own cars, they opted for a booth at Szabo's, a steakhouse at the north end of Newport. The straight-backed wooden booths were dimly lit and the clientele local. Their server, Delia, an older woman with permed hair, part of it dyed pink, looked like she ate there most nights. After efficiently taking their order and giving it to the kitchen, she disappeared behind the bar to get someone a Jack Daniel's.

While they waited for their steaks, Logan pulled out her laptop and they compared notes. As they were making a short list of people to add to their interview list, Delia arrived with their salads, which came with the meal. She frowned at Logan's computer and waited 'til she moved it over before she slid the bowls of iceberg lettuce topped with thousand island dressing and a handful of croutons in front of them.

Between mouthfuls of salad, Vern said, "You ready to do a solo? I think we can get more done if we split up tomorrow morning."

Logan stopped with her fork halfway to her mouth, "Solo? You mean, do an interview by myself?" She wasn't at all sure she felt ready for that.

"Yep," Vern said. "You gotta let go of the side of the pool sometime."

He pointed at Logan's still open laptop screen, then tapped on the second name on the list. "Amy MacGregor," he said, wiping dressing off of his moustache, taking a drink of his beer. "Not as close a friend to Brooke as Shelly, but they were in dance class together. Someone needs to talk to her, just to check the box. And it will give you good practice."

"Okay, sure," Logan said, feeling relieved it was an easy assignment. "I can do that. Should I call her tonight to see if she'd available tomorrow morning to talk with me?"

"Already set it up. I called her on the way over. She lives out in Siletz. You've got the address in the file. Tomorrow's her day off. She's expecting you at ten o'clock."

"Okay," she said. "What do you want me to ask her?"

For the next hour, after Delia cleared their plates and brought chocolate cream pie for Logan and rocky road ice cream for Vern, Vern helped her construct a list of questions, along with the general dos and don'ts of a basic interview. She would record everything, and he would go over it with her when she got back.

They said their goodbyes in the parking lot and agreed to meet back at the office in the morning to fine-tune her strategy before she drove out to Siletz to talk with Amy.

It was only eight o'clock when Logan got home, but it seemed later. She took Dixon on a short walk around the block with the flashlight. He must have availed himself of the doggie door while she was gone, because he only peed once, briefly, and she didn't see any accidents on the floor in the house.

Happy to see his human home, the labraheeler parked himself on top of her left foot as she sat in front of the fireplace and made her nightly phone call to Ben.

Good dog.

Dixon, not Ben.

SATURDAY, OCTOBER 12

Surprisingly, after some initial tossing and turning, Logan got a solid night's sleep and woke as the sun lightened the sky outside her window. After her run and a scalding hot shower, she got dressed and headed into Newport. As she passed Beverly Beach, she spotted a couple of gray whales off the coast, heading south. Larger numbers of gray whales didn't migrate back to Baja for a couple more months, but there were always a few resident whales who stuck around the area during the summer and fall. It was always a treat to see their waterspouts and if you were lucky, whole tails as they dove down into the water.

Electronics charged, she was at the dungeon, coffee made, reviewing Amy MacGregor's brief 2008 interview from the murder book when Vern arrived at eight-thirty. She wondered if he remembered it was his turn to bring sustenance. She smiled when she saw the greasy donut bag in his hand.

The 2008 interview had focused solely on what Amy knew about Brooke's relationship with Dylan, but Vern agreed with Logan that she should also ask about any other romantic relationships Brooke may have had, or other boys or men who may have shown interest or been rejected by the feisty redhead.

"Let her get comfortable with you. You're just a volunteer, verifying what's in the file, yada yada . . . ," Vern said. "I don't think she has anything to do with this or knows anything, but if anything in what she tells you today stands out as different from what's in here, make a note and we'll follow up."

While Logan gathered up her things to head out, Vern explained what he would be doing this morning.

"While you're talking with Amy, Gary's bringing over some maps. We'll be either here or in the conference room, exploring all of the ways in and out of that Riverview lot. Not as it is now, but before it was a lot, before those new roads were put in. That whole area has changed in the last sixteen years—trees cut down, roads built or improved, a few houses built across the river. Someone buried Brooke out there and Dylan's ranch is practically next door."

He sat back in his squeaky office chair, "But this time, we need to talk to people who lived around there, see who owned that land, who accessed it. Did Dylan ever graze his sheep there? Anyone else use it? Hunters or mushroom foragers—we're going to talk to everybody who may have seen anything."

Chapter Thirty-Four

Logan had no trouble finding the address but wasn't sure she was at the right place. No one answered her knock, so she rang the doorbell a couple of times. Vern had said Amy was expecting her. Maybe she had changed her mind or forgot about the appointment. Logan was about to leave when a short, round woman with chapped, red cheeks yanked open the door, pulling Logan inside.

"Sorry about that, but you have to come in quick before the inmates escape!" she laughed, shutting the door quickly behind her, pushing a strand of curly red hair out of her eyes. "Come into the kitchen," she said. "They'll calm down in a minute!"

The cacophonous chaos into which Logan had been welcomed was hard to take in all at once. To her right, by the fireplace, was a lined play pen filled with squirming, joyous puppies who very much wanted to get out of their puppy jail and come greet Logan. Then, from her left, an ear-splitting battle cry presaged the appearance of a pair of pint-sized warriors, racing through the living room to the back yard through the kitchen, followed closely by three wildly happy long-haired dachshunds, ears flopping, toenails scrabbling for purchase on the hardwood floor as they rounded the corner into the kitchen.

"This is nothing," Amy said. "I do day care, so during the week, I have four more! These two hellions are mine."

Logan could not imagine.

Miraculously, Amy—it was Amy who answered the door—got the troops under control by providing the boys and the dogs with a mid-morning snack. The puppies in the living room calmed down as soon as the new visitor was out of sight.

Amy was happy to answer all of Logan's questions and did not object to their conversation being recorded but had no new information. Yes, she and Brooke had competed together in Highland dance competitions, but no, they weren't particularly close. Brooke and Dylan were an item and, as far as she knew, Brooke had never been involved with anyone else.

Other than the yogurt pop Logan had accepted—just to be polite—when Amy was handing out snacks, she didn't have much to show for her morning's efforts. But she thanked Amy for her time and cooperation anyway and packed up to leave. She knew the drill this time, so was prepared for an explosion of barking as she tiptoed through the living room, but the puppies, most piled on top of each other, were fast asleep.

Adorable.

Once inside her car, Logan realized she still had a couple of hours before she needed to meet Vern and the team back at the courthouse. There wasn't time to go home, and she didn't need gas, but she could always eat.

Cruising down main street, such as it was, she spotted a brown, rectangular building with a row of windows topped with a sign that said Noel's Market. It looked clean and had enticing pictures of food in the windows, so she decided to take a chance. Turned out to be a good choice. Noel's was neatly stocked with a little of everything anyone would want or need, including a nice looking meat and deli counter.

After getting a roast beef with pepperjack cheese with everything on it, Logan grabbed a Coke out of the refrigerated case and a bag of chips, then went up front to pay for her lunch. The cashier said there was a picnic table around on the side of the building where she could find some shade. Taking his advice, she headed in that direction. The aroma of the roast beef and melted cheese was making her mouth water.

Anticipating her first bite, she rounded the corner of the building. A small picnic table was there, as the cashier promised, but it was already taken.

By Dylan Scarth.

Damn.

Her hands full, Logan nodded awkwardly and turned to walk back to her car.

"Wait," Dylan said. "Logan, right?"

Logan slowly turned back, not sure what she was supposed to do now.

"Yes, that's me," she said.

Dylan waved her over, indicating she should sit opposite him. He was dressed much as she had seen him before, in nondescript jeans, t-shirt, and a long-sleeved shirt. Ball cap on the table next to his lunch.

Slowly, she walked over and slid in, placing her lunch on the table in front of her. Hoping she wasn't too obvious, she checked to make sure there were people nearby. A mother and kids were walking past, and they were in view of the road and other businesses.

"Don't worry," he said. "I don't bite. This is the only place to sit."

"Thanks," she said, then added—because she couldn't help herself, "I thought you weren't talking to us."

Dylan looked at her evenly over his own sandwich, which he had almost finished.

"Well," he said, "I'm not talking to law enforcement." He carefully wiped his mouth with the paper napkin and neatly wadded the wrapper and napkin up, placing it into the paper bag on his left.

Logan waited while he took a drink of his Mountain Dew.

Folding his arms on the table, he continued. "You and that cop caught me off guard when you came to deliver the news about finding . . . Brooke's remains. But you're not a cop, are you?"

Logan shook her head. She couldn't answer right away because her mouth was full. (The sandwich was as delicious as it smelled.)

As soon as she swallowed, she answered. "No, just volunteering with the cold case unit. Scanning files—that sort of thing. Vern is in charge. He's training me. I have had all of two weeks experience."

She smiled, hopefully winningly.

"Mrs. Crawford helped me see things a little differently. She told me I should call you back, get my side of the story out there again. Looks like you've saved me a phone call. As long as you're here . . . ask away."

"Uh, okay" Logan said, reluctantly putting her sandwich down and pulling out her phone to record the conversation.

"No," Dylan said sharply. "I know how that works. Your cop boss will just try to trip me up between what I said back then and what I say now." He tugged down his shirt sleeves, refolded his arms and said, "No recording, but you can ask me anything and I will tell you what I remember. I want to find out who ended Brooke's life. I'll do anything I can to help. What do you want to know?"

Logan felt very much out of her depth, but this was a golden opportunity, one that may not come around again. She asked if she could at least get her computer from the car and take notes. Dylan nodded his assent.

Once she was set up, she began.

Chapter Thirty-Five

Logan took a second to settle her nerves.

"I know you covered this a minute ago, Dylan," she said, "but what made you change your mind? You seemed very adamant you didn't want to talk with us about all this last time we saw you."

"It was Mrs. Crawford's idea," he said. "Victoria Crawford, you met her."

"Yes," Logan said, "I was with Vern when he notified the family that Brooke's remains had been found."

". . . and the second time, when you went to tell her Brooke had been killed."

"Yes," Logan said.

Maybe it was the angle of the sun, but the long lines in Dylan's face looked like deep gashes carved by grief.

"You have to understand," he said, "this brought back all the bad memories of that horrible night and the days and weeks that followed. That whole year is just gone—one big black hole. I was so angry at the police for focusing on me. We tried desperately to find Brooke. Search after search. We wanted them to focus on that—to find her. Victoria helped me see that I was mainly angry at myself for not being there, for letting her ride home with Shelly. She said it was better for me to cooperate and help now that new people were working the case."

It suddenly seemed important to let Dylan tell the story his way.

"How about if we start from the beginning? How did you and Brooke first meet?" she asked.

Dylan gave a faint smile.

"Finally, a happy memory," he said. "We met at the Scottish Highland Festival in Salem. I was there with Rex . . . Scout's grandfather," he said, pointing with his chin to the dog she realized was waiting for him back in his truck. "We were hanging around until two o'clock when we were scheduled to give our sheepdog demonstration."

"You said we—did you have a partner in the business or a trainee?" Logan asked.

"No, I mean we as in Rex and I. Sheepdogs and their owners are more like partners. I give the commands, but once my dogs are in there up close with the sheep, they make some decisions on their own. They can see things I can't. I see the big picture. I watch them and they listen to me. It's all part of their training."

"That's cool," Logan said. "I didn't know that."

"Most people don't," Dylan said. "Anyway, Rex and I were getting some lunch when we heard the pipes start up—the bagpipes. People were gathering in the dance competition area south of the food courts. I looked over and saw three girls dressed in kilts step up onto one of the smaller wooden stages. They all bowed low at the waist, still keeping an eye on the audience, standing tall, waiting for their cue. When they heard the pipes, they started stepping!"

Dylan held one arm up, curved over his head, which looked rather comical. "They hold one hand up the air the whole time like this—very hard to do—could have been the sword dance, I can't remember. All I remember is the girl on the end. Even with her hair pulled back in that tight braided bun, you could see it was a coppery red. Big bright smile. She outshone them all. I don't think she even broke a sweat. She made it look easy. When the song ended—she won the contest—she jumped up and down, hanging onto that trophy, hugging her friends."

Logan could visualize a young girl's unbridled enthusiasm. Reminded her of her bubbly friend, Bonnie, back home, though Bonnie had bouncy blond curls, not red.

"Brooke loved winning, but she was happy even when she didn't," Dylan said.

"Later that afternoon, she and her parents came over to the field and watched Rex and me. When Rex had done his thing, Brooke showered him with kisses and he took to her, which was unusual, because Rex was a working dog and not too fond of females. She and her family asked me questions about Rex's training and before they left, Mrs. Crawford invited me to join them for Sunday dinner that weekend."

Logan's next thought was telegraphed across her face, even though she didn't verbalize it.

"It wasn't like that," Dylan said, "Brooke was only fourteen at the time, but I respected Brooke. At first I was just a friend of the family. Brooke and I were never alone together."

Logan wasn't sure what to think. Somewhere between fourteen and sixteen, Brooke must have blossomed into a young woman and hormones were probably stronger than whatever honorable intentions a twenty-year old young man and an impressionable sixteen-year-old girl may have had.

Dylan continued, "Victoria Crawford was like a mother to me. My own mother died young, and I was raised by relatives. I loved the Crawford's home, their family. I hadn't been around a family that still had both parents married. I helped Charlie with his homework sometimes, helped her dad with stuff around the house. I was there almost every Sunday. We saw each other at Highland festivals, and whenever they came out here. Brooke and her brothers loved to play with the lambs and Brooke was even learning how to work the dogs."

His next words came out in an anguished whisper, "It's like we were made for each other. We just got along so *well*. It all seemed like it was meant to be. I couldn't imagine being with anyone else."

For a few moments, Dylan didn't speak. Finally, he cleared his throat and refocused on Logan.

"So how did it go from friend-of-the-family to romantic?" she asked.

"I knew I wanted to marry Brooke someday, but there was no rush. The ranch keeps me busy. I was willing to wait. Just before Brooke's sixteenth birthday, her mother took me aside. She said she and Will, her husband, had talked about it. Said they understood what their daughter needed—and that was me. Steady, loved their daughter, and Brooke loved me. I could provide a good life for her. I thought I might have to fight for Brooke, assuming they would object to the age difference, but luckily, I didn't have to. They were all for it. Her sister, Mary, even helped me pick out the ring. It was kind of like I was marrying the family. I put the ring in her sweet-sixteen birthday cake. She wanted to get married the first weekend after she graduated high school. That made it a two-year engagement, but I didn't mind waiting. Brooke was worth it."

Logan stopped typing. "I am so sorry, Dylan," she said. And she was. It was obvious Dylan had loved Brooke deeply, but that didn't mean that he hadn't killed her. Intense love gone wrong was a great motive for murder.

Maybe Brooke started looking around, wanted to break off the engagement. Sow her wild oats. Go away to college for a few years before settling down. Even if—as Dylan claimed—she loved him as much as he loved her, all it took was one fierce fight, one moment of passion, one stab of jealousy . . .

Logan asked a few more questions, including having him summarize his movements the day Brooke disappeared, then saved her file and shut her laptop. She watched as he threw his trash away and got into his truck. He'd saved some meat from his sandwich for Scout. Gotta trust a man who loved his dog, right? But then again, Hitler loved his dogs, too, supposedly.

There was still a lot they didn't know about Dylan Scarth.

Chapter Thirty-Six

Back at the dungeon, Logan went over the main points of the interviews Dylan had given the police back in 2008, comparing it to today's notes. From what she could tell from her multiple readings of the reports, there were no discrepancies.

After typing her report, Logan sent it to the printer to be put in the murder book and then saved the electronic copy in the blue Brooke Louise Crawford folder she had created on her desktop. She noticed the other two files she had optimistically created when they first began their investigation, before the human remains discovered out in Siletz had been identified.

Rosemary Swanson and Eleanor Riley. She double clicked Eleanor's first. All it contained was the report from the visit she and Vern made to her husband's house. Well, he wasn't her husband now. He'd remarried. She remembered the interview as being mostly unproductive, except for getting the name of Eleanor's dentist. But at the bottom of that report she had jotted the chilling information the dentist's widow had shared about Eleanor's multiple trips to the office with her teeth bashed in—by her cop husband.

She and Vern had planned on pursuing that line of questioning further, but after they got the positive ID on Brooke, the other two cases had gotten pushed aside. Rosemary and Eleanor's names had even been erased from the white board behind Vern's desk, which was now filled with everything having to do with the Brooke Crawford homicide investigation.

Logan looked around the room. Even the two missing person's binders had been put back on the shelves. That just didn't seem right. She got up and retrieved the two binders, putting them out where she could see them on the table next to her desk. Yes, they needed to focus on Brooke's case now, but as soon as this was solved—and hopefully it would be—she'd start in on these two again. She was determined not to forget about Eleanor and Rosemary.

And while she was at it, she created a new blue folder labeled Margaret Nilsen, for Clay's sister. Since she ran away to San Francisco in 1966, during the wild and crazy Summer of Love, Logan had no idea what she would put in this folder, but it seemed only fair that Margaret, or Meg as Clay called her, would not be forgotten either.

She was just rereading her notes on her and Vern's truncated trip out to talk with Rosemary's father, George, when Vern and Grant came in with lunch. The aroma of grilled meat and warm bread filled the room. She closed her laptop and rolled her chair over to Vern's desk, glancing at the wall clock on her way. That roast beef sandwich from Noel's Market was a distant memory. She could eat.

Vern was already unloading the takeout bags while Gary pulled up a chair for himself. The bag said Gyro Newport.

Logan couldn't wait to share her news. Going for nonchalant, seasoned investigator, she first shared her brief interview with Amy, then casually mentioned her serendipitous meeting with their prime murder suspect, handing over the murder book opened to the appropriate page containing her notes for Vern's review. He quickly scanned her notes.

Without a recording and with no new facts to add, there wasn't much they could do with the information, but Vern approved of her handling of the opportunity. Not earth shattering, but it made her feel part of the team in a way she hadn't before.

After they inhaled their lunch, which was delicious, Grant threw away the trash while Vern made another pot of coffee. Once everyone had a fresh mug, Vern pointed to a map he had opened up with a pen, explaining what she was looking at.

"This is a zoomed out view encompassing Highway 20, Highway 229—the Siletz Highway—these are roads, this is the river and that," he tapped his pen on an area with rectangles indicating buildings, "is the Scarth Sheep Ranch. This is what it looks like now."

"Thanks to Grant here, this map shows what it looked like back in 2008."

Grant explained, "You can access Street View images and satellite imagery in Google maps and Google Earth, going back to 2007 with their time travel feature."

"Wow," Logan said. "How accurate is that?"

"Good question," Grant said. "Google maps has a horizontal position accuracy of around 2.64 RMSE, so about seven meters either way, but still, pretty accurate."

Logan wondered what RMSE meant but would ask later.

Vern continued, "As you can see, it was mostly woods and river at that time, not much development. It's still fairly rural out there. We wanted to see who could get in and out of the area where we found Brooke's remains, back to where she was last seen on Highway 20—somewhere between here and here, driving or walking, and how long each of those routes would take."

Grant nodded.

"So you're looking at the time frame between when Brooke started walking . . . ," Logan grabbed the murder book and flipped to the section that held the report of Shelly's interview, "and when she finally called her father to come get her—well, no, to the time he first stopped by the gas station to see if Brooke was there—then he drove the couple of miles to pick up his daughter. But, really, it is even longer than that, because we don't know where Brooke was or what was happening to her—we don't know when she was buried out there. It could have been that night or days or even weeks later if she was abducted and held somewhere first before being killed."

"Exactly," Vern said. "We've got our work cut out for us, so we start with the obvious suspect first, which brings us to Dylan Scarth."

Logan grabbed the report out of the printer and got her laptop. After she printed a copy for Grant, she found the time-line portion of her interview with Dylan this morning.

"Okay, Dylan said he got the call about the emergency from his neighbor around noon. It took him an hour-and-forty-five minutes to drive home. He untangled his sheep from the neighbor's fence—the neighbor verified that, but we can double check again. No one remembers the exact time that was, but they both said it probably took at least a half hour and another fifteen minutes or so to patch up the sheep before his sheep dog could get them back. Dylan drove his truck across the field toward home, guiding his sheep and the dog. That makes it somewhere between two-thirty and three o'clock when Dylan was last seen by anyone. After that, he claims to have been at home back at his ranch working, having dinner, etc. It wasn't until ten o'clock when the police came to tell him Brooke was missing and ask questions.

"And unless he drove another car, he had been home at least since nine-thirty that night because one of the cops made a note he felt the hood of his truck and the engine was cold," Logan added.

Vern jotted a note on his printout.

Logan turned to the section with Dylan's interviews and started running her finger down each page of the reports, looking for something. When she had gone through all of them twice, she looked up.

"Did anyone ever ask Dylan how he knew Brooke was walking down the highway? I mean, if he killed her, what made him drive out there? How would he have known the girls ran out of gas? Doesn't it make more sense that a stranger abducted her, someone driving down a lonely highway at night, looking for a victim? I know it sounds like a movie script, but isn't that what serial killers do?"

Chapter Thirty-Six

Vern added this to the growing list of unanswered questions on the white board but didn't seem alarmed no one had asked that question before—at least not on record in the murder book. He reassured her this was the norm for cold case investigations. At first, there was a flood of information, most of which was useless, but you never knew what was going to be important later, so you kept all of it. Eventually a clear picture would emerge of what really happened that night.

For their next fishing expedition, they decided to go talk with Shelly, the last person to see Brooke alive. Thanks to Gary, they had a recent phone number and address for Brooke's best friend. In the past sixteen years, she had only moved about an hour north of her childhood home in Newport to Lincoln City. A single mom with two kids, a boy, eight, and a girl, ten, Shelly lived a few blocks away from the Otis Cafe, a popular diner serving comfort food from 7:00 a.m. to 2:00 p.m. seven days a week, where she worked Fridays through Wednesdays and alternate Thursdays. Gary had subpoenaed her phone records along with Dylan's and Brooke's, but it would be a few days at least before they had those.

Grant stayed behind to put all of the new data they had into the PowerPoint for tomorrow's 9:00 a.m. team briefing. Vern and Logan drove up to Lincoln City.

Vern wasn't sure she would be home, but Logan assured him their chances were good.

"Single mom who just got home from waiting tables in a busy diner? Laundry and housework to do and dinner to get on the table, *and* an early morning shift tomorrow *and* kids? Trust me, she's home."

The sky was bright with thin, high clouds. Logan felt a definite fall chill in the air when they got out of the car and walked up the stained cement walkway to unit 39B, one of four apartments in this building. She was glad she wore her jacket.

A pot of geraniums whose stems had died back to a perky bouquet of black sticks graced the front of the royal blue door. There was a picture window, but the blinds were halfway down, and they couldn't see in due to the angle of the sun. Vern knocked.

Almost immediately, a thin, black-haired boy flung open the door. Looking up at them with light blue eyes, he shouted "Mom!" then ran back into the house, leaving them standing there.

His sister came to their rescue. "Our mom is home," she said firmly, daring them to disagree. "She'll be right here."

The tall girl didn't invite them in.

Logan approved of the training their mom had obviously instilled—not ever telling strangers their mother was not home. In this case, though, the girl was telling the truth.

A few minutes later, Shelly came to the door, barefoot, dressed in jeans and a sweatshirt, still drying her shoulder-length, red hair. When she removed the towel and tossed it over her shoulder, Logan could see one-inch roots at the scalp of a duller brown streaked with gray.

"Thanks, hon," Shelly told her daughter, "Chili's on the stove. You guys go ahead and eat. I'll be there in a minute."

Turning back to Logan and Vern, she stood in the doorway and asked, "What can I do for you? If you're looking for someone, the office is over there," she said, pointing to the unit next door. And if you're selling religion, I'm not interested."

Vern assured her they were not selling anything and introduced himself and Logan, telling her briefly why they were there.

Shelly's shoulders dropped.

"I don't watch the news, but I heard about that at work—about them finding Brooke—but no one said anything about it being a homicide," she said. She stepped back to let them in, directing them toward the couch in the living area.

"Let me get the kids settled and make sure the stove is off—I know it's early but they're always hungry—we can talk as soon as I get them fed."

Dinner instructions, dishes noises, chairs scraping. Shelly returned and sat opposite them in a side chair she dragged in from the kitchen.

"Okay, what do you want to know? I gave a bunch of interviews last time, when this all happened. I don't know what more I can tell you."

She seemed nervous but gave permission for Logan to record their conversation on her phone.

Vern went through the basic sequence of events, which she said sounded about right. "But you'll have to look at the original interviews. It's been so many years. I can't remember all the details now."

"You're doing fine, Shelly," Vern said. "Can you think of anyone Brooke had problems with? Another girl or another boy? Anything bothering her or any unusual things happen in the weeks or days leading up to the time she disappeared?"

"No," Shelly said, "Brooke didn't have any enemies, and she didn't have a 'mean-girl' bone in her body. Sure, some girls were jealous because she was . . . well, she was Brooke—you've seen her picture. She just kind of breezed through life. School was easy for her, dance came easy, too, and a boyfriend who adored her. Brooke had her future mapped out. Graduate, marry Dylan, and live on the sheep ranch. I swear, she never even got a pimple."

"Speaking of Dylan, what can you tell us about him? What was their relationship like?" Vern asked.

Shelly leaned to the left, so she could look into the kitchen to make sure her kids were still eating dinner.

Satisfied they were occupied, she continued, "Dylan and Brooke were made for each other. He was so good to her. Sometimes I don't think Brooke appreciated how good she had it."

Shelly paused.

Logan picked up on the hesitation. She decided to trust her instincts. Casting around the room, her eyes landed on a framed family photo of Shelly and her kids at the beach.

"You have a beautiful family, Shelly," she said, nodding at the picture. "Raising kids on your own can't be easy."

"You got that right," she said. "Well, sometimes. But they're worth it. Every minute."

"How long have you been raising them on your own?"

The boy poked his head around the corner and asked, "Is it okay if we go upstairs, now?"

"Did you put your bowls in the dishwasher?" Shelly said, turning around in her seat.

"Yes," her daughter answered, coming up behind her brother. "And I left the sharp knives out for you to do."

"Good girl," Shelly nodded, and the little boy let out a war whoop and they shot up the stairs—older sister taking them two at a time with her long legs, little brother scrambling up after her on all fours like a cat.

Turning to her guests, Shelly said, "Okay, we can talk now. They'll be on their computers or watching TV. Where were we?"

"I was asking how long you'd been a single mom, doing all this by yourself," Logan said.

Shelly looked at the picture Logan had referenced on the wall, "Still in the process, legally," she said, "On again, off again. Things were okay until he stopped paying child support last year. I finally got an attorney—it's an ongoing battle. I'm sure you don't want to hear about all that."

She pulled a drawer open in the end table next to her chair and pulled out a pack of cigarettes. "You mind?" she asked.

Neither Logan nor Vern objected.

They waited for her to light up, inhale deeply, and exhale slowly. She reached back into the drawer and rummaged around, taking out a creased 5x7 portrait of their family, this one with the dad still in the picture. Dressed in their Easter best and beaming smiles this photo was obviously taken during happier times.

"That's Donny—everyone thought we were the 'per-fect fa-mi-ly'," she said.

"I hear you," Logan said. "I had a husband like that once. Things aren't always as they seem."

Vern gave her a sidelong look. She would have to fill him in sometime about her first marriage.

Shelly placed the photo carefully back in the drawer and fidgeted with her cigarette.

Logan leaned forward.

"Shelly, was Dylan and Brooke's relationship as happy as it seemed? If there is anything you need to tell us about that, now's the time," she said.

Shelly stubbed her cigarette out in the small bowl they could see now she used as an ashtray and glared at Logan. For a minute, no one spoke.

"Turn that off," she said.

Logan tapped the surface of her phone, stopping the recording.

"How much trouble would I be in if I didn't tell the police everything I knew?" she asked. "I have kids. I want to do the right thing, but they come first."

Logan let Vern take that one. She had no idea.

He answered directly but carefully. "Unless you were a witness to Brooke's murder or knew what happened after the fact, or have any direct evidence," Vern said. "I think you're on solid ground. It depends on what you know. What didn't you tell the police sixteen years ago?"

Shelly rubbed her face with her hands. "This is where I should ask for an attorney, right?"

They waited to see if she would.

Finally, she said, "Okay, I don't have any evidence, and I didn't see anything, but there are a few things I left out when I talked with the cops."

Chapter Thirty-Eight

When Shelly didn't say anything, Logan decided to give her some encouragement.

"Whatever you can tell us will help. Once we have all the facts, we can hold the right person accountable. It's not up to us to decide what's important and what's not."

"You're right, I know. I can't imagine Dylan ever hurting Brooke on purpose. If something happened it must have been an accident. But Dylan and Brooke had been fighting," she said.

She let that dangle out there for a minute. Vern was taking notes since Logan's phone was not recording.

"Brooke was growing up. She didn't like Dylan's 'big brother' attitude. He was used to being the adult and Brooke the child in their relationship," she said. "Brooke started fighting back. Not in a big way, just making her own decisions sometimes, choosing the opposite of what Dylan wanted even if it was something small like whether to get the cod or the halibut fish and chips."

"Had they ever gotten into a physical fight, even a small one?" Logan asked.

"No," Shelly said, "nothing like that. And half the time, Brooke gave in anyway. But Dylan didn't like it."

"So what happened the day of the festival?" Logan asked. "Did they have any arguments that day?"

"Not until he got that call from his neighbor about one of his sheep getting into the neighbor's field," she said. "The one ewe had gotten tangled up and Dylan had to leave right then."

"When was that?"

"Around noon—he came and found me and Brooke at the food court and said he had to leave, but even with the drive to Siletz from McMinnville and back and handling the emergency, he'd be back by 4:00 or 5:00 at the latest to give her a ride home like he always did."

"What happened next?" Logan asked.

"Well, Brooke blew a gasket, that's what," Shelly said, "Completely overreacted, telling him to stop treating her like a child, that she was perfectly capable of getting a ride home on her own."

"Did anyone overhear the fight?" Logan asked.

"No, we were sitting on a picnic blanket under a tree, away from the food booths. That's when I said Brooke could ride home with me. I didn't want to get in the middle of it—Dylan was just being a good boyfriend—but I had my mom's car and said I could give her a ride home, no problem. We both lived in Newport. It wasn't even out of my way."

"What was Dylan's reaction to that?" Logan asked.

"He said there was no way he was letting her ride home with me," she said. "Nothing personal, he told me, but two flakey girls driving alone was not a good idea."

"I have to admit I sort of deserved that—I was a little flakey. I mean who isn't at that age? It was a miracle my mom let me borrow her car that day. I'd let it run out of gas before."

Shelly got another cigarette out and lit it.

"I wish she hadn't, now," she whispered.

"Anyway," she said. "Brooke won that argument and Dylan stomped off to take care of his emergency back at his sheep ranch. Brooke and I left the festival when things wrapped up around five.

"There was a wreck on the 18. That's why we were on Highway 20 instead of Highway 101 when my mom's car ran out of gas."

"What time was that?" Logan asked.

"I don't know. It's in the record somewhere, but I know it was just beginning to get dark. We popped the hood up, but only one or two cars came by, and no one stopped, so finally Brooke offered to walk down the road and get gas. We knew there was a Pac Pride not far away. We got the gas can out of the trunk and last I saw her she was walking away from me on the side of the road.

"I waited and waited, but when she didn't come back after a really long time, I started to panic," she said. "I couldn't call my parents because they would never let me drive my mom's car again and I needed it to get to work at the grocery store the next day. I knew Brooke had been gone long enough to walk there and back more than once, so something must have happened.

"I didn't want to call Dylan because this would just confirm what he thought of me and her, but there was no one else to call," she said.

Logan unconsciously sat up straighter.

"What happened next?" she asked.

"Well, it rang, but Dylan didn't pick up," she said. "I tried texting him, but he never responded. The cell service was spotty out there in Siletz, still is, but it did ring, so I thought he was probably ignoring me—us—still mad at Brooke."

"I finally gave up and called my dad," she said.

She took a long drag of her cigarette. "Later, when Brooke went missing, I thought maybe Dylan wasn't answering because somehow they'd gotten into a fight, and he'd found her and accidentally killed her!

"But I decided not to say anything because I hadn't gotten through to him, hadn't talked with him on the phone," she said. "He wouldn't have known where we were."

Anguish in her eyes and voice, she looked up at Logan, "Now that I know her body was found near his sheep ranch . . . I still can't imagine Dylan did this, but now I just don't know."

Tears spilled out onto Shelly's cheeks. She wiped them away and put her cigarette down in the ashtray.

Logan reached out and took the woman's hands. "I know this must have been difficult for you, Shelly, but you did the right thing."

When she let go of Shelly's hands, another question occurred to her. "Didn't those calls show up in your phone records back then? Didn't the police look into that?"

"They never asked me for my phone," she said.

But they definitely would have looked at Dylan's, Logan thought, but didn't remember seeing anything like that in the murder book. She looked over at Vern. They needed to see those phone records.

Chapter Thirty-Nine

While they were waiting for the phone records to come in, Logan and Vern decided to look at any possible men or boys who may have caught Brooke's eye or vice versa, no matter how briefly. Any reason for Dylan to become enraged enough with jealousy to become violent.

Vern took the dance teacher to see if she or any of her other students knew of any boys Brooke spent time with other than Dylan. Logan decided to circle back to the school interviews.

The only name that had come up there, even tangentially, was Brooke's lab partner, Lamar. Frank Salazar, their biology teacher, said Brooke and Lamar were not romantically involved, but it could have been one-sided, a silent crush that Brooke used to tease Dylan with, or Dylan found out about. Salazar mentioned that Brooke and Lamar had worked on their project together a few times after school. Maybe they'd met other times as well.

It was late, but they reached Gary at home, and he said he would be able to track down Lamar's contact information and recent work history online fairly easily.

Logan got Gary's email Sunday morning at home after her run with Dixon. After zipping him a thank you, she sent it to the printer, and copied Vern so he could add the information to the murder book. Refilling her large mug with hot coffee, she retrieved the printout and returned to the kitchen table to read it.

The rumors of substance abuse Cheryl had heard were accurate. Lamar had drug and alcohol problems after high school, a few drunk and disorderlies, DUIs, lost his license for a while. Couldn't hold a job. Finally, in 2016, he checked himself into Safe Harbor, a detox and rehab facility north of Siletz. He'd been clean and sober ever since—or at least hadn't been arrested for anything since. He worked more or less steadily crewing on various fishing vessels docked in Newport. Married since 2018 and had two boys, five and seven years old.

After clearing it with Vern on the phone, Logan decided to take a chance that Lamar would be home on a Sunday. Securing the house, she made sure Dixon had plenty of fresh water and access to the back deck. Scratching him behind the ears, she promised that if the weather held, they'd have another long run when she got back.

Her phone battery ran down talking with Ben last night, so she plugged it in to charge as she drove south to Newport. As she broke out of the trees at Beverly, she took in the spectacular view. She'd lived here for almost six years now, but the rugged beauty of the Oregon coast still had the power to thrill her. Brilliant white foam capped navy blue and jade waves rolling onto the broad, flat stretch of beach or smashing up against jagged black, rocky cliffs. Seagulls wheeling overhead. The colors and clouds constantly changing. It never got old.

Following her GPS, ten minutes later, she pulled up to a large, boxy house in need of a paint job several blocks east of Highway 101 in a working-class neighborhood. Older model cars, trucks and SUVs parked in most of the driveways or could be seen through open garage doors. 1204 5th Street's shallow front yard was dominated by a large pine tree of some kind, its roots pushing up the driveway. The ground directly beneath the branches was bare, overgrown brush of salal and mounds of heather and rosemary filled the rest of the space.

On the left of the driveway two large garbage cans sat in front of the narrow, gated end of the fenced back yard. A "beware of dog" sign was on the fence. Logan didn't hear or see one as she walked up to the front door, but when she rang the bell she heard a dog's toenails scrabble on the hardwood floor as it came around the corner to greet her. The golden retriever mix she saw through the glass window on the side of the front door, wagging its tail furiously and barking its head off did not look a dog she needed to "beware of"! unless she was afraid of being licked to death.

Gary had sent along a mug shot of Lamar, so Logan recognized the man who answered the door, although he looked a lot better now. For one thing, his eyes weren't bloodshot, and his dark hair was cut short. Clear-eyed, about 5' 11", wearing typical Oregon garb, he was of average build with a neatly trimmed moustache and beard. She heard sounds of children playing in the background.

After identifying herself and why she was there, Lamar invited her in, but said, like everyone else, he didn't know how he could help. His wife, Stephanie, brought out coffee and said if Logan was hungry, she hadn't put the hashbrown casserole away yet and there were a few pieces of bacon. Just to be polite, Logan accepted.

After inhaling her second breakfast in two bites, Logan wiped her mouth on the napkin provided and asked Lamar to tell her whatever he could remember about Brooke. It was the beginning of the investigation; they were talking with anyone who knew her. She emphasized her volunteer newbie status and said he would be helping her out by bringing her up to speed.

Stephanie went to take care of the kids and Lamar said sure she could record their conversation, but he didn't have long. He'd promised to take the kids to the Oregon Coast Aquarium.

Sundays were locals' day, and they wanted to get there in time to see them feed the sharks.

"When did you first meet Brooke?" Logan asked.

"I don't remember ever meeting her. I just always knew her. Most of us kids knew each other all through school," he said. "I mean, if you grew up here."

"So you were in the same classes, went to the same parties, that kind of thing?"

"Some, yeah," he said.

"Were you and Brooke friends?" she asked.

"Well, kind of, sure," he said.

"When you got to high school, did you have any classes together besides biology?"

"No, just biology. I was retaking it, and Brooke was an advanced student," he said. "She was a junior and I was a senior," he said.

"Did you guys ever go out? Date?"

Lamar set his coffee down on the table. "No, nothing like that. Brooke was with Dylan. We were lab partners. That's all."

Logan tried a few other angles, but Lamar had nothing more to say. Decidedly less friendly now, he placed his hands on his thighs and pushed himself up. "Look, I hope you don't mind, but I've got to help get the boys ready. The aquarium opens soon. I wish I could help you, but I really don't know anything."

His wife came around the corner from the kitchen. "One for the road!" she said, handing Logan a baggie with several thick bacon slices in it before going back to round up her kids.

Sitting in the car, chewing a thick piece of pepper bacon, Logan studied the house a minute before starting up the engine and backing out onto fifth street. Lamar knew something, but she didn't know what. Somehow she needed to get the man to talk.

Chapter Forty

Lamar was at the aquarium, but his mind was not. The boys didn't notice, but his wife did. He apologized and made an attempt to pay attention and be more present with his family, but for the most part, he failed. Timmy wandered off once and he didn't even notice until his wife went and grabbed her son before he climbed into the tidepool exhibit.

When they got home, disgusted with her husband leaving all the parenting up to her, Stephanie stomped upstairs to give the boys their baths before a late lunch or early dinner. Timmy wanted to play with the motorized plastic fish they got him from the gift shop. Lamar let them go.

Steph had every right to be upset with him, but he couldn't help it. The more he thought about Logan McKenna's visit that morning, the worse he felt. Finally, he shouted another apology up the stairs and said he was going out to the garage to work on those pantry shelves she'd been wanting. Hopefully that would help dig him out of the hole he had dug for himself today. And he would work on those shelves, as soon as he made a call.

Entering the garage through the laundry room, he shut the door behind him and flipped on the light. He looked around and sighed. He really needed to get out here and clean this place up. Stephanie's car fit on one side, but the other was so full of junk he had to park his truck in the driveway.

Weaving his way through some empty Costco and Amazon boxes he needed to break down, he pulled out a step stool and sat. He stared at his phone for a few minutes. Before he could change his mind, Lamar dialed a man he hadn't spoken to in years and wished he didn't need to talk to now.

"Hello?"

"It's me, Lamar."

"Hey buddy, long time no hear. What's up?"

His old friend's confident, casual tone really pissed Lamar off. He must have heard about Brooke's remains being found but was acting as if Lamar was calling to suggest going out for a beer. What an asshole!

"The police were out here this morning."

"That doesn't sound good," the man said. "I thought you'd cleaned up your act. What'd you do, fall off the wagon? If you need bail money, no can do . . ."

Damn it! He was misunderstanding on purpose. Classic.

Lamar struggled to keep his voice calm, "Look, cut the crap. You need to come clean about what happened with Brooke. They said it's a homicide investigation now. . . . I don't know how they know, but she was asking all kinds of questions . . ."

"She?" the man asked.

"Her name's Logan McKenna. She's not an actual police officer; she's working with the cold case unit. They're working with the cops on this."

"Okay, so what does this have to do with me? She didn't come knocking on my door," he said.

Lamar heard Stephanie clomp down the stairs and go into the kitchen. She was obviously still mad at him.

Lowering his voice, he fiercely whispered, "Look, she was here, in my home, with Steph and the kids! They're talking to me, but they should be talking to you! You need to talk to the police—tell them it was an accident."

Hoping he could cajole him into making the call, Lamar added, "It's been a long time, but they're close. They're going to figure this out. You need to go to the cops. You can tell them it was an accident. You didn't mean to hurt her."

The man cut him off, his voice turned to ice.

"What did you tell her—this Logan woman?"

"Nothing! I swear," Lamar said. "But I don't think she believed me. I think she'll be back."

Lamar thought of all the years he had lost in that miserable pit of depression and his futile attempts at dulling the pain with alcohol and drugs.

It hadn't been easy, but he'd crawled out of that black hole and slowly rebuilt his life. He couldn't lose all that now. He still went to meetings and one of the twelve steps was about honesty. Until now, he had hoped that didn't include telling anyone what happened that night, but now that Brooke's remains had been found, he knew he could no longer remain silent. Brooke's mother had a right to know what had happened to her daughter.

The thought of all he could lose was overwhelming.

But just as he was about to give in to despair, a powerful wave of peace washed through him. He would have to trust that Steph would stay with him when the whole truth came out. That he wouldn't lose her or his kids.

"I can't do it," Lamar said. "I won't cover for you."

The man barked a harsh laugh. "Go ahead—who are they going to believe? An upstanding member of the community or a used-up drug addict who can barely keep food on the table for his family? I'll tell them you did it and now you're blackmailing me! How long do you think that nice little wife of yours will stand by you when I describe how you attacked Brooke and when she wouldn't give in, you killed her?"

"But that's not true! You know it's not—you're twisting everything!"

Lamar squeezed his eyes shut. He knew there was no sense arguing. This guy hadn't changed. He was never going to tell the truth. He probably didn't know how. Everyone thought he was such a nice guy, but he would do what was best for himself, just like he'd always done.

Then Lamar remembered. There was only a slim chance the evidence would still be there after sixteen years—he'd have to check first, but if by some miracle it was still there the police would have to believe him! His next few words were critical. He had to convince this guy he would do as he said. He forced his voice to sound defeated.

"Okay," he lied. "You win."

"Good boy, Lamar," the man said. "This will all blow over, you'll see. They've got no way to pin this on either of us as long as you keep your mouth shut."

Chapter Forty-One

Ray tapped his phone thoughtfully, then leaned back in his chair, steepling his fingers. For several minutes he sat perfectly still, staring out the window. His body may have been still, but his mind was processing. With quantum speed, he flipped through each piece of information, each probability, each course of action.

One thing became very clear. Lamar could not be trusted. That weakling was going to spill his guts—what an idiot.

He sat a few minutes longer, making sure he had considered all options.

It would be Lamar's word against his, but still, he couldn't count on things going his way. It would only take one judge to believe Lamar instead of him. No, he couldn't take that risk.

Mind made up, he rummaged in his bottom desk drawer for his old keys. They were right where he left them. Snatching his current car keys off their hook by the door he slipped on his jacket and dropped the old keys into his pocket. He glanced at the clock, mentally calculating his moves and how much time each task would take.

If he left now, he could get it all done. He'd wait until dark, but in the meantime he needed a few supplies. He should have done this a long time ago, but better late than never. By tomorrow morning, no one would ever be able to connect him to Brooke's murder. In fact, if all went as planned, that case would be closed for good. Who knows? He might even come out the hero!

Chapter Forty-Two

When Logan got into the office, she started a fresh pot of coffee and looked at the calendar on the wall. Day four? It could not be day four already! She went back to her desk and checked her phone. *Damn.* Vern pulled the Lincoln County Major Crimes team together last Thursday, October tenth and this was Monday, so yes, this was day four. That meant they only had one more day to join forces and resources to find Brooke's killer and they weren't even close. They had some promising leads, but it would take a lot longer than another twenty-four hours to find this guy.

But when Vern started the morning briefing, he had good news. Largely thanks to the local paper keeping Brooke's story front and center—including her high school picture, encouraging anyone who had any information to contact the cold case unit at the Lincoln County Courthouse—the county commissioners had given the team a few more days. But, Vern emphasized, unless they got something concrete in the next day or so, they would pull the plug and dump the case back in Vern's lap. Couldn't justify the expenditure.

With that kick in the butt—as if they needed additional motivation—they all got down to business. Going around the table, Vern had each team member report out what progress, if any, they'd made so far on their assignments with Grant displaying pertinent documents on the overhead monitor.

Barb went first. Since the FBI had the expertise on serial killers, her assignment had been to see if any had been operating in the area during the time Brooke went missing, was murdered, and buried by the river.

". . . Some of you may remember Jeremy Brindle. He was active roughly between 2006 and 2010. Brindle's favorites were young blondes—seven that we know of, but one was a strawberry blonde, could be considered a redhead."

Logan immediately thought of her daughter, Amy's strawberry blonde hair.

Barb continued, "He had a defined geographic area—Toledo to Salem—several were women with car trouble on Highway 20, so that fits."

"Method?" Vern asked.

"Strangulation, blunt force trauma, one was shot point blank in the face. When he was done with them, he stuffed their bodies in trash bags and left them on the side of the road to be discovered. 'Brindle's Bundles' the press called them."

She paused, looking disgusted, then continued reading from her notes. "Brindle's at Oregon State—over in Salem," she added for Logan's sake, "on death row where he belongs. We have his DNA, but we have nothing to match it to, yet, for Brooke."

She continued, "The second killer, nicknamed the River Strangler by the media, is thought to have operated for a longer time, possibly as early as 2003, still at large. This guy targeted a wider age range, too, twenties to thirties, all heavyset. Mostly brunettes, but one was a redhead. His victims were assaulted, strangled, and drowned—usually, but not always in that order. As far as we know, he did not bury any of them but let them loose in the Siletz River after he killed them."

"Could be the second guy . . . " Gary said. "But . . . Brooke was only sixteen . . ."

They mulled over the likelihood, decided to add that piece to the puzzle but continue following other leads. Monson was up next.

Monson reported he had been successful in getting Nici Vance to take a second look at Brooke's remains. Her preliminary analysis of the skull fracture was blunt force trauma, and she had a pretty good idea what type of weapon was used but wouldn't say more until she got it under her microscope. She promised to get to it Friday, but so far he hadn't heard from her.

While he was talking, his phone rang. Holding his finger up in the universal 'wait' signal, he put his phone on speaker and answered.

"Monson here," he said.

A cheerful young woman's voice came over the line. "Hi, Detective Monson, I'm glad I caught you. This is Tina Lalor, over at Oregon State Forensic Anthropology Department? I'm one of Dr. Vance's lab techs. She wanted me to let you know we did that extra analysis on your skull, and it verified her original observations. If you've got an email, I can send the summary over. The full report is coming to you snail mail."

Monson gave her Grant's email address so he could project it on the monitor when it came in.

"I was supposed to send this over to you guys on Friday, but the old fax number didn't work, then we got slammed Saturday, so this is the first chance I've had to call. I hope I'm not too late. Dr. Vance's said it was important—a homicide investigation—wanted you to have it right away. I—"

Monson managed to interrupt her with thanks from the team and a promise to let her know if he didn't receive the full report in a day or two.

"That's great," Tina said, sounding very relieved. "Let me know if you have any questions . . . and hope this helps you nail the guy."

Grant opened the attached report and adjusted the contrast so everyone could read it.

Summary of Findings: The skeletal remains exhibit a depressed fracture on the right parietal region of the cranium. The fracture is consistent with blunt force trauma.

Detailed Observations:

1. The fracture measures approximately 4.2 cm in diameter and displays concentric and radiating fracture lines, indicative of a high-energy impact.

2. Microscopic analysis of the fracture site revealed the presence of metallic fragments embedded within the bone tissue. These fragments were identified as ferrous in composition, suggesting the use of a metallic object.

Interpretation: The pattern and morphology of the fracture are consistent with an impact from a blunt object with a relatively small surface area. The presence of metallic fragments strongly supports the hypothesis that the object was metallic in nature. While the exact weapon cannot be conclusively identified, the characteristics of the injury are consistent with tools such as a hammer or similar blunt metallic instruments.

Conclusion: The evidence suggests that the individual sustained a fatal injury caused by a high-energy impact from a metallic blunt object. Further analysis or corroborative evidence (e.g., matching tool marks or weapon recovery) would be required to identify the specific weapon.

Now all they needed to do was find a hammer with Brooke's blood on it. Like that was likely. After sixteen years, Logan doubted the killer would leave something that incriminating laying around. Still, it was one more piece of information.

Chapter Forty-Three

Gary went next.

"The phone records for Shelly back up her claim that she tried to reach Dylan at 8:37 p.m. and again at 8:43 p.m., with a text between at 8:39 p.m."

"That's great!" Curtis said. "We got him in a lie."

"Unfortunately, not quite," Gary said. "They can't tell for sure if Dylan received the calls and text or not."

"Why not?"

"He claims he never saw the calls or text, or he would have answered. Without a body, they did not have enough evidence to take his phone. He showed it to them, but he could have deleted the calls and text first."

If Dylan received the calls and text, did he ignore them because he was out murdering Brooke?

Logan ran her finger along the timeline in her notes. If he had known where to look, Dylan could have picked up Brooke on the stretch of highway between Shelly's broken down car and the gas station, murdered her, buried her, and gotten back to his place before 9:30 so his engine would be cool when the police arrived. It was possible. But is that what happened?

Grant pulled up maps on the big screen wall monitor so Vern could point out the points of egress and ingress Dylan could have taken and the approximate time each would take to drive. Walking wasn't practical because he wouldn't have had time to carry her in, bury her, and hike out afterward. Of course he could have killed her there, but why would they be out by the river in the first place?

"So," Logan said, "Playing devil's advocate, if we assume for a minute that Dylan is telling the truth and never received the calls or text—" She looked at Gary. "How would Shelly have dialed and heard the phone ringing, but Dylan not hear it on his end? Is that possible?"

"Given where they were and cell phone coverage at that time," he said. "It's possible."

He nodded to Grant to pull up the next slide. "My contact at the phone company sent me this. I asked for all the possible reasons why the call rang but didn't go through."

- **Network Delays or Issues**: The caller's network may send a ringing tone even though the recipient's phone hasn't actually been notified yet. This often happens due to delays in connecting through the recipient's network.
- **Do Not Disturb (DND) Mode**: If the recipient's phone is on DND or a similar setting, it might silently reject the call. The caller would still hear ringing during the connection attempt.
- **Phone Powered Off or Out of Range**: Sometimes, a network will still generate a ringing tone for the caller while trying to locate the recipient's phone. If the recipient's phone is off or out of service, it might not ring at all, but the caller might still hear the ringing for a short time before the call fails.
- **Simulated Ringback Tone**: In some cases, the caller's carrier generates a "fake" ringing sound to assure the

caller that the call is being processed, even if the recipient's phone isn't ringing yet.

Gary gave them time to read through the list. "It's unlikely Dylan would have had his phone on do not disturb. From the records, he was always available and in touch with Brooke almost constantly throughout the day. And from what both he and Shelly said, he was protective—or controlling, depending on how you view that—of Brooke and would want to keep the line open."

While the rest of the team continued discussing cell phone technology, Logan let her mind sift through the options. She started with what she knew already. Dylan and Brooke had been in a fight. That may be why there were no phone calls between them when that would have been the natural thing for him to do. Going by past history, they would have spoken on the phone on her way home. But this time, they hadn't. At least there was no record of it. She quickly calculated the odds. No, she doubted there would be that many glitches in the cell phone coverage system.

Logan let her mind continue to travel down that thread. Dylan could have received the calls and text from Shelly but not wanted to talk to her. It made sense that he would be angry or at least irritated with her for encouraging Brooke to ride home with her and not wait for him. Encouraging Brooke's growing independence.

Logan warmed to this idea. If Dylan killed Brooke, the question had always been how would he know where she was? He wouldn't. But if he was lying about seeing Shelly's text telling him about them breaking down on Highway 20 and Brooke walking into town to get gas . . .

"Can we get a subpoena for Dylan's phone after all these years? Based on Shelly's claim?" Logan asked.

"Already on it," Gary said. "If we're lucky, it will show at least one of those calls or texts made it through."

A video of how that night could have unfolded began forming in Logan mind.

Dylan was older, used to being in charge. He could have driven out to 'rescue' Brooke to show her she needed him. Stubborn and feisty, the new Brooke could have refused his help, they argued, got in a fight and he accidentally killed her, panicked, buried her, and went home to play the innocent fiancé.

Then reality sunk in. The pieces fit, but she had absolutely no physical evidence. Not enough probable cause to get a search warrant and how would they even know where to start? Dylan's truck, his home, the barn, a tarp? How would he transport her? And would he still have the same truck after sixteen years? That would be beyond stupid.

She wanted to share her thoughts with the team, but realized they were premature. She wasn't about to throw a half-baked theory out there and have it shot down. As it rightfully would be.

Logan was next in line around the table. Startled out of her reverie, her face turned red when she realized Vern had called her name twice before she realized he was talking to her. He must think she was an idiot.

"Sleeping Beauty's up next," Vern said, with a good-natured grin. "Dylan Scarth didn't want to talk with anymore of us cops, so Logan got a one-on-one with him Saturday."

To her great surprise, no one gave her a hard time about wool-gathering in the meeting. Maybe they understood that sometimes you needed to let your mind loose to make unconscious connections your conscious mind couldn't make.

Besides, Logan was happy to have something concrete to share with the team. Even if she couldn't deliver the smoking gun, it felt good to be adding even a scrap or two of information to the murder book that would come together and eventually lead them to Brooke's killer. Like Vern was teaching her, it was all about building an ironclad case one piece at a time.

Chapter Forty-Four

Vern stayed behind to talk with Grant, so Logan left the conference room and went to open up the office. She wanted to add Gary's phone report and a few other documents to the murder book.

Finally, they were getting somewhere. It would just be nice to know where. It seemed the more evidence they gathered, the less they knew. At some point, she hoped all of this new evidence would begin to whittle down, not expand, their suspect list.

She was carefully lining up the holes to the binder rings to add Barb's FBI report when the landline rang. Since Vern wasn't there, Logan snapped the rings shut and picked up the receiver.

"Hello, Lincoln County Cold Case Unit," she said.

For a few beats there was nothing but silence. She was about to hang up when a robotic voice said, "Hello, is this Logan McKenna?"

Logan wondered who would be calling her but tried not to sound like a newbie. "Yes, this is Logan, how can I help you?"

"I have information about a case you are working on. Brooke Crawford. Do you have something to write this down on? I don't have much time and I'm only going to say this once."

The caller was obviously using some kind of voice altering software. She couldn't even tell if the robotic voice was male or female. She had no way of recording this call, either, so she grabbed a yellow lined pad and a pen and said, "Yes, okay, I'm listening. Can you tell me who's calling?"

"No. Just listen. You need to go to 1724 SW Greely. There's a big garage in the back of the property. Bigger than a residential garage. Has a roll up door. For storing big equipment. You got that?"

"Yes, 1724 SW Greely," Logan said. "What's in the garage?"

"A 2006 Chevy Silverado. Green. I checked. It's still there. The idiot never got rid of it. He cleaned it up, so I don't know if you can still get anything, but on TV they say blood's hard to get rid of. I hope so. Look on the floor and the seat in front—on the passenger side . . . If you find any blood, it will be Brooke's."

Logan knew she had to keep him on the line. She needed a name.

"Okay, thank you for calling this in. Can you tell me how Brooke's blood got in the truck? Were you there? Whatever you witnessed, you need to come in and give us a statement, help us catch this guy," she said.

Crickets.

Fearing he would hang up, Logan stuck her neck out and added, "Even if you were a part of it somehow, if what you told us leads to an arrest, that might help you . . ."

Click.

Damn!

Pulling her computer over, referring to her scribbles, Logan's fingers flew over the keyboard, typing up every word of the conversation she could remember while it was still fresh in her mind.

When Vern came in, Logan tore off the piece of paper she wrote the address down on and handed it to him.

"Anonymous call came in through the landline. Don't know why, but they asked for me," she said.

"Male? Female?"

"Couldn't tell, they altered their voice. Sounded like a robot. He says there's a truck there with possible traces of Brooke's blood on it," she said. She filled him in on the few details she'd been given as she pulled up the address on Google maps. Then she started pelting Vern with questions.

"Are all calls to the courthouse recorded automatically, or do we have to request that? Is there any way to trace that call? For future reference, is there any way I can record an incoming call from here—type in a code or something? Is that legal? I mean, can we do that?"

Every time the case took a new turn, Logan realized how much she still needed to learn.

Vern answered her questions in order, "No, the calls aren't recorded, but we may be able to find something," he said, calling Gary, giving him the time and length of the call, which Logan had the presence of mind to note on the yellow pad while they talked.

"Can we trace it?" Logan asked.

"The number of each incoming call to the courthouse shows up on our caller ID unless the caller blocked it. Since they were savvy enough to use voice altering software, they probably did block it, but we might get lucky," he said. "Gary will call us back if he gets anything. In the meantime, where's our truck?"

"Oh, of course," Logan said, turning her computer screen so he could see it. If she had written the address down correctly and if the anonymous caller was telling the truth, there was a truck with traces of Brooke Louise Crawford's blood on it smack dab in the middle of an industrial area of Newport, OR. That lot had probably been a rural area at one time, but according to Google maps, it was now surrounded by a lumber store, a storage facility, and a wholesale grocery outlet.

Gary came in with a thumbs up, "Got it," he said, writing the number of the phone on the white board. "Only one call came in to the main number during that five or ten minute time period. This has to be it."

"What happens if it's a burner phone?" Logan asked.

"We'll check locally to see if we can track down where it was purchased," Gary said. "Hopefully they used a credit card, and we can find them that way. But even if they paid cash, we can narrow down where they called from with cell tower triangulation . . . then there's the carrier's metadata . . ."

Vern interrupted Gary to fill him in on the content of the tip. Logan finished typing and printed out several copies of her report, including the phone number at the top. One for the binder, the others for the team.

Adrenaline surging, Logan grabbed her jacket and started toward the door, "Your car or mine?"

Vern pulled her up short. "Hold on, Bosch. Even if we found a green, 2006 Chevy Silverado sitting in that garage just like the caller said, any decent defense attorney would eat us for lunch. I know it's frustrating, but we need to do everything by the book—and that means taking the time to get a search warrant."

Logan sat back down. She may have been pouting.

"Yeah," he said. "I don't like it either."

"Can we at least have someone watch the property so the killer doesn't move the truck?" she asked.

Vern gave her a sad smile, "You have the budget for that? Because I don't."

While Gary went to work on writing the warrant, Vern called a contact of his at the DMV to see what vehicles were or ever had been registered to a Dylan Scarth in Lincoln County. He also added "land recorder's office" on the white board. Gary said he would take that one. The County Recorder's Office had property records.

Logan's hopes rose again.

STONE COLD

If a 2006 green Silverado turned up as being registered to Dylan, even if it had since been sold, a judge would *have* to sign a search warrant, and they'd have him! And if that was Dylan's piece of property, they could throw away the key.

The vibrant Brooke Crawford, a human being full of promise, had been in the stone cold ground for sixteen years and until now, the killer had gotten away with it. He hadn't even bothered covering his tracks, which really made Logan angry, but that arrogance might be his downfall.

Justice may be late to the party, but she was coming, and Logan couldn't wait to be there when she arrived.

Chapter Forty-Five

Over lunch, which was soggy sandwiches from the vending machine in the basement and sodas from the sister machine next to it, Vern and Logan reviewed the new information that the team had gathered and then worked through the pile of calls that had come in from the new tip line.

Victoria Crawford had been busy. Once she got over the initial shock of her daughter's remains being found, she set up a dedicated anonymous tip line manned 24/7 for the next two weeks by concerned citizens and a few temps. She hadn't even had to use GoFundMe. A local business had forked over the cash, and she'd used her connections at city hall to have it established there at the courthouse in a spare office. Notably, she hadn't coordinated with Vern, but since the police never found her daughter sixteen years ago, why would she put all her trust in them now?

In a way, Logan couldn't blame her. If it were Amy in that grave, Logan would do everything within her power to find her killer, no matter whose toes she stepped on. At least the tip line volunteers were recording all calls and sending them to the cold case unit. Logan was listening to one, now. Vern was calling someone back who thought they might have seen something.

Vern put his call on speakerphone so Logan could hear the tipster's full-volume tirade.

"We need a safe town! This is just another example of those short-term rental people coming down from Portland and doing whatever the hell they want! I'm not trying to tell you how to do your jobs, but what you need to do is look at all those rich city people—find out which ones came out to the coast that weekend when it got too hot where they were—they still do! And it's getting worse! They take over! Block the highways, flood the restaurants . . ."

Logan rolled her eyes. Vern was much more patient than she would have been, taking the woman's name and thanking her for calling in.

Logan was about to play back the next recording when a well-dressed man with thinning blonde hair leaned into the office, smoothing his ice blue tie.

"Hello! Is this the cold case unit?" he asked, pausing in the doorway.

Five-ten, mid-forties. Twenty pounds and twenty years had softened his jawline and padded his frame, but he was still a good looking man.

Vern got up to greet their visitor.

"You've got the right place. How can we help you?"

The man walked in, extending his hand to Vern, "I'm Ray," he said, "Ray Hagerstrom, a friend of the Crawford family. I helped Victoria get that dedicated land line set up. I wanted to stop by and see if there is anything else you need. Flyers, anything. You may not know what you need yet, so would it better for me just to write a check or . . .?"

At first, Logan couldn't place the name, then she remembered this was the kid Cheryl told her about, the local boy made good—Ray Hagerstrom, successful businessman and philanthropist.

The man began reaching into his back pocket, presumably for his wallet.

Vern waved it away. "We appreciate your generous offer, Mr. Hagerstrom, and will keep it in mind. If you would like to distribute flyers around town or in the neighboring towns in Lincoln County, I'm sure the Crawfords would appreciate that. I can't think of anything else we need right now."

"If you're sure," Ray said, "Let me know if you change your mind."

Smoothly handing Vern his business card, he said, "All of my numbers are on there. If you think of anything else, let me know."

"Will do, Mr. Hagerstrom," Vern said.

"Please," Ray said, flashing a winning smile, "just Ray, my father was Mr. Hagerstrom."

Turning serious, he paused at the doorway and turned back, "You know, we were all devastated when Brooke went missing—the whole town. We searched, but no trace . . . That family has been through so much. We know the police did everything they could—not questioning that." Looking Vern in the eye, he added, with a catch in his voice, "It's just not right, that girl's murder being unsolved all these years."

Logan gave Vern a wide-eyed look and mimed a police stakeout, stabbing her finger silently at the Google map location still on her computer screen and then at Ray's back as he rounded the corner to exit the office. In spite of Logan's poor Charades skills, Vern got it.

"Mr. Hagerstrom," he called out. "Ray!"

"Yes?"

"I just thought of something. If you're serious," he said, "there might be one thing you could help with."

Without sharing any details of the investigation or exactly how the money would be used, Vern explained that since the overtime budget had already been stretched to keep the major crimes team active, they could use some funding to pay off-duty officers on an as-needed basis for various tasks and costs associated with the investigation.

Ray was ready to write a check, but Vern said he'd have to get approval from upstairs first and then work out the administrative and banking details. Ray said not to worry, he knew every councilman and woman by first name. He would take care of that. Vern gave him a number. Ray didn't bat an eye. Didn't even ask for an accounting of how the money would be spent. They shook on it.

"We appreciate the support," Vern said. "Hopefully this will help nail this guy."

Logan did the math in her head. She guessed what an hourly rate for the officers might be and figured the amount Vern asked for would probably fund twenty-four-hour surveillance coverage on the property—two guys in a car—for at least a week.

Yes! That would give them time to track down the truck and property ownership, while waiting for a search warrant to come through. If they got lucky.

When Ray left, Logan and Vern sat down and worked out the shift schedule. The rate of pay would be generous, so Vern knew he'd have no trouble finding officers to fill the time slots. Ray said it might take a day to get things organized, but by tomorrow he should have things set up with the city council and the bank. As soon as it was finalized, he would give Vern a call.

That meant the first shift could start as early as tomorrow afternoon!

Chapter Forty-Six

By mid-afternoon, Logan and Vern had the schedule hashed out. Before Vern left to go down the hall and talk to the powers-that-be, he told Logan she might as well take the rest of the day off. After the initial flurry of calls, the tip line had slowed way down and there wasn't much more they could do, anyway. Better to start fresh in the morning.

Logan would have been happy to put in a few more hours, but Vern was right—there wasn't much to do until they had a search warrant. Besides, last night when she talked with Ben on the phone, he said he planned on flying home later this week. His nephew was doing well and about ready to take over the project.

Logan wanted to do something special for Ben's return but knew her limitations in the kitchen. Any welcome home dinner she attempted would probably send him to the ER. Maybe she'd make reservations at Side Door. Ben loved the rack of lamb, and she could get the ribeye.

That decision made, she rolled into the driveway and went inside. Twenty minutes later, she had changed into her running clothes and was across the highway, heading north, with Dixon's compact form trotting beside her. The dog was more than thrilled to be released from house arrest early. He knew that meant he'd get a good play session in at Fogarty.

He wasn't wrong.

When they arrived at the small crescent beach, Logan let Dixon off leash to take full advantage of what he considered to be his personal playground. There were a few other dogs already there, all ones Logan had seen before and knew got along with Dixon—a chihuahua, a big, black doodle of some kind, and a chocolate lab, so she didn't worry about any aggressive incidents. Dixon had excellent recall, so if any strange dogs arrived, she could call him over and hook him up again. Max, on the other hand, wasn't nearly so well trained. They were working on it, but she doubted Ben's goofy English Cream Golden Retriever would ever match Dixon's lightning response to obedience commands.

Sitting on one of the flatter rocks—she knew better than to trust any of the huge driftwood logs as those could easily roll over on you without warning—Logan zipped up her jacket against the cool breeze but enjoyed the warmth of the sun on her face. Fall had officially arrived almost a month ago, but there were still days like this with dark blue waves rolling in, puffy white clouds scudding across a cornflower blue sky and the whole picture framed by rugged, black rocks. She would never get tired of this.

She'd have to check the tide tables and see when the next biggest negative low tide would be at Christmas and mark it on the calendar. Her grandson, Ian, loved exploring the tide pools—they all did—last summer they had even seen a baby octopus. Which reminded her, she needed to check with Amy on Ian's shoe size—she wanted to get him a pair of non-slip reef booties so he could navigate the slippery rocks more safely next time they came.

It was almost five o'clock by the time they got back to the house. The slanting rays of the sun suffused everything with a golden light, causing the windows to flash a fiery yellow as she jogged up the steps. Last year, Ben had planted a rhododendron from Thompson's nursery to the right of the front door. It's gorgeous, fat deep red blossoms had graced the entrance all summer and there were still quite a few blossoms to greet her now.

Relaxed and happy as she unlocked the front door, Logan heard her phone ring. Still slightly out of breath, she answered. It was Belinda, Clay's wife. She'd gone huckleberry picking this morning and had been making preserves all day. She made more than she and Clay needed, so if Logan would be home for a while, she could pop over and deliver a few jars. Did she want any?

Did she? Duh! Logan's mouth watered just thinking of the sweet, rich taste of Belinda's huckleberry anything and said yes, she was home and would trade her a glass of wine and a visit in front of the fire for a couple of jars.

Even though they were from different generations, Logan enjoyed the woman's company. She reminded her of Tava'e, the Samoan coffee shop owner and her good friend back in Jasper. Both women were the warm, fuzzy mothering type Logan had missed growing up.

Logan showered and changed into a roomy dark green sweatshirt and pants and had the wine poured and a plate of crackers and cheese ready just as Belinda arrived. The temperature had dropped significantly since the sun went down, so they sat in front of the fire to enjoy their glasses of pinot noir.

Dixon did a fly by—nuzzling Belinda's hand for treats, but when none were forthcoming didn't hold it against her. He went back to Logan and plopped down on the rug beside her, keeping a watchful eye on the two humans in case one of them tossed a goodie his way.

Chapter Forty-Seven

When Belinda heard that Ben was coming home in a few days and Logan was still tossing around ideas for something special to do for him, she went out to the car and brought back a small bucket of fresh huckleberries. "I only have a few left," she said, handing her offering to Logan. "But there are enough to make an excellent pie."

Seeing the look on Logan's face, Belinda rummaged in her purse for some paper and a pen and excitedly jotted down a recipe. Handing it to Logan, she said, "Trust me, it's easy as pie!" She slapped her thigh and laughed at her own joke and said to call her if she had any questions.

Logan accepted the bucket of huckleberries and the recipe but wasn't hopeful. Just because she had XX chromosomes, it didn't mean she could pull this off. But she didn't want to disappoint Belinda, so kept her mouth shut.

Belinda either ignored or didn't notice her discomfort. Hugging Logan, she said her goodbyes and hustled home to make dinner for Clay—probably something simple like Beef Wellington and Baked Alaska.

Not for the first time, Logan wondered why she hadn't been blessed with any traditional female skills. It wasn't just that her mom was not around. An accountant who preferred her office to the kitchen, her mother was not exactly a domestic goddess herself. Still wasn't as far as Logan knew. She checked out the slim offerings in the pantry.

She had already polished off all of Ben's premade frozen meals, so dinner was a can of chili and some questionable hot dogs that had gotten pushed to the back of the deli drawer in the fridge. Using the rest of the block of Tillamook cheddar, she smothered beans and dogs with several slices of cheese and zapped it all in the microwave. It was delicious if she did say so herself.

She sprinkled some extra cheese on Dixon's kibble and tossed the last hot dog his way, which he caught mid-air. Not sleepy yet, she gave him his after-dinner walk and then went back into the living room, pulling Bella out to play while her dog took up his place on the rug.

Other than the crackling fire, the house was quiet, full of the stillness in which Logan always felt the urge—and the space—to compose or play music. Sometimes the music rushed in and presented itself whole, and she could barely write it down fast enough. Other times, like tonight, thin fragments tickled her brain, floating by—single notes, phrases, harmonies—she had learned over the years to trust the process and let it come to her instead of chase it.

She was lost in the music when her phone rang. The fire had died down and the windows were dark. She looked at her phone. The area code was local, but she didn't recognize the number.

"Hello?" she said.

"Am I speaking to Logan McKenna?"

Logan immediately tensed when she heard the robotic voice that called the cold case unit this morning. Grabbing her pen, she flipped a page on the tablet she'd been making notes on and jotted down the time.

"Yes, this is Logan, who's this?"

"That's not important," the voice said. "Why haven't you arrested him? I told you where the truck is, but nothing's happened! Didn't you believe me?"

Logan wasn't sure how much to say. She settled for honesty.

"Yes, I do believe you, but they—the police—need a search warrant to look in the garage and what you told me isn't enough to get one," she said.

Cursing on the other end. "Why?"

"But we're trying. We've got a plan to gather enough information to get a judge to sign one and . . ."

"There isn't time! Don't you get it?" the caller said. "When you were here, you said you wanted to help! I thought you might be someone I could trust . . ."

Logan immediately caught the caller's blunder. *When I was there?* She wondered if he realized what he had said. He was on a roll, now—increasingly panicked—and didn't seem to have noticed.

". . . I'm putting my life on the line here. You don't know this guy, what's he's capable of . . . my family . . . if he finds out I talked to you . . ."

Logan thought quickly then decided to risk him hanging up. She used her firm mom voice.

"Okay, I want you to listen to me. Take a breath. I am going to ask you a question, but don't hang up on me. Okay?"

The caller said nothing. So far so good.

Logan took the plunge. "I got the anonymous call at the office this morning with the robotic voice, but I also spoke with a good man yesterday. A real man who cares about his family. Is that you? Is this Lamar?"

Silence.

"Lamar, if this is you and there is anything more you can tell me that would give us enough probable cause to get a search warrant or even to arrest this guy, you need to tell us. You need to come down to the station and make this all official. There are people who can help. It's the only way to stop him and protect your family."

The next voice Logan heard was Lamar's. He must have turned off the voice altering software.

"I can't! I can't go anywhere near the police," he said. "I didn't hurt Brooke, I would never hurt her or anyone, but I was there, I was involved. I think that makes me an accessory or something—I can't go to jail and lose my family!"

Logan felt completely out of her depth, but she wanted him to keep talking. If she could get him to tell her what happened, Vern would know what to do with it.

"Okay," Logan said. "You don't have to do anything you don't want to do. But why don't you tell me the story, over the phone? There may be a way later for my boss to meet you somewhere and get your official statement without anyone knowing."

"Lamar?"

Chapter Forty-Eight

Logan held her breath, her whole body tensed, waiting for Lamar to say something, keeping the tenuous thread of hope alive. Dixon picked up on the tension and jumped up, sitting at attention in front of her, ready to launch into action if she needed him. She motioned with her free hand for him to lay back down, which he did, but he kept his head raised and his eyes on her.

Finally, Lamar spoke.

"Okay," he said. "I guess I can do that. Maybe if you know more you can get him. And even if you can't, I've been carrying this around for years. Not that I'm blaming my problems with alcohol and drugs on what happened—that's all on me. AA teaches you that. Taking responsibility is the only way you can get sober and stay that way. It's one of the twelve steps."

"I've heard that," Logan said. "It sounds like AA helped you turn your life around."

"Yes," he said, "it did. And I did all the steps all the way, except one—the one about asking forgiveness from those you've harmed. I rationalized that since I wasn't the one who killed Brooke, I didn't have to go to her family and tell them what I knew, but I should have. Of course, I can see that now. But so much time had passed and then I met Stephanie and now we have the boys. I talked myself into being quiet because going to the police would have hurt my family and that would be causing harm, right?"

He let the end of that pleading question hang. When Logan didn't say anything, he went on.

"But really, it was me, being selfish. It was me I have been worried about—I was thinking of myself. Losing them would hurt too much. I didn't want to lose my family."

Logan sensed how hard it was for Lamar to admit this, exposing himself to whatever punishment would come his way when the police heard his part in Brooke's murder, whatever it was.

"You are only human, Lamar," Logan said. "What matters is that you're doing the right thing now."

Logan knew this was true, but at the same time, she hoped that this man would not be punished along with the killer just because he was afraid all these years. She didn't know enough about how the law worked to reassure him, so she didn't. She hit record on her phone and plugged it into the charger as Lamar began his story. She knew the recording couldn't be used in court if it came to that, but at least this way Vern could hear it. "Go ahead, Lamar, tell me what happened," she said.

"Ray and I were friends . . ."

Ray? Lamar couldn't possibly be talking about Ray Hagerstrom, the same Ray who was helping finance efforts to track down Brooke's killer. Or could he? Knowing any interruption might stop Lamar's telling of the story, Logan held her questions until he was finished.

". . . we knew each other all through school. It was the start of our senior year. It was a Saturday. We had just done a small job for Ray's dad out in Philomath—a side job off the books, the customer paid cash. My mom was a single mom, so I appreciated Ray including me. The guy paid well. I didn't have wheels, so

Ray drove his work truck. His dad gave Ray the Silverado when he bought a new one. The green one I told you about. Ray's dad did construction and they were pretty well off financially, but not nearly as comfortable as Ray is now.

"I don't know the exact time, but it was getting dark. We were almost to Toledo when we saw Brooke walking along the side of the highway. A few minutes earlier we had passed a car pulled off to the right. I thought we should stop to see if they needed help, but Ray said no, they didn't have their car hood up and they would if they needed help. Ray wouldn't have stopped to help anyway."

Lamar took a shuddering breath, "We came up behind her. I knew it was Brooke because of her hair. It just lit up bright red in the headlights. She carried one of those red metal gas cans with a spout, so I assumed that must have been her car on the side of the road back there, or someone else's, and they ran out of gas.

"There weren't any other cars on the highway right then, so Ray slowed down and cruised along beside her. He lowered my window so she could hear him."

"What did he say?" Logan asked.

"Nothing good. Ray was an asshole and so was his dad. Not many people knew, but his dad had confederate flags and Nazi stuff in the basement. Ray hated anyone brown or black, but in particular, Ray hated Indians. It never set right with him that Brooke was engaged to one, so he had me lean back and yelled out the window, 'Dylan have you doing squaw duty now? Your car runs out of gas, and he makes you walk into town?' Stuff like that. He offered to give her a ride, but she flipped him off and kept walking. Ray had asked Brooke out before, but she always turned him down. I know he was embarrassed that she turned him down again in front of me."

Chapter Forty-Nine

"So he changed his tactics. Said he was just kidding; he didn't want her walking on the highway at night—it was dangerous out here. Just wanted to help, to keep her safe—stuff like that.

"I was really surprised, but she stopped, looked at me and the inside of the cab, like she was considering his offer.

"Ray must have thought she didn't think there was room in front, so he told her not to worry, I'd get in back and she could sit inside. Plenty of room. I got out of the cab so Brooke could get in.

"She looked back down the highway at where she'd left the car, then up at the direction of the gas station where she was headed, made up her mind and climbed in. I didn't even need to help her. She firmly placed the gas can between her and Ray. She waved me to get in-said I didn't have to ride in the back. So it was Ray driving, Brooke in the middle on the bench seat, and me by the door."

Logan wanted to clarify something.

"Okay, but they interviewed the gas station attendant that night. He said he never saw Brooke, never filled any gas cans that night, and made no mention of a green truck," Logan said. "I know because I read the file."

"That's because we didn't make it that far. Before you get to the station, there's a turnoff to the Siletz Highway, Highway 229. When we got there, Ray turned right. Brooke's eyes went wide, and she blurted out something like 'What are you doing?' I was wondering the same thing.

"He told her to relax; it was just a short detour. He pointed to a six-pack of beer on the floorboard the guy we had just done the work for had given us as a bonus. We'd planned on drinking that back at his dad's place. He said something about, 'You need to relax, let your hair down, thought we'd take a minute to enjoy ourselves, then I'll fill that gas can for you—I'll even pay for it—and get you back in less time than if you walked.'

"But Brooke wasn't having any of it. She was furious! She yelled at him to pull over, but Ray laughed and kept going. Now I knew he wasn't kidding around. This was no joke. I froze, but Brooke didn't. She scrabbled over me to reach the door. I think she would have thrown herself out of the truck even if it kept moving.

"But Ray kept ignoring her, pulling off onto a smaller road, or really just a narrow grass and gravel track. There were no street signs or lights or anything. I could only see a few feet ahead, just as far as the headlights went. We were in the middle of nowhere, but I knew we must have been near the river. I couldn't see it, but I could hear it.

"When Ray turned off the headlights it was totally dark. No moon and it must have been cloudy, too because I don't remember any stars, either. I'll never forget the change in Ray's voice. Even now, it feels like ice in my gut.

"'Relax, Brooke. We're just going to have a little fun.'"

Logan saw the horrible scene clearly in her mind. Brooke must have been terrified, with no way to escape.

"The next few minutes are all jumbled, but Brooke was doing everything she could to get away from Ray, clawing at the door. I pushed it open and sort of fell out. I reached back to help Brooke. She was reaching for my hand and our fingers touched, but Ray grabbed the belt on her jeans and dragged her back in. I'll never forget the terrified look on her face or the crazy look on Ray's. It was like he was possessed or something.

"Ray was on the wrestling team and worked a lot of construction with his dad, so with almost no effort, he flipped Brooke over onto her back."

Lamar's voice lowered to a whisper.

"He held her down with one arm and undid her jeans with the other. Brooke's fighting back only seemed to excite Ray more. I remember shouting something like 'What are you doing? Are you crazy? Stop! You're hurting her!' but I didn't pull him off her. I just froze.

"Brooke wasn't giving up, though. She fought like a wildcat, kept yelling 'Get off me!' while blindly groping the floorboard with her right hand, looking for something to use to defend herself. She shoved the six-pack out of the way and found Ray's toolbelt. He always left it inside the cab so it wouldn't get stolen out of the back.

"Several of the tools fell out onto the floorboard. She managed to grab the hammer and swung it up at him. But she didn't have good leverage and couldn't see to aim, so it only managed to connect with his left arm and side. That just made him go into a rage.

"It was a cold rage, though, made my skin crawl. In two seconds, he easily wrested the hammer from Brooke's grip and brought it down on her head—hard. It looked all bashed in on one side. I am ashamed to say that instead of rushing to stop him, I threw up. It all happened so fast. He'd attacked her right in front of me and I had done nothing."

Chapter Fifty

"There wasn't very much blood, so I thought maybe she was still alive. I kept saying we needed to call an ambulance or drive her to the hospital right away in case they could save her, but Ray said, 'And tell them what, Lamar? That she accidentally banged her head on a hammer?' Then he reached over and grabbed the top of Brooke's head by the hair and waggled it back and forth to demonstrate his point. 'Nope, this little rag doll's done for. No more high step dancing for this little Raggedy Ann!'"

Logan couldn't imagine seeing something like that, let alone what kind of cold, evil person could murder someone so easily and without even a twinge of conscience.

"Anyway," Lamar said, "it was obvious Brooke was dead. She just lay there, still, her right arm flung out, her hand open. The only thing moving was her hair. She had beautiful hair. It kind of spilled out of the truck and brushed the ground. It was awful and beautiful at the same time.

"I finally sort of came to and again said we should call someone, but Ray said no. He got a shovel out of the back of the truck and threw it to me. When I sort of backed away, Ray laughed and told me I had no choice. I was in this as deep as he was. He motioned to the edge of the river where the ground was softer. Said we could bury her over there and then go home. No one would ever be the wiser."

Logan thought of where Brooke's remains had been found—out by the Siletz. In this aspect at least, Lamar's story checked out. Besides, there was no upside to him lying about this.

"What happened next?" she asked.

"I started digging while he got some work rags wet in the river and cleaned up the blood on the seat and floorboard. Like I said, there wasn't much blood. Brooke had really thick hair-maybe that kept the scalp from bleeding a lot, I don't know. But he hit her hard enough to bash in her skull and kill her, that's for sure. Her head was kind of caved in on one side. Just thinking about it . . .

"Later, after . . . I had him drop me off at my house. He wanted to order a pizza to go with the beer, like nothing had happened. Unbelievable. Anyway, when I said 'No, thanks,' he warned me again not to say anything and drove off."

"Do you remember about what time that was—when he dropped you off at your house?" Logan asked. "When did you hear about the search party?"

"I don't know," Lamar said. "It was late, probably nine or so. I took a hot shower and tried to wash it all off me, but . . ."

"Did you join the search party?" Logan asked. "I think they started looking for Brooke around ten o'clock."

"No," Lamar said. "Not that night. Of course Ray and I weren't supposed to know Brooke was missing, but the next morning word got out. My mom heard about it—one of her friends called her. She had to work that day, so I went and joined the search party. I felt like an idiot."

Logan didn't know what to say.

"Anyway, the longer this went on with us not saying anything, the harder it got," he said.

"What happened with you and Ray?" Logan asked. "Did you ever talk about what happened?"

"Nope," he said. "I stopped hanging out with him, started avoiding him at school. Luckily we only had one class together. He called me a couple times with jobs, but I made excuses. Money was tight but there was no way I could ever work with him again.

"I managed to make it through the rest of that year and graduate, but I was already really messed up, super depressed, and drinking. I'm ashamed to say I raided my mom's purse more than once to buy alcohol."

"Weren't you too young to buy alcohol?" Logan asked. "How'd you get it?"

"Much easier than you'd think. Everyone knows someone who has an older brother or an uncle who'll get it for them. At first, you sneak whatever alcohol you can find in the house, but when you want more, you need a connection. I got work at the docks and in a couple of years I was old enough to buy my own anyway."

"How'd you get sober?" Logan asked.

"Stephanie," he said, without hesitation. "About six years after I left school, I finally hit bottom. I'd lost another job, was basically homeless. Couch surfing, but even that friend threw me out. I put myself in rehab again. This time at Safe Harbor. They've got a great program, and I was ready to do the work.

"I'd been out about a week, looking for work at the docks when I met Steph—her dad has a fishing vessel, *Pelican's Paradise*. I don't know what she saw in me, but she helped me through—was strong when I was weak. And here we are, nine years later. I'm different now."

The last sentence had a defensive edge to it, like he hoped Logan would believe him.

"How well did Ray clean up the blood on the seat?" she asked. "And why would he have kept the Silverado all these years?"

"You'd have to know Ray," Lamar said. "Ray thinks he's the smartest guy in the room. He knew I wouldn't talk and there was no other connection between him and Brooke. I think he just felt really confident he was in the clear. As far as the blood, I don't know if he used anything else on it when he got home, but even if he did, the CSI techs on TV are always finding enough blood to get DNA from, right? I think there's a chance there will be some left. At least I hope so."

Logan tapped her phone to stop recording. She appreciated Lamar telling his story, but she had a pretty good idea that without physical evidence, even his official statement would not be enough to arrest Ray or even bring him in for questioning. Without physical evidence, it would be Lamar's word against Ray's, but maybe it would be enough to get a search warrant for the truck, which hopefully would give them the blood. Brooke's DNA plus Lamar's story would give them what they needed to put Ray Hagerstrom away for a very long time. She hoped.

After explaining this to Lamar, he agreed to come in the next morning and make an official statement with Vern.

"I'm glad in a way," he said, "getting all this out in the open completed that last step. Feels good."

They agreed to meet at the courthouse the next morning at 8:45 a.m. Logan had her ID now, so she would walk him in to meet Vern, so he wouldn't chicken out. She hoped Lamar's voluntary contribution to solving the case would mean Vern wouldn't arrest him on the spot as an accessory or something. But Lamar didn't ask, and she didn't bring it up. He sounded at peace, now that he'd made up his mind, willing to risk even the most negative consequences in order to do the right thing. Logan didn't know if she would be so brave.

She shook off her unproductive thoughts and dialed Vern.

Chapter Fifty-One

Lining up everything he might need on the kitchen counter, Ray checked each item one more time before placing it in the small duffel. The SIG Sauer, one he'd picked up in Portland that could not be traced back to him, was fully loaded and ready to go, although he hoped he wouldn't need to fire it. He had a foolproof plan, but was prepared for whatever contingencies might arise. Duct tape and zip ties were useful for so many things.

The last object was small, weighing not more than an ounce, but was the most critical item for the success of this morning's mission. He had to laugh. He never used the word "mission" anymore. It had been years since he'd been in the army, and then only for one tour of duty, but it's funny how naturally that word came back to him, along with that mindset and focus. And what he had to do this morning definitely qualified as one.

And like any other mission, he would be in and out in minutes, maybe even seconds, then would never have to worry about this problem again. He'd taken care of the first half of his problem last night. Everything had gone smoothly. This was the last loose end.

Securing everything carefully in the duffel, he pulled a large, all-weather jacket on over his baggy sweatshirt and workpants. All of the items he wore this morning he'd purchased at a Goodwill in Corvallis, including the boots and ball cap. Loose fitting, generic. Nothing anyone would remember.

Satisfied with his preparations, he grabbed the duffel, went out the front door, locking it behind him—there were thieves and criminals everywhere; you couldn't be too careful these days. He lived in a rural area between Newport and Depoe Bay, so was not concerned about being seen by nosy neighbors.

He shivered. His thrift-store jacket was crap. As soon as this was over, he'd stuff it in the trash where it belonged.

This early in the morning, the sun hadn't made her appearance yet and the air still clung to the night's biting cold. Pearls of dew hung on the tips of hemlocks and cedar branches. Rubbing his hands on his upper arms to get warm, he walked to the rear of his truck—the older one without the vehicle graphics. Bending down, he scooped up some mud and smeared it across the license plate, then did the same for the front. He knew this town and didn't expect to be caught on any CCTV cameras, but still. Pleased with his preparations, he tossed his duffel bag in first then got in himself. Cranking up the heat, he revved the engine a bit and pulled onto the empty highway heading south.

Twenty minutes later he turned into a lower-income, working class neighborhood. Quarter-acre lots, but homes were a mix of manufactured and stick, many with rusting metal sheds, toys in the yard, and one or more vehicles up on blocks. Some were nice. Lamar's wasn't the worst. He parked across the street and one house down. Slouching in his seat, he settled in to wait.

The fishing vessels Lamar crewed on often left in the pre-dawn hours, so Ray was relieved to see that Lamar hadn't left yet. His truck was parked in his driveway and all the upstairs windows were still dark.

His plan was to take Lamar in his truck while the wife and kids were still in bed. Right in front of the garage was the perfect spot. Overgrown escallonia hedges on either side of the long driveway shielded it from the neighbors' view and the house across the street was for sale. They had a Ring camera above the front door, but it was aimed to catch porch pirates, not murderers in the driveway.

Unzipping the duffel, he got ready. He put the handgun in his left jacket pocket and the loaded hospital syringe in the other. Carefully. He was wearing disposable latex gloves, but he couldn't afford to prick himself with that needle.

As the sky lightened and lights came on in the house, he started growing concerned. Other households would be waking up soon and he didn't want to have someone come out and ask him what he was doing there. He was just about to leave and try tomorrow when the front door opened, and Lamar came out.

Slipping out of his truck, quietly pressing the door shut, making sure his ball cap was pulled low and his sweatshirt hoodie was pulled up, Ray stuffed his hands into his pockets and started to jog across the street. Luckily, third grade training kicked in and he automatically looked both ways before crossing.

A large, rumbling trash truck came around the corner, almost running him over, and stopped in front of Lamar's to collect and empty the three bins that had been hidden behind the overgrown hedge. Quickly getting back in his truck, Ray pretended he needed something from the jump seat behind him, averting his face as Lamar backed out of his driveway and drove by.

What was weird was that Lamar wasn't heading toward the docks.

Chapter Fifty-Two

The next morning, Logan walked into the kitchen and groaned. The small bucket of huckleberries Belinda had gifted her with yesterday sat expectantly on the counter, the recipe tucked underneath. She'd forgotten all about them. Well, hopefully they wouldn't spoil before she could attempt making the pie. How long did huckleberries stay fresh, anyway? Should she put them in the fridge?

Logan sighed and took a look at the recipe. Flour, butter, berries . . . she probably had all that, but what did 'cut cold cubed butter into flour' even mean, exactly? Cut with what? Scissors?

Hoping the berries would still be useable when she got back, Logan got Dixon's breakfast and her own. She was showered, dressed, and in the car by 8:00 a.m. She promised Dix a run when she got back tonight. No pie and no run. She was a terrible pie maker *and* a terrible dog mom!

A dingy sky, almost the same dull gray as the asphalt, was almost indistinguishable from the rocky cliffs. A turkey vulture slowly circled above the trees.

Last night after hanging up with Lamar, Logan called Vern to update him on the exciting new developments. They agreed that

Ray's brazen attempts to insert himself into their investigation, actively joining the search party back in 2008 and offering help now with a straight face, lent credence to Lamar's assessment of his old friend.

Ray Hagerstrom was their guy, an arrogant sociopath who saw himself as free to do as he pleased without fear of being caught. Up to and including leaving a truck with the victim's blood on it in a storage garage.

It made Logan wonder if he was more than that—maybe a psychopath. Had he killed other women over the last sixteen years? She didn't know the precise psychological label, but whatever he was, this new information opened up a lot of avenues to explore.

She just hoped they could get a judge to sign a search warrant once they had Lamar's official statement in hand.

Since it was a Tuesday and the weather was crappy, traffic was lighter than usual in Newport. Every local—of which Logan was now one—was happy to see winter coming and the tourists going. As she passed the Chevron station she realized she needed gas but decided to wait until later. She wanted to make sure she was in the parking lot before Lamar arrived so he didn't chicken out and leave if she wasn't there. They'd agreed to meet at 8:45 a.m. Vern was already in the office, getting everything ready to take Lamar's official statement.

As she pulled into the courthouse parking lot, she glanced at the clock. Good. She was ten minutes early. Plenty of time. She'd park somewhere where Lamar would see her car and keep the heater running while she waited.

Most of the spaces nearest the courthouse itself were already taken, so she backed into a space in the last row next to a blue Honda where she could see the entrance to the lot. She wished she had asked Lamar what kind of car he would be driving. She'd just have to keep an eye out.

STONE COLD

Glancing around the lot, her eye landed on a brown Toyota truck parked between an eight-passenger van and a black Ford F150. Dwarfed by the two much larger vehicles, the little truck made her smile. A couple of minutes later, the sun shifted, illuminating the inside of the vehicle, silhouetting the outline of someone leaning against the passenger side door, their head resting on the window. Probably just some guy sleeping, but something didn't feel right. Who napped in their car in the courthouse parking lot?

With a rising sense of alarm, Logan quickly got out of her car and started jogging over to check. Several people were walking from their cars into the building. No one else seemed to have noticed the person inside the Toyota.

Coming up from behind on the passenger side, Logan told herself not to overreact and lightly knocked on the window. She didn't want to frighten anyone if they woke up and saw her invading their privacy.

"Hello?" she said, looking inside.

It was Lamar. His skin looked clammy and when she yanked open the door, his limp body almost fell out. Propping him up with one hand, she felt for a pulse with the other and yelled, "Somebody call 911!"

Almost immediately, a heavy-set woman with wiry gray curls materialized at Logan's side. Gently but firmly moving Logan aside, she leaned into the cab, felt Lamar's skin, lifted his eyelids quickly with the side of her thumb, then checked the side of his neck for a pulse. It looked like she knew what she was doing—maybe she was a nurse—so Logan stayed out of her way.

Reaching into her voluminous shoulder bag, Florence Nightengale extracted a small spray bottle and quickly squirted something into Lamar's nose.

"Overdose," she said. "He's breathing, but just barely. If he doesn't respond in a minute, I can give him another dose."

"What is that?" Logan asked. "Are you sure that's what's wrong with him?" She was hoping whatever she'd given him wouldn't harm him.

"Pinpoint pupils, clammy skin, sleepy or passed out," the woman said. "Overdose."

Logan didn't want to argue with her, but she was worried. "I know this man—at least I met him recently. As far as I know, he's been clean and sober for a while. Are you sure it's not a heart attack or something? I don't think he was using drugs anymore."

"Well, even if it's something else," the woman said. "The Narcan won't hurt him, so better to give it than not. The EMTs will figure it out when they get here."

Logan was relieved when she heard the sirens.

"Good," the woman said, keeping one hand on Lamar's shoulder to steady him, introducing herself. "Sandra, Sandra McCall. I work in the building."

"Logan, Logan McKenna."

A few seconds later, an ambulance wailed into the lot, disgorging two EMTs who hit the ground running, gear in hand. Logan and Sandra moved aside and waited on the sidewalk to give them room to work in the tight space.

She was hoping Lamar would come to, revived by the dose of Narcan the woman had given him, but he didn't move, let alone open his eyes, even when the EMTs got him onto a gurney for transport. She watched until she lost sight of the ambulance, although she could still hear it racing toward the hospital, lights and sirens clearing the road ahead as it went.

Show over, the courthouse onlookers began to disperse. Logan gave Vern a call. He said he'd be right out and asked her to stay with the truck until he got there.

Logan had almost forgotten about the woman who'd administered the Narcan to Lamar. She didn't know if Lamar would survive, but she wanted to thank her, anyway. She looked around and spotted her on the sidewalk, hoisting her bag up onto her shoulder.

"Sandra!" Logan called out, before she was too far away to hear her. "I just wanted to thank you again for stepping up like that. A lot of people wouldn't have gotten involved."

Sandra waved off the compliment.

"Oh, that was nothing," she said. "I'm just glad I could help."

"You were very well prepared. Do you always have Narcan with you?" Logan asked.

Sandra hesitated before answering. The creases in her softly lined face deepened as she smiled sadly.

"Teddy," she said. "My grandson. He was such a good kid." She roughly wiped away a tear with the back of her hand.

"Two years ago that beautiful boy died of an accidental fentanyl overdose. They told me that if he had gotten a dose of Narcan in time, he would have survived. Now, I never leave home without it. No one else should ever have to lose someone they love to drugs."

Before more tears in her eyes could fall, Teddy's grandma turned and briskly walked up the sidewalk toward the court-house entrance.

Chapter Fifty-Three

When Vern got there, Logan filled him in on the details of this morning's events. He listened intently.

"So Lamar didn't say anything before they took him to the hospital?" he asked.

"No," Logan said. "He couldn't talk. He wasn't even awake. Sandra—the grandmother—said usually one dose brings an overdose victim around. He didn't respond at all. I assume the EMTs tried again in the ambulance, but I'm not sure."

Vern got on his cell and left a message for the EMTs at the nurse's station in the emergency room to call him as soon as they got there with Lamar. Either tell them he died or hopefully see if he was able to be revived.

Standing in the parking lot, she and Vern went over the possible explanations for Lamar's drug overdose. Without too much trouble, they came up with several.

Option One: Suicide. After telling Logan the whole story of what happened, Lamar had become depressed and anxious over what the fallout would be with his family and the law once the story of his involvement and years of silence came out and decided to end his life rather than face the consequences of his actions. As a former drug addict, he would know where to get what he needed.

Option Two: Accidental overdose. Lamar took drugs not to kill himself, but to take the edge off the stress he was under making this formal statement to the police and possibly losing his family or going to jail for his part in Brooke's murder.

Logan had read an article in the NYTimes about how recreational drugs were often laced with fentanyl without the buyer's knowledge. Maybe that happened to Lamar. He bought some other drug to help him through the morning, not realizing it was laced with something lethal. Apparently it only took a very small amount of fentanyl to kill you. And it did it very quickly.

Logan thought that option was more likely than suicide, given the peace she heard in Lamar's voice last night once he'd made up his mind to come in this morning and give them a formal statement.

Option Three: Murder. Option three was tough. Ray could have realized Lamar wasn't going to keep quiet and decided to shut him up permanently. That would fit with what they now knew of Ray's ruthless nature, but how would he know where to find him? Lamar was terrified of Ray. There was no way he would have called him up and told him he was going to the courthouse this morning to rat him out. No, that didn't add up.

Vern's opinion was that Lamar had chosen option two, taking the edge off with a street drug and accidentally overdosed.

"He had a long time to stress about what he told you last night. Probably was a nervous wreck by morning. A former drug user, he'd know where to get his hands on what he needed to get calm. Just his bad luck he got a hot shot."

As much as she didn't like this option, Logan had to admit this was the most probable sequence of events. But something about the scene that didn't fit.

"Lamar wasn't driving!" she said. "He was in the passenger seat when I found him."

Vern looked at her with raised eyebrows.

"If Lamar was alone and just wanted to take a hit of something to calm his nerves before he came in, why was he in the passenger seat? There'd be no reason for him to be there, right? He would have just taken whatever it was, then gotten out of the car when I got there and walked in with me."

Vern considered this.

"But that *would* make sense," Logan said, "if Ray killed Lamar and wanted to make it look like a suicide. Lamar being overcome by guilt for murdering Brooke and maybe even worried he was about to be arrested, blah, blah, blah."

Vern was nodding his head, "Okay, but how'd he get Lamar into the passenger seat and, even more important, how would Ray know where to find him? Lamar talked to you late last night. As you said, there was no way for Ray to know about that call. Lamar certainly wouldn't have called Ray and told him he was coming here this morning."

"I don't know," Logan said. "He could have followed him here from home."

"Yeah, maybe . . ." Vern said.

She knew her argument was weak, but she wasn't ready to believe Lamar had attempted suicide or taken the easy way out and given himself a little Dutch courage and accidentally overdosed.

Vern screwed his face up in concentration, then called over a couple of uniforms and instructed them where to cordon off the crime scene.

Pulling his ball cap down more firmly on his head, he turned to Logan and said, "If this doesn't work, McKenna, I'm taking it out of your allowance."

Logan grinned widely. They might still have to send some evidence they collected up to the OSP crime lab for analysis, but they could do some things here. For now, Vern said they could park the truck in their garage to preserve any evidence and make sure collection protocols were followed. Logan was most interested in finding out what the syringe they'd found on the floorboards contained. If it was meth or some other recreational drug laced with fentanyl, that made an accidental overdose most likely. If it was straight fentanyl, it could go either way—accidental OD or murder.

Vern called Monson. "Yeah, if we're not out here, we'll be in the conference room . . . If Ray was anywhere in or around this truck, we could clear two cases . . . attempted homicide today and for the 2008 case, with Gary's magic pen, I think we'd have enough points to convince a judge to sign off on a search warrant for that truck . . ."

Yes!

Excitement surged up Logan's spine. Finally they were getting somewhere. In her bones, she knew Ray was guilty of both crimes. There had to be physical evidence somewhere. No one was that careful. She was surprised at the fierce anger that filled her just thinking about the casual cruelty with which Ray had stolen innocent lives and his arrogant assumption that he would continue to get away with it.

Chapter Fifty-Four

After the area was taped off, one officer resumed his normal duties, while Officer Daniels was assigned to man the entrance, logging everyone in and out. This record, along with all the reports from detectives and techs would eventually be added to Brooke's murder book. Daniels made sure everyone grabbed plastic gloves and booties to cover hands and shoes before he let them into the cordoned off area.

The parking lot soon bustled with looky-loos watching evidence techs going over every inch of the Toyota truck—which was registered to Lamar—and the exterior of nearby vehicles. Logan saw Sam standing outside the barrier, but just barely, interviewing Daniels. The courthouse was Sam's regular beat, so she was first on the scene and included it in her morning online post.

Vern interrupted Logan's thoughts. Looking at the cars inside the crime scene tape he said, "Hope these guys aren't in any hurry to leave. We are *not* going to be popular today."

Logan nodded then got back to her wishful thinking.

If they found even a scrap of physical evidence that showed Ray had been inside or even just touched Lamar's truck . . . All they needed was one good print. Or for Lamar to wake up and testify to Ray's attacking him—if that's what happened. Too many ifs.

"Have the EMTs gotten back to you yet?" Logan asked Vern, who was talking to Monson—in person now. Monson had just donned his plastic booties.

"Not yet," Vern said. "Go ahead and call the ER—you need the number?"

"No, I got it," Logan said, already dialing.

The ER nurse who answered was slightly miffed that Logan wasn't calling with an injury of her own, but when Logan said she was calling for Vern, the woman became much more cooperative.

"No, sorry, they left already," she said. "Had another call . . . No, your guy didn't come around—even after multiple doses."

"He died?" Logan said. "Lamar's dead?"

"No, but he didn't wake up either. He is alive, but he can't breathe on his own. They put him on respiratory support. They called his wife and got permission to intubate. She's on her way here now. Sorry, but I really have got to go. It's crazy right now. This isn't for the public, okay? Tell Vern he can call later."

"No, of course, that's fine," Logan said. "You've been a tremendous hel—"

The nurse hung up before Logan could finish thanking her, but Logan got it. The woman had shit to do. And Logan had the information she needed. Lamar was alive—if barely—and fighting for his life. He just couldn't tell them what happened . . . yet. She filled in Vern and Monson.

5:30 P.M.

The major crimes team had been at it for hours. Once the truck had been towed to the lab for further examination by the techs and the scene released, Vern, Monson, and the rest had adjourned to the conference room where they'd been going over the case step by step, clarifying details, forming and discarding theories.

They had new information, but nothing concrete to verify Lamar's version of Brooke's murder in 2008. When and if Lamar ever recovered from the overdose, he could tell them what happened. Until then, they would have to work with what they had. Which wasn't much.

Finally, Vern sent everyone home to their families for the night. He would call them in the morning once they had any solid news about Lamar.

In the meantime, the off-duty officers would begin their first surveillance of Ray's property in thirty minutes for the first shift—six o'clock to midnight. The second set of officers would cover midnight to six. Their instructions were to observe and record only. As of now they were not to confront the suspect.

They'd keep up the surveillance as long as Ray Hagerstrom's money held out. Vern estimated a week. Logan loved the irony of Ray paying for his own surveillance. No one held out much hope that this would yield results, but it was worth a shot. Who knew, maybe two off-duty cops sitting in their unmarked vehicle ten yards from the entrance would catch Ray drive his green 2006 Chevy Silverado out of his garage, preferably dripping blood out the back as it glided past them.

Right.

The courthouse had mostly emptied out by the time Vern locked up the conference room and they made their way toward the dungeon. Logan never thought she'd be so happy to enter the dingy, low-ceilinged space, with its flickering fluorescent lights and ugly office furniture castoffs. But it would be quiet, and after all the activity today, she could use some of that.

Vern went in first, deftly tossing his ball cap onto Murdock's skull as he walked by. Rubbing his own head with both hands, he put the murder book on his desk and plopped in his chair. Putting his boots up on his desk and his hands behind his head, he leaned back for a good stretch. Logan admired his balancing skills, knowing just how far to go without tipping backward.

Equally exhausted, Logan dropped into her own chair and finished off a bottle of water she had left there yesterday. It wasn't cold, but she didn't care.

The evidence techs would continue meticulously going back over every print and every gum wrapper and bit of trash they had collected this morning, but so far, even though they'd put a rush on it, they had nothing. No prints inside or outside of the truck that didn't belong to Lamar or his family. Any stray prints not belonging to Ray would be saved but were not helpful unless they came up with another murder suspect. On the off chance Dylan was still a suspect, they had compared some of the outlying prints to his, but didn't get a match.

No witnesses. Not even any useful CCTV footage.

Parking lot coverage was minimal to begin with—nobody expected any kind of major crime to occur within steps of a building crawling with law enforcement. And the camera that was aimed in that direction was blocked by the panel van between the Toyota truck and the entrance. There had been a fair amount of foot traffic—people coming and going from the courthouse that morning, but none of them looked like Ray. If he had been there, he had done a great job of blending in. They'd keep reviewing the footage but didn't have much hope. All Ray had to do was slap on a hoodie and a ball cap and not look furtive. He'd look like half the guys in Newport.

They did have that one phone call from Lamar to Ray. The phone company would have a record of it, but not the content. But by now, Ray would have had plenty of time to come up with a good story to explain that call.

Chapter Fifty-Five

Since most of Dixon's beach runs had been shortened or skipped this week, Logan made sure to give him a long, fast one the next morning, with extra time at Fogarty for him to chase seagulls and play chicken with the waves. By the time they got home they were both panting and dripping wet. It felt great! As she headed into the shower she realized how much she needed those sessions, too.

When she arrived at Pirate's for the weekly Cormorant Coffee Club's confab, Sam and Jean were already there. Ordering her usual, Logan grabbed her coffee and joined them at the picnic table by the window. Sam, her ever-present laptop already open, was trying to squeeze information out of Jean about what happened yesterday.

"I already have the basics, Jean," Sam said. "My contact at the hospital filled me in. It was an overdose. Fentanyl. Big one. Would have killed him if that woman hadn't given him a dose of Narcan, but . . ."

Jean calmly shook her head and stirred some honey into her hot tea. Logan wasn't a tea drinker, but she loved the aroma of jasmine wafting her way.

"You know I can't tell you anything, Sam," Jean said, "even if there was anything to tell."

Sam let out a huff of frustration but didn't give up.

"I know you can't tell me anything *officially*, and you know I won't use your name," she said, fingertips poised over her keyboard in hopeful anticipation. "You can be an unnamed source."

"Nope," Jean said.

"At least give me a hint. I can do my own research, but would I be wasting my time if I did some digging? Something doesn't sit right about this. The courthouse parking lot is not where an addict usually chooses to shoot up. According to my sources, he had been clean for years, didn't do drugs anymore. This just doesn't add up."

Jean ignored Sam's accusing glare.

Placing her spoon beside her mug, she said, "The only thing I can do is verify it was an overdose. No other drugs besides fentanyl showed up on the tests. No alcohol. And," she said, pointedly including Logan in her report, "no sign of struggle or other foul play. No skin beneath his fingernails, no bruising, nothing. I can't speak to his sobriety—and this is off the record, Sam—Lamar gave himself that injection."

"Got it," Sam said, accepting defeat if only momentarily, "So you know the who and how but not the why."

"Right."

Jean took a long drink of her tea while the three friends thought about the man hanging onto life in the ICU. Jean answered Sam and Logan's next questions before they could ask them.

"They won't know if he'll make it, or if he suffered brain damage until he wakes up. They ran tests. CT scan shows some cerebral edema—brain swelling—but his EEG results were inconclusive. They've got him on diuretics and steroids to reduce the inflammation. Getting clearance for oxygen therapy. But it doesn't look good."

Hope for the best but expect the worst, Logan thought. That had been one of her dad's favorite pieces of advice whenever she was worried about something.

Logan was bursting with unshared information. She really wanted to tell Sam and Jean what she knew and what she suspected had happened to Lamar, but even though she could probably have safely shared Lamar's phone call with Jean and stayed within professional boundaries, she knew talking to a reporter, even one who was a trusted friend like Sam, would violate the trust Vern had put in her. If Vern found out, he'd cut her loose from the cold case unit—and rightfully so. Then she'd never be able to help nail Brooke's killer or find out what happened to the other missing women in the cold case binders gathering dust back in the dungeon.

No, until she knew more, she'd have to keep her mouth shut.

Not her strong suit.

Before she put her foot in her mouth, Logan stuffed it with a big bite of the breakfast burrito Kathy had just brought over and let Jean turn the conversation to other topics. Miss Magnolia, Sam's two-and-a-half-year old terror was proving to be as strong-willed as her mother. Last week when they thought she was down for the night, the little Houdini escaped from her crib, defeated the child-proof lock on the bottom bathroom drawer and got into Sam's old makeup kit from her high-power news anchor days in Olympia. It held a jumble of half-used bright lipsticks and other heavier makeup she didn't need here on the more casual Oregon coast.

After diligently applying slashes of 'Apple Red' lipstick to most of her naked little body—Magnolia had removed her nightclothes and proudly strutted into the living room to show her parents how pretty she was. She didn't understand why her mother let out a yelp and her father came rushing over to save her.

"In the dark it looked totally like blood! We thought she'd found a razor in there," Sam said.

Listening to Sam, Logan was very glad Amy was grown, and she didn't have to deal with those adventures anymore.

The clouds had cleared by the time Logan got on the road, and it was turning into an unseasonably warm October day—which for the central Oregon coast meant the temperature was in the high sixties. Logan lowered the windows and enjoyed the ocean air, knowing that in a couple of hours, it would probably cloud up again, dropping temps back into the fifties and forties. Spotting a streak of low, dark clouds on the horizon, she mentally added the probability of rain.

When she got to the office, after dropping off an old-fashioned glazed on Vern's desk, she got her third cup of coffee and sat down. They were just updating the whiteboard, discussing next steps in the investigation when Ray knocked on the open door and took a tentative step inside.

"Hi," he said. "Do you guys have a minute?"

Ray looked uncharacteristically anxious. Nothing like the confident, in-charge businessman persona he had projected before.

Logan was grateful Vern's face remained impassive, not giving away the fact that after Lamar's confession, Ray was their prime homicide suspect. She hoped her own face was as unreadable.

"Sure," Vern said, "pull up a chair, Ray."

Ray rolled one over, positioning it in front of both Vern and Logan's desks. Clasping his hands in front of him, he looked like a recalcitrant third grader called into the principal's office. When he looked up, there were dark circles under his eyes and they were bloodshot.

"Okay, shoot," Vern said, his face neutral. "How can we help you today?"

"I know I should have come forward earlier, but I didn't have any evidence, only suspicions. But now, with Lamar attempting suicide in the parking lot, there are some things you need to know."

Logan couldn't wait to hear what he had to say.

"I can't believe Lamar fell off the wagon. I actually helped get him into rehab the first time he went—paid for his treatment. But this," he said, nodding at his phone, "I can't ignore this. I feel sorry for the guy, but . . ."

"Why don't you start from the beginning," Vern said. "How did you and Lamar know each other?"

Ray dragged his hand down his face, then told his story. "Okay, but you've got to know it never occurred to me that Lamar could have anything to do with Brooke's disappearance, let alone murder, until I saw this text."

Vern waited for him to continue. Logan wanted to take notes but was afraid to interrupt the flow of this new information.

"Lamar and I were friends in high school," Ray said. "A few days before Brooke's disappearance, he borrowed my truck to go fishing. Chevy Silverado. That was my work truck, but I didn't have any jobs that weekend—I used to do construction work for my dad sometimes—so I said sure. When he brought it back, there was some blood on the seat. He said he snagged his leg on some blackberry brambles and sat in the passenger seat to hunt for a first aid kit or at least a Band-Aid in the glove compartment. He had tried to wash it off, but it was still a little stained. It was an old truck, no big deal, so I never thought about it again. But now . . . I don't know what to think."

The man looked up, stricken.

"What if Lamar killed her? He had the truck for several days before and after she disappeared. He returned it with blood on the seat . . . I mean, I don't know why I didn't put two-and-two together at the time. It just didn't cross my mind. What would Brooke be doing in my truck with Lamar?

"We were all busy searching for Brooke. My mind was totally focused on that, and Lamar—you never think someone you know could be capable of something like that. Maybe it was an accident?"

These last few words sounded desperately hopeful, like he was grasping at straws for his friend's sake.

"Where is the truck now?" Vern asked.

Logan knew Vern was weighing this new information, measuring it against the story Lamar had told Logan, trying to decide who to believe. She hoped Vern wasn't buying it.

"That's just it," Ray said, huffing with frustration, "I sold it years ago—the guy who bought it never paid me the rest of the cash, so we never transferred the title. I shouldn't have given it to him until he paid all of the money, but he said he really needed it for work. I'm just a softie sometimes. I wrote it off as a business loss."

"So you have no idea where it is now," Vern said.

"Not a clue."

How convenient.

When Ray left, Vern said he didn't take either Lamar or Ray's stories at face value. Yes, he agreed Ray was a jerk, but that didn't make him Brooke's killer.

Their job was to follow the evidence and right now they didn't have any.

Logan agreed to keep an open mind, but inside, she was leaning toward believing Lamar. So she did take some pleasure in knowing that Ray was paying to have his own garage watched. If his truck was parked inside that garage, he wouldn't be able to sneak it past their round-the-clock surveillance.

With no new leads to follow, Vern told Logan she might as well take off. If anything broke loose or they got lucky and Lamar gained consciousness and was able to communicate, Vern promised to give her a call.

On her way out, Logan almost went back to grab the other two missing persons binders on her desk. She could work on them at home.

Torn between what she wanted to do and what she was supposed to do—which was not to take anything confidential out of the building—Logan hesitated. Vern had gone to the men's room, so she could probably sneak the two binders out, but she'd given her word. With a sigh, Logan hoisted her computer bag up on her shoulder. A woman of her word, she would resist temptation . . . for now.

Chapter Fifty-Six

By seven-thirty the next morning, the sun was up and so was Logan. After taking Dixon for another good run, she showered and changed, then grabbed her laptop and headed into the kitchen. Yawning deeply, Dixon did a downward-facing-dog full body stretch, butt in the air, then, trotting into the living room, found a triangle of sun on the hardwood floor, curled up, and promptly went back to sleep.

Ben would be home tomorrow—Friday. Since today might be her only day off, Logan planned on using it to get the house back in shape before his return. That included replenishing the pantry and filling the fridge with Ben ingredients.

Pouring herself more coffee, Logan sat at the kitchen table and logged into their Fred Meyer's grocery account. After cobbling together a shopping list from the last few orders Ben had placed for pickup, she opened the fridge door and tried to visualize what fresh fruits and vegetables were usually in there. She pulled out the produce drawer and removed its only inhabitant, a limp celery stick and two bendy carrots.

Yuk.

She added carrots and celery to the list. Which reminded her they needed onions, too. Those were the three vegetables Ben always had on hand. He needed them to make mirepoix. The only reason she knew that term was from her French foreign exchange program mother back in high school, who was an excellent cook. Mirepoix, she'd said, was equal parts diced carrots, celery, and onions. The cooking lessons didn't stick, but the term did. It apparently was the basis for almost every soup, stew, or casserole in France.

Next she added green beans, chicken, a couple of rib eye steaks, and romaine lettuce (she'd forgotten to water Ben's garden as often as she was supposed to, and the formerly perky greens had all wilted). Before she logged out, she threw in some of her favorite essentials: ice cream, Reese's Peanut Butter Cups, hot dogs, and sea salt and vinegar kettle chips. Ben kept the staples pantry stocked and Logan never went in there, so she assumed they still had plenty of rice, pasta, flour, sugar, backup spices, and salt.

So far Logan had successfully avoided dealing with the bucket of huckleberries on the counter, but before she left for Freddie's, she broke down and called Belinda for help. The kind woman said she'd could come over later this afternoon and walk her through Pie Making 101. Logan secretly hoped Belinda would take pity on her and take over the process in exasperation, but a personal guide was better than nothing.

Mid-week and mid-month, Freddies wasn't very crowded, so Logan was in and out with her groceries by noon. She was just finding room for the ice cream in the freezer when her phone rang. It was Vern.

"How soon can you get to Big Creek Reservoir?" he asked. "You're gonna want to see this."

Logan shoved the ice cream into the bottom drawer and opened the map icon on her phone to type in the location.

"About twenty minutes. Address?"

Making sure she didn't leave out any food items that needed to be refrigerated or frozen, Logan grabbed her purse and car keys. She went back to give Dix a scratch behind the ears and tell him she'd be back soon, made sure he had fresh water, then flew out the door and jumped into her car.

"Upper Big Creek or Big Creek Reservoir Number 2 should get you here," Vern said. "Once you get to the water, keep driving, you'll see us. Big tow truck, couple of divers, a K9 unit, and hopefully a big, wet truck."

Logan froze, stunned.

"You got the truck?!" she said. "OMG! How?!"

"Easier to show you than tell you," Vern said. "I'll explain it all when you get here. Make sure your phone's charged. While I'm supervising the haul out of the truck, I need you to take the K9 trainer's interview. They're the ones who found it."

"On my way!" Logan said.

Following her GPS, Logan headed south. As she drove, she wondered how Ray had gotten the truck past the surveillance team. I mean, they were parked right outside with a full view of the old garage and the driveway, the only way in or out of that property.

Then she remembered. Consecutive shifts of off-duty cops had been sitting on the house since late Tuesday, but Lamar had called her Monday night and overdosed in the courthouse parking lot early Tuesday morning. Ray must have figured out sometime before then that Lamar was a loose end and already moved the truck, before Vern could get all the approvals to get the surveillance teams in place.

So far, Ray had always been one step ahead, but maybe this time they got lucky.

Logan pressed the gas pedal a little harder.

Chapter Fifty-Seven

At first, a solid wall of trees and brush blocked Logan's view of the water, but eventually there was a break on her right. A small road opened onto a gravel pullout which she assumed had been created for people to access the water for fishing or other recreational purposes.

Today, the area was filled with a big tow truck and numerous law enforcement personnel gathered around their prize, a dripping wet, green Chevy Silverado, water still streaming out from the cab. Logan grinned. She had never seen a more beautiful sight!

Vern, head and shoulders taller than anyone else, yelling above the mechanical racket, was helping the tow truck driver and another man disconnect hooks and straps used to pull the Chevy up and out of the reservoir. Disconnecting her phone from its charger, Logan slipped it into her jacket pocket, pulled on a ball cap, and got out of her car.

Vern warned her he might be busy when she got there making sure the divers followed chain-of-custody protocols for every step of the retrieval and making sure it was all on video, so leaving the truck to Vern, Logan looked around for the K9 trainer and her dog. Spotting them over by a large rock, shaded from the bright sun by a thick stand of mixed conifers that came right to the water's edge.

When she got within a few feet, the sleek Doberman who had been watching her approach perked up and barked, vigorously wagging the stump of his tail.

"Kraken!" Logan said, delighted to see the beautiful animal, and of course, the smiling woman behind him.

"Hey, Oletta!"

Clad in jeans and boots, with a thick blonde braid hanging over her right shoulder, Oletta leaned against the back of her SUV, hat beside her.

The two women hugged, and Oletta let Logan give Kraken a treat, then put him in a down-stay at her feet so they could get to the reason Logan was here. Oletta had put the major crimes team in touch with Chuck and his cadaver dog, Roux, the one who successfully located Brooke's remains out in Siletz, so she already knew Logan was volunteering for the cold case unit.

They caught up for a few minutes while Logan got set up, laying her phone on the rock where it could pick up their voices—hopefully without too much noise interference. When she was ready Logan established the basics—names, time, and place, then let Oletta relay the morning's events.

She began with the obvious question, "How did you find the truck?"

"Well, first of all, I didn't find it, Ruby did," she said, pointing back at her SUV to a crate containing a small, light-colored shepherd of some kind, who looked out at them with intelligent, hazel eyes.

"Ruby's my latest," she said. "Two-year-old Belgian Malinois. Other than dobies, they make the best search and rescue dogs. Small, agile, and super smart."

Oletta went on to explain that the local search and rescue group, already small, only had access to one cadaver dog and she was often called out to other areas, so Oletta had volunteered to train a new one.

"What's the difference between a cadaver dog and a regular search and rescue dog?" Logan asked. "You told me once, but I can't remember. Why can't they both do the same job?"

"Cadaver dogs only search for dead people," Oletta said. "Or what's left of them. Like blood, bones, clothing remnants. They're trained totally differently. Search and rescue dogs are trained to follow scent trails given off by live humans. Cadaver dogs are trained to recognize the specific odors of decaying human tissue or remains."

"Ruby here tested the best out of her litter. I've been working with her a couple of months so far. And believe me, what this girl did today was simply amazing."

Logan let Oletta continue.

"We got here early. I wanted to train when the water was calm and there wouldn't be a lot of people around, no distractions for now, while she's still in this stage of her training. I left Kraken in the car and Ruby in her crate, then rowed out and placed three canisters of human tissue and blood about forty yards out, suspended at varying depths, before coming back to get her. She usually gets the easy ones, the ones closest to the surface. This time I'd put one of the canisters pretty far down. The scent rises, but the deep ones don't give off much scent by the time it bubbles up to the surface.

"Ruby got all three, bam, bam, bam—one right after the other!"

"How do you know when she finds it?"

"Her alert is one bark and a pointed stare at the spot."

"Then what happened?"

"Well, every dog is different. Ruby's reward is belly rubs and her favorite treat for each successful find. When we were done, I decided to take a minute to enjoy the peace and quiet. It's beautiful out here. I rowed out a ways and just sat and closed my eyes to enjoy the stillness. I had my hand resting on Ruby's back when I felt her body stiffen. She went to the edge of the boat and barked once, staring down into the water.

"I thought I messed up and it was leftover scent drifting from one of the submerged canisters, so I started rowing back to shore, but she would not give up. Finally, I looked over the edge into the water and not thirty, forty feet down I saw what looked like the top of a truck cab—Chevy Silverado. Lane used to have a Silverado. The view of the bed was murky, but I could see it. Wasn't sure of the color with the reflection in the water, but thought it was either blue or green. If it had been in a deeper section of the reservoir, or if it hadn't been such a calm morning, I'd never have seen it at all.

"With Ruby alerting, I called it in as a possible DB," she said. "The dispatcher's boyfriend is a sheriff's deputy, so she knew the Newport PD had an unofficial BOLO out on a 2006 Chevy Silverado. She called it in, and they called your guy, Vern. He got here first, with the tow truck right behind him. Everybody was here, including the divers, within an hour."

Logan tapped the screen on her phone to end the recording, then both women looked over at the dripping truck. Someone had opened both cab doors. Empty. No dead body.

Oletta looked disappointed, but Logan wasn't surprised. If this was Ray's truck, Logan knew the only thing they'd find— if they were lucky, were remnants of Brooke's blood on the passenger seat where she'd been killed.

She wanted to tell Oletta that her dog, Ruby hadn't failed, that she *had* alerted to blood, but knew as long as the investigation was ongoing, she couldn't tell her friend anything. At least for now.

When and if, by some miracle, traces of Brooke's blood with viable DNA had survived for sixteen years, Logan was going to not only tell Oletta the whole story but also buy Ruby the biggest beef steak ever!

Chapter Fifty-Eight

After Oletta and her dogs left, Logan walked over and joined Vern. They talked with the divers while they packed the last of their gear. Most everyone else had already cleared out. Vern offered Logan a bottle of water from the trunk of his car. She gratefully accepted.

With Ray's truck hauled off to the OSP crime lab to be taken apart by their best forensics techs, there wasn't much either Vern or Logan could do until the lab came back with results. Vern said it would probably take a day or so to totally dry the truck out, even using industrial fans. At that point, whatever the evidence techs were able to glean from the interior of the truck would undergo further analysis. If the stars aligned, they'd get some viable DNA and it would match.

He doubted they would hear anything until early next week, even with the rush he had put on it. In the meantime, he had Gary get started on an arrest warrant for Ray. They would fill in the blanks later should they get lucky and find enough evidence to get a judge to sign one. The rest of the team would stand by. He sent Logan home with the usual "keep your phone charged" request and then went home himself.

The worst part was that they couldn't tell the family they were close, that they might finally have found Brooke's killer. They couldn't risk getting the family's hopes up only to bring them crashing down if they couldn't prove Ray had done it.

By the time Logan got home, the adrenaline that had kept her going all afternoon had drained away. When she went to unlock the door, it pushed open before she could insert the key. In her hurry to get to the reservoir earlier, she must not have locked it. Oh well, at least Ben wasn't here to witness her lax approach to security.

Kicking off her boots, she sloughed off her jacket and hung it on a hook next to Dixon's leash. Speak of the devil, Dix came running in from the back deck to greet her. Getting down on the floor, Logan took a few minutes to roll around and wrestle with her dog before heading in to shower.

As she passed by the kitchen, a mouthwatering aroma of freshly baked goods wafted her way. She followed her nose. There on the kitchen table sat a beautiful, still warm, lattice-topped huckleberry pie. And next to it, neatly draining on a dish towel were the mixing bowls and spoons and other utensils used to make it.

Damn!

She'd forgotten all about Belinda coming over this afternoon.

Logan quickly called to apologize for not being here this morning and thank her friend for turning the bucket of berries into a beautiful pie. "I really didn't intend for you to make it for me," she said, "but I'm glad you did. It looks a whole lot better than anything I would have produced."

"Happy to help," Belinda laughed. "No trouble at all. You just take care of that man of yours and give him a hug from us—it was good of him to go help his nephew out."

Logan agreed Ben was a keeper. She really needed to tell him more often all the things she admired about him. For now, she would do the next best thing and clean the house from top to bottom and make reservations for dinner at Side Door tomorrow evening. Which she did.

Later that night, after her shower, Logan curled up in her favorite chair in front of the fire with a short glass of Maker's Mark—one ice cube—and returned Ben's call. She'd missed it earlier when she'd been in the shower.

Enjoying the warm, deep sound of her husband's voice, she settled in to listen to Ben describe Max's latest adventures. That dog had definitely been a handful.

"Max didn't get car sick," Ben said, "but he did sit panting in my ear for most of the trip. Also, at almost every stop, he made every attempt to jump out of the passenger side window to play with any child and dog who came within ten feet of the car."

With his happy prance and feathery, waving-flag tail, Max made friends with everyone. At the last McDonald's stop, Ben said, a little boy gave Max his cheeseburger, onions and all, before his mother could stop him. Max happily gobbled up the unexpected treat. That *did* result in an almost immediate rejection by Max's gastrointestinal system, which unfortunately splattered on the mom's shoes as she tried to pull her child away from impending disaster.

Picturing her sweet husband valiantly trying to clean up the mess with flimsy fast food napkins with one hand, hanging onto Max with the other, all while profusely apologizing to the mother and offering to pay for the little boy's lost cheeseburger, Logan almost squirted whiskey out of her nose.

The rest of Ben and Max's afternoon had been much less eventful. They made it as far as Willows, CA, a small town on the I-5, stopped at a grocery store for a deli dinner, then checked into a just barely decent motel. The thermometer read ninety-two degrees, Ben told her, too hot to take Max for anything more than a short potty walk behind the motel, so they were in for the night. After the long drive, Max was already stretched out on the bed beside him, fast asleep. Ben planned on getting on the road early and hoped to be home by four o'clock.

Logan wrapped her robe around her and wriggled deeper into her chair. She listened to the motel's struggling A/C and Max's soft snores in the background as Ben's voice grew soft and husky, telling her how much he missed her.

A little shiver of anticipation ran up Logan's spine. No matter what time Ben got home, she planned on serving a little dessert before dinner . . . and she didn't mean pie.

Chapter Fifty-Nine

After enjoying his welcome-home dessert Friday night, Ben declared the rest of the weekend a mini-staycation. No work, just fun. So that's what they did. Tidepooling, BBQing in the backyard, watching old movies, a hike up Driftwood Creek, and catching a great bluegrass band at Beachcrest, followed by a full-moon stroll on the beach.

The weekend passed quickly, too quickly, but by Sunday night, Logan started worrying about Brooke's case again. She knew Vern would call if there was any news from the OSP crime lab about Ray's truck, but she couldn't sit here waiting for the phone to ring. Even if all she did was work on scanning old cold case files tomorrow, she needed to go into the office.

***

When Logan left the house in the morning, her family didn't even notice. Ben was happily digging in the garden with Max underfoot, and Dixon lay on the back deck, supervising.

And she'd been worried about deserting them.

After stopping for a freshly-ground bag of Left Coast coffee, she drove south, pulling into the courthouse parking lot twenty minutes later. Her mind flashed back to last Tuesday morning, seeing Lamar slumped against the window in the passenger seat of his truck, barely alive. She'd have to call again today and see if she could find out how he was doing.

Shaking off the memory, she gathered her computer bag and keys, locked her car, and headed into the building. She hoped Lamar made it. And not just because he would be able to testify against Ray. Yes, they wanted Ray to pay for murdering Brooke and attempting to murder Lamar, but Logan wanted this young man to live for his own sake, for his future, his family—his wife and children. He had worked so hard to deal with the horror he had witnessed sixteen years ago and been forced to live with ever since.

She hoped he would pull through, but as each day passed, Logan felt less and less confident. She had already checked several times this week, but as far as she knew, Lamar's condition remained the same.

When she got into the office, determined not to feel helpless, Logan got the coffee going and cleared her desk of all but the three cold case binders they had been working on.

- Brooke Crawford, age sixteen, 2008.
- Rosemary Swanson, age seventeen, 1986.
- Eleanor Riley, age thirty-two, 1984.

When the coffee was ready, Logan got up and zapped her pastry for a few seconds in the microwave, filled her mug, and took it all back to her desk.

She had started in on her bear claw when Vern called and said he would be a little late this morning. He had to take Rocket into the vet. The young dog had managed to get into it with a big old raccoon in the backyard and Rocket did not come out on top. The dog was current on his rabies shots and Vern didn't think he needed stitches, but he wanted the vet to give him a once over and make sure.

Logan totally understood. She told him she'd hold down the fort until he got there. He said he'd call if he heard anything from OSP.

She decided to set Brooke's murder book to the side for now and focus on the other two cold cases, see if she could make any headway on those while she waited for Vern.

She pulled over Rosemary Swanson's binder first, opening to the chronological record log in the front. She remembered Vern explaining that this document tracked investigative actions in order. Her and Vern's interview with the uncooperative George Swanson, Rosemary's father, was the last entry. She flipped to that page and reread Vern's report. It was well written. She was grateful she had such a good mentor. It was obvious he cared about each and every one of these missing girls.

When the remains in Siletz were identified as Brooke's, this case had been dropped, but maybe they should try again. They still needed to try to find Rosemary and George's DNA; it might help.

Logan scribbled a note to herself on the yellow pad and moved onto the next report, the one she had written of her brief conversation with Cheryl Meece at the high school.

Cheryl's memories of the good student turned troubled teen were sharp and clear, considering the number of years it had been since the girl went missing. Cheryl was amazing. Logan finished reading, sat back in her chair, and thumped her pencil on the edge of her desk.

What would cause a teenage girl to run away? George was obviously an overly strict father, but was he worse than that? Had he sexually abused his daughter? Cheryl hadn't alluded to that, and she probably would have if she'd suspected it.

Logan flipped through the previous reports in the binder. No record of that either, but they may not have had adequate evidence to bring those charges against the man.

Was Rosemary still alive or had she died? Was she perhaps a victim of one of the serial killers Barb said were operating in this area during those years? Dead or alive, Logan was determined to find her and bring her home. George may not care, but the file mentioned an older brother. She didn't know if Rosemary's brother was still in the area or even alive himself, but if he was, he would probably want to know what happened to his sister.

Chapter Sixty

ROSIE

Digging her keys out of a large, canvas bag with an orange and black Oregon State Beavers logo on the side, fifty-five-year-old Rosie Swanson unlocked the door to her office and flipped on the light. Cedar House didn't serve breakfast until eight, but she liked to come in early, before Sally and her crew started making breakfast in the kitchen.

Hanging her jacket on a hook by the door, she unpacked her bag at her desk. Wallet locked in the bottom drawer, laptop and coffee thermos on top. She looked around and sighed. What her office really needed was new carpet, new paint, and probably a new ventilation system, but remodeling was not a priority in the budget. There were better ways to spend the limited funds she was able to funnel their way.

But first things first.

Scooting her chair back a few inches, she took a deep breath and shook out her arms. Positioning herself on the edge of the seat, aligning her head, shoulders and hips, she placed her feet flat on the ground, hips' width apart. Tucking her stomach in and her pelvis under, she sat as tall as she could, visualizing someone pulling her straight up as if by a string at the top of her head, lengthening her spine. Finally, she rested her hands loosely on top of her thighs, palms up, alleviating any strain in her shoulders.

When she felt centered, she closed her eyes, breathing slowly in through her nose, then breathed out even more slowly, keeping her mouth closed.

With each breath, her heart rate slowed and she felt more grounded—heavier in her body. After about five or ten minutes—she wasn't rigid about time, she rose and did three "sun salutations," a sequence of stretching and strengthening yoga poses she had learned in her first stint at rehab, nearly ten years ago. Relaxed and ready to work, she stowed her yoga mat against the bookshelf and briefly touched a small, white porcelain statue of a gentle, robed woman before returning to her seat.

People often mistook the female figure as a representation of the Virgin Mary, but the vase she was holding from which the water of compassion flowed identified the simple figurine as a depiction of Kuan Yin, the Buddhist Goddess of Mercy. Rosie never corrected anyone. Both females embodied unconditional motherly love, which is what Rosie felt when she looked at it.

As she opened her laptop, she heard the muffled clanging of pots and pans in the kitchen. That had been her first job at Cedar House. Every recovering addict chose an area to put in a certain number of volunteer hours as part of their program. She hadn't wanted to scrub pots and pans, but it had been better than scrubbing toilets, so she'd signed up for kitchen duty as the lesser of two evils.

But that training gave her the skills she'd needed to get a job as a short-order cook, which helped her pay her way through college. After those years lost to living on the streets, Rosie was in her mid-forties before she completed her BA in Psychology. Next came her masters. She'd been a licensed social worker for four years, now, and the director of this shelter for two.

Her first love was still one-on-one counseling, and she did her utmost to reserve ten hours a week on her schedule for that, but unfortunately, most of her time had to be spent dealing with administrative issues or raising money to keep this place afloat. The city chipped in, but local companies and private donors kept the doors open.

After taking a break to help serve breakfast—she always made time to connect with each resident, offering a few words of encouragement here, a touch on the shoulder there, or a listening ear—Rosie returned to her office and for the next couple of hours tackled her inbox.

Most of the emails were people she corresponded with regularly: donors, city councilmembers, and local businesses she nagged for donations. So when she saw an email from Oregon State Hospital Memorial marked urgent, she almost deleted it as spam, but the subject line caught her eye.

Re: DNA Family Matches, Response Requested

Rosie read the email through three times. The sender had attached a photo.

Brushing a couple of tears from her cheek, Rosie unlocked her bottom desk drawer. Retrieving her wallet with shaking hands, she carefully removed the worn black and white photo with white, scalloped edges and held it against the image of the woman on her computer screen.

The photograph Rosie had carried with her all these years was not well focused and the woman's image on the computer was fifty pounds heavier and had a vacant look in her eyes, but she did have dark hair, and those eyes . . . could it be?

She reread the email again.

Dear Ms. Swanson,

My name is Regina Fredericks. I am a volunteer with the Oregon State Hospital in Salem. I have some important news to share with you, but before I do, this story needs a little context.

In the 1980s, the Oregon State Hospital in Salem was deinstitutionalized. The hospital staff at that time did the best they could, but those patients who did not have families to take them in or make alternative arrangements for them were sent either to East Oregon Hospital in Pendelton or to private foster homes. Some of these patients—many indigent and unhoused—had no identification on them when they were admitted, so OSH had no way to contact any remaining relatives they may have had.

For the past twenty years, I have been searching through genealogical records attempting to connect these patients, most of whom have since passed on, with their remaining relatives. I have had some success, but it wasn't until the last decade that genealogy sites like 23andMe became popular. More and more people added their DNA to the database, seeking out birth parents or just building their family tree. I now have a powerful tool at my fingertips. DNA forever changed forensic genealogy!

I can explain more when and if you would like to meet, but in the meantime, I am very happy and pleased to let you know that a parent/child match has been made between you and a woman who was a former patient at OSH. This would not have been possible if you had not also submitted a sample of your own DNA, so we assume you did so in hopes of locating her or other relatives.

I know this is a lot to take in all at once, so when you are ready, feel free to call, text, or email me and I can tell you more. In the meantime, I have attached the only photograph we have of the woman we believe was your mother. She was one of the patients taken into a foster home—a good one from all appearances.

Unfortunately, your mother passed away in 1998 and the couple who took her in are also deceased, but their daughter, Tess, who was a child at the time Loretta (this is the name they gave her at the hospital, since she had no ID when she was admitted), sent us this photograph and is happy to answer any questions you might have.

She assures me that although your mother had fairly severe cognitive limitations when she knew her, she was happy and content. Loretta passed away peacefully in her sleep in her foster home at the age of forty-nine. She was thirty-four years old when she became a patient at OSH. I have included Tess's contact information below, next to mine.

There was also a second match. Not parent/child, but someone who shares a lesser percentage of DNA with you. Just thought you would want to know. They have also opted in to be notified, so you can log into the site and contact them if you wish . . .

Chapter Sixty-One

Rosie looked again at the small, black and white photograph in her hand. She remembered the day she found it.

It was Christmas 1985.

She was in her room avoiding her father, who was working his way through his first holiday sixpack, but, finally, she had to come out to start dinner. Pete wasn't there. He must have been at a friend's house. George was in his usual spot, slouched in his easy chair, watching a football game. Another hour and he'd be passed out. She was an expert at gauging her father's level of inebriation.

Rosie shivered involuntarily. The memory of that day came rushing back. She remembered every detail in vivid color and detail.

Without taking his eyes off the TV, George growled something about not forgetting to put the pineapple rings on the ham, then added, "Even your mom, the slut, remembered to do that."

Rosie clenched her fists, angry tears spilling down her cheeks. She was so tired of having to listen to every poisonous word he spit out of his mouth, without being able to fight back.

She looked to her right, searching the meager collection of family photos on the wall for a picture of her mother she knew she wouldn't find. There were no photos of her mother anywhere in the house.

Although she used to ask often when she was younger, George refused to explain why her mother left or if he knew where she was now, just that she had run off when Rosie was little, abandoning all of them.

Most of the pictures on the family photo wall were of her brother, Pete, in various sports team uniforms as he grew up. There was only one picture of her. Ironically, it was a photo of George holding her in his arms when she was about three. His curly, coal black hair and bushy eyebrows contrasted with her wispy, white-blonde pageboy haircut and blue eyes. She often wondered if her mother took that picture.

Her dad looked happy. They both did. He must have loved her once. She wondered when everything changed—and why.

For a moment, she froze, feeling all the hurt. All the years of unanswered questions boiled up within her. Acting on pure emotion, she snatched the framed picture of her and her dad off its hook and threw it across the room, shattering the protective glass cover as it hit the opposite wall.

For a second, they both froze, then George launched himself out of his chair and came after her. She turned and ran, but he caught her in the hall before she could reach the safety of her room. She knew better than to yell—he didn't like it when the neighbors called the cops. So she curled into a ball and took her beating, silently, triumphantly! It had been worth it.

She remembered laying there until she heard the screen door slam and the engine of George's car start. Then she eased herself into an upright position and made it into the bathroom to clean up.

Lifting her sweatshirt, she twisted around to assess the damage on her back and grimaced. Nothing was broken, but from shoulder blades to butt, she was covered with angry, red welts. *Gotta hand it to the man,* she thought. Even drunk, the asshole could aim. He never left marks where they would show.

She sighed and lowered her shirt back down. *At least he'd be gone for a while,* she thought. *That was something.*

Splashing her face with cold water, she dried her hands on a towel and went into the living room to sweep up the broken glass, at least put the picture back in its frame before starting on dinner.

After picking up the largest pieces, she swept the rest of the shards into the dustpan and then used a damp paper towel to get up the small pieces that might cut the bottom of someone's feet.

The frame was slightly skewed, so before hanging it back up she popped off the cardboard backing with a butter knife in order to straighten it out. When she did so, a smaller black and white photo that had been tucked in back floated down to the floor.

Carefully picking it up by the edges, she held it up to the light. In it, a young couple posed in front of a diner, made out of an old train or something. 'The Salem Diner' was spelled out on a sign that ran along the top. Looked like the kind of place that sold real milkshakes, thick burgers, and piles of crispy fries.

The scrawny, blonde boy on the right wore a short-sleeved white shirt, a stained apron tied around his waist, and clunky black shoes. His chin-length, stick-straight hair was tucked behind two big ears, framing a goofy face. A thin, striped paper hat like she'd seen cooks wear on that old sitcom *Happy Days* was folded into his apron in front.

The grinning young man had his arm slung around a pretty brunette's shoulders. The top of her head only barely came up to his chin. The girl's dark hair spilled across her narrow shoulders from under her waitress cap, framing a heart-shaped face with smiling eyes.

Something in Rosie clicked.

With growing excitement, she flipped the photo over. On the back in faded blue ink, someone had scrawled "Me and SB" and beneath that, "1969."

It was still there, although almost illegible now.

She didn't know who SB was, but Salem was only an hour and a half north of here . . .

Going into the kitchen where the light was brighter, she had carefully examined the picture of the woman again. There was no doubt. The heart shaped face, the slender build. The woman's face in this picture was the same one that looked back at her every morning in the mirror. This was her mother! And the man? Well, she wasn't tall like him, but if he was her father, that would explain her white-blonde hair that neither Pete nor her dad had.

In fact, that's when she realized it would explain why she didn't look like George at all, the man she'd known as her father all these years, and, even more enlightening, why he hated her.

So many thoughts swirled through her mind she couldn't sort through them all right then, but she knew one thing for sure. She was going to find out.

As soon as she could save up enough money for a bus ticket she was out of there!

Unfortunately, when she finally got to Salem, there was no trace of her mother. The diner in the photo wasn't even there anymore. Totally unprepared for this scenario and too stubborn to call home for help, she soon ran out of money and luck.

Rosie sighed. Everything went downhill from there. It had taken her seven years, but with the help of Cedar House, she had clawed her way out of that hole. She wanted to get in touch with Pete to let him know she was okay but had no idea where he was living now.

She tucked the photo back into her wallet then looked at the photo on her computer screen again.

DNA didn't lie. But how could the doughy, middle-aged woman sitting on the old nubby brown loveseat, staring out at her with that unfocused look possibly be the same happy young woman in the photo? And if she was, how had she wound up in a mental hospital without any ID?

Chapter Sixty-Two

Logan was reading through Rosemary's file one more time when Vern came in, talking on his phone. Striding across the office in just a few long steps, he put his phone face up on his desk while taking off his jacket and tossing it toward his chair. He missed.

"Yes," he said to whoever was on the other end of his conversation, "I'm here. I just got into the office. Can you start over? I've got you on speaker. Go ahead."

A woman with a well-modulated voice did as instructed.

"Well, like I started to say, it took until Saturday afternoon for the fans and dehumidifiers to do their job, but once the interior of the truck was dry, we were able to get in there and search. We did find human blood on both the passenger seat and floorboard."

Logan did a silent cheer and Vern leaned forward with an intense look on his face. The woman continued.

"We also recovered a metal ballpeen hammer, Craftsman," she continued. "Size and shape fits the imprint in the skull that caused the blunt-force trauma that killed the victim."

"Where was it?" Vern asked.

"The hammer was in a leather tool belt, along with other loose tools in a locked toolbox in the bed of the truck. And before you ask, the hammer and blood from the interior have been sent over for testing. We have our own people, just down the hall."

Vern let out a breath and sat back, "How long?"

"We put a rush on it, so shouldn't be too long. I'll call you as soon as I hear anything, but I thought you'd want the preliminary report."

"Yes, thanks," Vern said. "Call anytime, no matter what time it is. We have a lid on the story for now, but as soon as the news gets out that we found this guy's truck, he'll bolt."

She promised.

"Why wouldn't he have gotten rid of the hammer? What kind of idiot keeps the murder weapon?" Logan asked, then answered her own question. "An arrogant one. It's the same reason he kept the truck. He was so confident he had Lamar under his thumb, Ray never thought anybody would come checking."

While they waited, Vern thanked Logan for remembering coffee. Filling his mug, he brought it over to her desk and listened while she brought him up to date on her review of the Rosemary Swanson file.

She was just running her DNA-gathering ideas past him when Vern's phone rang. It was the lab.

"That was quick," Vern said.

"Yep," she said, "You must be living right, Vern."

Vern smiled.

"I have good news and bad news, which do you want first?"

Vern didn't hesitate, "Gimme the good."

"Well, the blood on the passenger seat belongs to your murder victim, Brooke Louise Crawford."

"You're sure?"

"Yes, Vern, you can take it to the bank."

A broad smile spread across Logan's face.

"What's the bad news?" Vern asked.

"You don't have a murder weapon. At least not that we can prove. We can't say without a doubt this ballpeen hammer was the one used to smash in Brooke's skull. There were traces of blood, but only a very small amount—and degraded too much for testing. Could have come from anything. He could have banged his thumb with it. The full report is on its way, but I'll be here for a while if you have any questions."

Vern thanked her and got off the phone, a pensive expression on his face. Logan didn't understand why he wasn't more excited.

"We got him, right?" Logan asked. "I mean, isn't blood on the seat that matches the murder victim the evidence we've been waiting for?"

"It is solid physical evidence," Vern said. "But it doesn't convict or clear Ray. It gets us closer, but we're not there yet."

Logan still looked confused.

"Think about it. All we know is that Brooke's blood was found inside Ray's truck, not who put it there."

It took a minute for that to sink in. She'd forgotten about Ray's version of what happened that night. His supposedly reluctant sharing of Lamar borrowing his truck and bringing it back with blood on the seat. She'd been so wrapped up in nailing Ray she'd forgotten all about his visit to the dungeon last Wednesday. She realized how effective that seed of doubt he'd planted had been.

That slippery bastard.

While appearing to not want to tell on his friend, Ray had skillfully steered the homicide investigation away from himself, toward Lamar. Which was nonsense!

Unless of course, Lamar *was* Brooke's killer.

All of this made Logan's head hurt. There had to be something she could do.

She spent the rest of the day scanning old cold case files. Around three, Vern left to pick Rocket up from the vet. The little dog would be fine, but the vet had given him several stitches and kept him there for x-rays and blood tests just to make sure. Logan promised to lock up before she left.

A few minutes later, she was halfway out the door herself when she remembered one more thing she could check before going home. Returning to her desk, she found the phone number she was looking for and dialed.

Chapter Sixty-Three

Hooking her foot on the bottom ring of her office chair while she waited, Logan's knee bounced up and down. Logan hoped not everyone had gone home for the day. When someone answered, Logan breathed out a sigh of relief.

"Forensics, Rafferty," a man said.

Logan recognized the name. He was one of the evidence techs who had worked the crime scene out in Eddyville last year with Jean. Hopeful he would have the information she needed.

Identifying herself first as a volunteer for the cold case unit working with Vern, Logan asked if they had finished processing the truck they had sent over Tuesday morning, the one involved in a possible homicide investigation.

"The one we towed from the courthouse?" Rafferty said.

"Yes," Logan said.

"Well, most of the prints belonged to the registered owner or members of his family, but . . . um, is Vern there?" he asked.

"No," Logan said. "Vern's out of the office right now."

"Well, tell Vern to call me when he gets in," Rafferty said.

"That won't be until tomorrow morning," Logan said, "and we really need the information now if you have any. What other prints did you find?"

She was getting irritated with this guy's stalling.

Rafferty's voice took on an official tone, with a streak of underlying snark.

"Nothing personal, ma'am, but this is information I can only share with an official law enforcement officer and that's not you."

Logan knew this wasn't true. She had passed her background check, but instead of arguing with him, she sweetly asked him to send his official report to Vern and ended the call.

She didn't know if she'd ever get used to some members of law enforcement refusing to deal with her—either because she was female or because she wasn't a member of the club. But she couldn't let it get to her if she was going to do this job.

She decided to make an end run around this guy.

She called Dr. Pullman's Family Practice and left a message. Rafferty couldn't refuse to cooperate with the Lincoln County medical examiner.

When Jean was through with her last patient, she returned Logan's call. Logan explained what she needed.

"Got it," Jean said.

Two minutes later, she called back.

"Good news. Rafferty says they got a print. Well, a partial, anyway."

"You're kidding!" Logan said. Then she pulled her expectations back to ground level. "Did they get a match?"

"Yes, they did," Jean said. "Ray Hagerstrom was in that car with Lamar. In the driver's seat."

"You're kidding!" Logan said. "Wait, can you hold on a sec? Let me get Vern on. This can't wait until tomorrow!"

After a couple of tries, Logan successfully added Vern to the conference call. That way he could hear Jean's explanation, too.

"Where was the print?" Vern asked. "I would think Ray would be too smart to make that kind of mistake. He must have worn gloves or his prints would be on the door handle if nothing else."

"The partial was on the seat adjustment lever under the driver's seat. My guess is that Ray used latex rather than heavy duty gloves, enough to leave a partial print. They sent it up to OSP and with a little work, one of their print techs was able to raise the ridges and get a match."

Logan interrupted, "And you're sure it's a match?"

"99 percent positive. They ran it through AFIS and got a hit. Your boy was in the army."

"You're welcome," Jean added, just as Vern and Logan were profusely thanking her.

***

Lamar said he hadn't interacted with Ray in years, so with this new evidence placing Ray firmly in Lamar's truck when he had no reason for being there, combined with what they had already, Golden-Pen Gary was able to craft a convincing warrant for Ray's arrest and find a judge willing to get out of bed at midnight to sign it.

Logan would not participate in the actual raid planned for the early morning hours, but she offered to stay and help in any way she could as the team prepared. Vern appreciated the support and for the rest of the night, Logan served as fast-food-orderer, copier, and general gopher, doing whatever tasks needed to be done as everyone hustled to get ready.

When she called Ben to let him know she'd be late, he wasn't happy about it but thanked her for letting him know and said for her to call him when she was leaving and he'd have dinner or breakfast ready for her when she got home.

At two-fifteen in the morning, Vern gathered the team together for one last review, going over maps, approaches, and communication protocols.

Standing in the back of the room sipping on the last of her coffee, Logan was impressed. She couldn't think of anything else they could do to prepare. The only way Ray Hagerstrom was going to escape answering for his crimes was if news leaked that they were onto him.

If even a whisper got out of his truck being hauled out of the reservoir, or that the blood found inside had been identified as Brooke's, or that he left a partial fingerprint inside Lamar's vehicle when he tried to kill him at the courthouse . . .

Anxiety began to crawl up Logan's spine. There were too many points of weakness here. Ray had already proved he was willing to ruthlessly eliminate anyone who stood in his way. She looked around the room at the major crimes team members she'd grown to admire as she'd gotten to know them in recent weeks. Barb, the FBI agent who had kindly included her at the crime scene when Brooke's remains were recovered, Monson, whose steady nature and intelligent mind she had come to respect, and all the others. She fervently hoped all of them came back alive and unharmed from this operation.

Logan looked up at the clock. It was almost three in the morning. The SWAT team leader was wrapping up his instructions, his tone calm, direct, and professional.

"Alright, listen up. I want you to stay sharp, watch each other's backs. This guy's dangerous, but we've got the advantage. Move in fast, move in clean, and we'll all get to sleep in our own beds tonight."

One of the younger officers couldn't stifle his enthusiasm. Punching his fist in the air, he shouted, "Let's go get 'im!"

Logan hoped more experienced officers would be out in front.

As she watched the SWAT team check their gear and head to their vehicles, she couldn't suppress the nagging worry that Ray had been tipped off somehow. Putting herself in a murderer's mind was not a comfortable place to be, but she forced herself to do it anyway. How would Ray react? What would a cold-hearted killer do if he were cornered?

Chapter Sixty-Four

While everyone else left to confront the beast in his lair, Logan drove to the hospital. Ray had tried to kill Lamar once already. In Ray's mind, Lamar was the only loose end left. He might want to finish what he started, angry at his old friend for turning on him. Without Lamar's testimony, with a good lawyer, Ray might still believe he could get away with Brooke's murder. He didn't know they had that partial print—evidence of him being inside Lamar's truck.

She didn't know if Ray was brazen enough to attempt to get to Lamar in the ICU, but she wanted to at least warn the nurses on that floor to keep an eye out. Maybe they could add some hospital security. She didn't know if it would help, but this was one thing she could do before going home and waiting to hear how the raid went. She would have called Vern and asked if he could post one of the off-duty officers outside Lamar's room, but Vern was a little busy right now. Maybe after.

As she drove through the almost empty streets of Newport, Logan listened to the soporific hum of wheels on the pavement. She lowered the window for a few minutes and shook her head in the blast of cold air. Now that all the excitement was over, exhaustion was setting in. She began to second guess her decision to make this side trip on her way home.

Ray had most likely already been rousted out of bed—handcuffed and on his way to jail in the back of a patrol car. No reason for her to go play cop at the hospital. But it was only a few blocks away.

Since she was almost there already, Logan decided to pull in, park, make a quick run upstairs, leave her message at the nurse's station, and then go home to her warm bed—and Ben. Try to catch a few hours' sleep. Once they got Ray to the station, Vern would call her.

The main hospital entrance was dark, so she drove around to the emergency room entrance. The brightly lit interior made it easy to spot. In spite of the early hour, it was surprisingly busy. She couldn't see any patients inside waiting to be seen, but there were quite a few cars in the parking lot. As she cruised by, looking for a space close to the entrance, a woman dragging a little boy by the hand was going in, as an impatient man pushed past her to exit the building.

Rudely pushing past the mother and boy, the man looked up, his face momentarily illuminated by the light of the Emergency Entrance sign. Logan froze! It was Ray. In the same instant, he recognized her, too. Not wasting a second, he bolted to the right, away from her and into the darkened end of the parking lot.

Logan's heart tightened. Was she too late? Had Ray already killed Lamar?

She circled around looking for a place to pull over to call Vern, get him over here, but before she could make the call, Ray came roaring up behind her, almost blinding her with his brights. She swerved to avoid impact but needn't have bothered. Ray wasn't interested in her.

Straddling a large, black motorcycle, crouched forward like Tom Cruise, short hair whipping in the wind, he blew right past her, flying onto Highway 101 heading north.

Toward Portland. Toward the airport.

No!

Logan had nothing to stop him with, but she knew someone who did. Acting on pure instinct, Logan cranked her wheel hard to the left. Wishing she was driving a Porsche instead of a Hyundai, she made as tight a U-turn as her SUV would allow, then floored it. Keeping Ray in sight, but staying about two blocks behind, she scrabbled for her cell phone and called Vern.

As she listened to his plan, she forced herself to slow her breathing so she didn't hyperventilate. It wasn't completely dark, but the streets were almost deserted. The only illumination came from stoplights and a few neon signs.

By the time Ray was approaching the Fred Meyer intersection, Vern instructed Logan to fall back. Law enforcement would take it from here and Logan was happy to let them.

Slowly letting her foot off the gas, Logan kept Ray's motorcycle in view until she saw Vern's white RAM truck pull out a couple of lights ahead of Ray's northern progress on Highway 101, just before Walmart.

Ray saw him in time, started to turn onto a side street, but a patrol car cut him off in that direction. Not missing a beat, Ray gunned his engine and did a one-eighty, almost laying his bike down on the pavement as he did so. Then he was racing away from Vern—directly toward Logan!

With Vern coming up on his right, but staying behind him, and the patrol car flanking his left, Ray was essentially boxed in, being herded down the road.

Seeing lights in her rearview mirror, Logan saw a sheriff's car barreling toward them, lights and sirens flashing. They were still several blocks away, but Logan realized if she didn't move, she was going to get caught in the middle.

Time to get the hell out of dodge!

Yanking her wheel to the left, Logan stomped on the gas pedal and aimed for the sidewalk, but not in time. Before she could reach safety, there was a horrendous deep thud as Ray smashed directly into her car. Squeezing her eyes shut, Logan cringed. The sounds of screeching metal tore through the air as the bike scraped along the side of her car, then twisted, before being dragged several yards.

Not anticipating Logan's move, Ray had veered to the right to go around her, but instead, unable to brake in time, had crashed directly into her car. Without a helmet.

***

It wasn't until the sun rose several hours later that the police cleared the scene and Ben tucked Logan into his car and drove her home. Her car had been towed for repairs, but Ray's motorcycle, along with Ray, were beyond repair. Not wanting to have that image in her brain, Logan had avoided looking at his body when the EMTs took what was left of him away.

The EMTs insisted on getting her checked out by an ER doc, but as soon as she could, Logan corralled a nurse and asked about Lamar. Her main fear was that Ray had gotten to him already—that she was too late. The nurse didn't know, but seeing Logan's concern, said she'd try to find out.

From what they could piece together later from CCTV footage and witnesses, Ray, dressed in scrubs he'd picked up along the way, managed to get up to the intensive care unit without being detected, but he couldn't even get close to Lamar's room, let alone quietly slip in and kill him.

Far from lying there comatose—a helpless victim—the video feed showed Lamar sitting up, awake and talking with his doctors, while other medical personnel hustled in and out of his room. Not wasting any time, Ray had gone back to the first floor, ditching the scrubs in the elevator.

Watching the video, Logan was repulsed by the stone cold look on Ray's face. The casual disregard of life, friendship, or decency, all of the things that make life worth living for most of us, and his determination to do whatever he felt necessary to protect himself, the rest of the world be damned, was something Logan hoped she never would understand.

Chapter Sixty-Five

THANKSGIVING MORNING

Barely avoiding knocking Logan off her feet, Dixon and Max streaked through the living room and out onto the back deck, barking their heads off, in a loud game of chase Max was sure to lose. No dog on the planet was as fast as Dix. But Logan didn't mind. It was better they got their zoomies out now, before their guests arrived. She would run the vacuum again right before everyone got here around 3:00 p.m. There were football games on all day, but the big one the guys wanted to watch didn't start until four-thirty, so they'd have time to stuff themselves with Ben's turkey and all the trimmings before topping it off with pie and coffee in front of the TV.

Checking to make sure the guest bathroom had fresh towels, Logan looked around the room and recounted the chairs. The long folding table Ben brought in seated up to eight. She ticked off her guest list: Sam and Tim, Clay and Belinda, her and Ben. All good. Belinda said they might bring someone, so she had another couple of place settings and chairs on standby.

Chores complete, Logan went into the kitchen to see if Ben needed any help with dinner. If he did, he wisely did not accept any from her. The delicious aroma of roasting turkey made Logan realize how hungry she was. Ben was skipping lunch, but Logan needed at least a little snack. Hunting in the fridge, she spotted a glass container of last night's lasagna. Hesitating for only a second, she dished the whole thing into a large bowl and zapped it in the microwave. If anyone asked, she was just making room in the fridge for today's leftovers.

Taking her booty into the living room to enjoy, she plopped into her favorite chair in front of the fire and dug in. She was mid-chew when her phone rang. Luckily, she had left it on the end table next to her when she was setting up the chairs.

Swallowing quickly, she reached over and tapped the screen to answer.

"Hello?"

"Hello," a woman's said, "Is this Logan McKenna?"

The voice sounded familiar, but Logan couldn't place it.

"You probably don't remember me," she said, "This is Beth. We only met once, but I wanted to call and let you know you were right about Nate."

Now she remembered. Beth was the new Mrs. Riley, Nathan Riley's second wife. She and Vern met her when they went out to interview Mr. Riley about his first wife, Eleanor Riley's disappearance and obtain her dental records.

Eleanor's dentist's widow had told them her husband reported Eleanor's injuries when Nate knocked her teeth out, but no one had ever followed through on that report, and had, instead, covered up for Nate because he was a police officer at the time. Out of necessity, this case had been pushed aside as she and Vern focused on Brooke's homicide investigation, but Logan hoped they could get back to it soon.

Beth spent the next few minutes unloading, telling Logan all about the years she'd suffered at her husband's hands. Logan tried to envision how awful Beth's life must have been. Turning the volume up, she murmured, "I am so sorry, Beth. Do you need help? Are you calling from a safe place? We can come pick you up . . ."

"No, I'm out of here," Beth said, "I've been making plans for a while. I don't think Nate will be able to find me. I just wanted to ask you not to give up on Eleanor. I didn't know her, but I hope she got away somehow, too. And if she didn't make it, I hope you nail that bastard to the wall."

Logan promised.

Going back into the kitchen to reheat her lasagna, Logan reached around her husband's waist and hugged him fiercely. He looked surprised but didn't ask for an explanation. Sometimes words weren't necessary.

Logan thought about calling Vern to update him about Beth, but then she remembered Vern was somewhere over the Pacific Ocean, winging his way to Kauai. He and Portland's whip-smart medical examiner, Cyndi Birdwell, had been seeing each other for about a month. Since neither had family in the area, he said they'd decided to spend the holiday together in Hawaii. And while his master was away, Rocket was in doggie paradise out in Eddyville at Oletta's K9 Adventure Camp.

Chapter Sixty-Six

By three-thirty, everyone had arrived, with bottles of wine and side dishes to complement the feast. Somehow, they all fit around the groaning table, including Clay and Belinda's plus one, making Logan glad she saved an extra place setting and chair. After Clay said grace, Ben brought out the turkey, carving it at the table. A Norman Rockwell-worthy scene.

The sun dipped below the horizon, pulling the daylight behind it. Blue sky faded to a soft charcoal gray. The humans inside were too busy eating and visiting to notice.

For the next hour, wine and conversation flowed freely, guests and hosts alike talking to, over, and around each other. When everyone was stuffed, Logan and Sam cleared the table while Ben made coffee and lined up the pies down the center of the table. The game didn't start for another thirty minutes, and everyone was still talking, so they stayed at the table. Belinda asked how Lamar was now that Ray was no longer a threat.

"Lamar's doing great," Logan said, "home from the hospital, still moving slow but the doctors say he'll make a full recovery. And the DA's not pressing charges. The fact that Lamar almost paid with his life for coming forward now, seemed punishment enough for his not turning Ray in at the time."

Sam's husband, Tim, asked, "So whatever happened to Dylan? Wasn't he suspect number one before they got Ray?"

Logan's mouth was full of pie, so Sam fielded this one, "Dylan's in the clear, of course. Totally exonerated. The family never thought he did it, even though everything pointed to him before, but they were shocked to learn it was Ray who killed Brooke. All this time they thought he was their friend. He seemed so sincere."

Swallowing her pie, Logan said, "He fooled a lot of people for a long time."

The game was about to start, and the men started migrating to the couch and chairs around the TV. Logan helped herself to the last slice of Belinda's huckleberry pie.

Belinda was a football fan, so they shooed her out of the kitchen to watch the game with the guys. That left three women sitting convivially around the kitchen table, Sam, Logan, and Clay's surprise holiday guest, Rosie Swanson.

Logan was still trying to wrap her head around the fact that the blonde pixie with the sparkling blue eyes, sitting across from her, drinking coffee and laughing at something Sam said, was the same angry teen who had glared out of her 1986 yearbook photo through kohl-rimmed eyes.

But even more of a shock was when Clay proudly introduced Rosie as his niece! It took a while, but by the time the meal was over—and after asking innumerable questions—Logan finally understood the basics of how the two were related.

***

Back in October, on Logan's suggestion, Clay had submitted his DNA to the same database in hopes of locating his sister, Meg, who had gone missing in 1966. He never expected to hear anything back, but within a few short weeks, he was notified of a sibling match. He thought at first a mistake had been made because the name they had for the woman in the database was Loretta. He learned from Rosie this was the name his sister had been given because no one knew who she was.

Rosie then explained her chapter in this saga. She also had received a notification of a familial match with Loretta, but hers was a parent/child match. Loretta was her biological mother.

The OSH forensic genealogy researcher also matched Clay's DNA with Rosie's at about twenty-to-thirty percent of DNA. Normally, this could indicate anything from grandparent/grandchild to half-sibling, but since Meg's parent/child match with Rosie was definitive, as was Clay's sibling match with Meg, the uncle/niece relationship became clear.

Rosie did some more digging and was able to piece together at least some of her mother's story.

Through a newspaper article written about the diner before it closed, she obtained the name of several original employees the reporter had interviewed. One of them, Curtis, a night manager and fry cook, lived with his son's family in Corvallis and agreed to talk with her. Curtis remembered Rosie's mother from the picture, who was going by the name Addie. And the blonde young man was her boyfriend, Jack, nicknamed Speed Bump, SB for short.

Rosie remembered their conversation word for word.

"Your mom was the prettiest thing. Everybody loved Addie. But she only had eyes for SB. SB and Addie got engaged just before he got sent over to 'Nam. It wasn't but a few months later she got that telegram. Just about killed her. Sank right down to the floor in the middle of the lunch rush.

"She was pretty sure she was in the family way by then, with you, but she wasn't showing yet, so I let her keep working. And then there was George. George had been after her ever since SB left. Just would not leave her alone. He worked as a mechanic down the street and saw her walking to work. He had a little boy already. Guess he thought he'd plug a nice, strong woman into the wife and mother slot and be done. He sure needed one. That man didn't know how to raise a child.

"Next thing you know, Addie says yes, and he moves her out to a small town on the coast, Newport, Oregon. She called once to let us know she was okay and that you'd been born. Said you had the same blonde hair as your dad. She also said George was none too happy about that.

"He knew you weren't his. She said she'd call again when she could, but the diner closed down the next year and everybody scattered. My guess is your mama was working to save money to come back and get you and something must have happened before she could."

Logan gave Rosie a minute to compose herself while she got everyone some more coffee.

"So what year was your mom admitted to Oregon State Hospital?"

"The researcher, Regina, said the records don't show a month, but it was sometime in 1973," Rosie said. "She was admitted from the hospital—that's where they brought people when they didn't know who they were, but she doesn't know why she was in the hospital originally."

"Well, that fits," Logan said, "You were born in 1969, and you have vague memories of her when you were little—before she left, like that guy Curtis said, she probably went back to Salem to find work and then send for you. Probably got work as a waitress, even though the old diner had closed. But before she could send for you, she got into an accident that damaged her brain . . . if she didn't have a car, she could have been hit by one on her way to work or walking to the store."

"But wouldn't they have called George or someone? Wouldn't they check for ID if she was admitted to a hospital?" Rose said.

"Not if she was going under a different name. She was hiding from George, right? Maybe she didn't have any ID on her. Probably rented a room off the books with someone, no record.

She may not have decided whether she needed to change her name permanently or not," Sam said.

"At least we know it now—Margaret Adeline Nilson. It warms my heart knowing she gave me her middle name. My full name is Rosemary Adeline Swanson." Rosie said. "And as soon as I can I'm changing my last name legally to Jensen."

Softly, she added, "That was my real father's last name. Jack 'SB' Jensen."

Logan and Sam agreed that was an excellent idea.

Chapter Sixty-Seven

Logan tried to imagine the series of events that led to Rosie's mother getting lost in the system all those years.

Sam summed up what Logan was feeling. "That is so unfair! Somebody should have tried harder to find out who she was before just sticking her in a state hospital!"

Rosie put her hand on Sam's arm and said, "Thanks Sam, but it's okay. When I first found all this out, I was pretty angry, but I had the opportunity to talk with Tess, the daughter of the couple who took my mother in when the hospital was deinstitutionalized. Some of those people landed in places that could or would not give them the care they needed. My mother was one of the lucky ones. She was placed in a kind, loving home where she lived peacefully for fifteen more years, then died in her sleep. I hope I'm that lucky when my time comes."

Logan and Sam looked at each other. Rosie was obviously much more spiritually advanced than either of them.

Sam put her coffee mug back onto the table a little too hard and almost shouted, "Well if I could time travel, I'd go back and kick some institutional butt! Oh, and George butt, too!"

Tim hollered from the living room, "Everything okay in there?" which made all three women burst out laughing.

When Rosie could talk, she said, "I already visited George and gave him a piece of my mind, Sam. I'm not *that* much of a saint!"

"What about Peter? Does he ever visit George?" Logan asked.

"Pete said he saw George a year ago," Rosie said. "He didn't elaborate, but I get the feeling they aren't that close anymore."

Rosie had told them during dinner that she had located her older brother out in Bend. Since he hadn't changed his name, with a little help from a private investigator, he had been fairly easy to find. Logan wondered if Pete and Rosie planned on being in each other's lives now that they were reconnected but was afraid to ask. Sam wasn't so shy.

"Until you found that picture, you thought Pete was your biological brother all those years. But he's still your stepbrother. Have you seen him?" she asked.

"We haven't met in person yet, but that's in the works. Although we don't have the same biological mother—Pete's mom died in childbirth—you're right, we were raised together. My mom was his stepmother for several years before she left, so she's the only mother he ever knew. He was ten at the time, so he remembers more about her than I do. He wants me to come visit. Pete's married, got five kids and four dogs, but insists on me staying with them. Says there's always room for me. He wants me to come for Christmas, so I've got some shopping to do for all my nieces and nephews. Two nephews, three nieces. I've met them all on FaceTime, so I know what they're into, but I work with adults, so I have no idea what to buy them."

After Rosie gave them the names and ages of the five children and the interests she knew about so far, Logan made a list on her computer. Pulling up several online stores, the three women spent the rest of the evening brainstorming, coming up with great gift ideas.

✳✳✳

Later that night after everyone had gone home, Logan turned off the lights while Ben added another log to the crackling fire. Then, mutual missions accomplished, they plopped down on the couch. Bellies full, Dixon and Max were already stretched out on the rug in front of the fireplace, fast asleep.

As the moon rose above the trees and started her nightly journey across the sky, the dark settled all around them. Pulling Logan close, Ben kissed the top of her head. She nuzzled his neck, then lay her head on his shoulder. For a long time, neither of them spoke, but sat gazing into the flames, which flickered hypnotically.

How did they get so lucky? They had a warm home, good friends, loving family, decent health, and thanks to Ben's careful saving and her music videos, a little extra to pursue their passions and help family and friends. Today was truly a day of Thanksgiving and Logan silently promised herself never to take any of her blessings for granted.

Before she drifted off to sleep, Logan's mind wandered back to Beth. Logan hoped she made it and that wherever she was now, she found safety, love, and happiness.

Beth hadn't asked for any help for herself. Her only request was that they never give up on finding Eleanor. It was an easy promise to make. These cold cases got under your skin. Logan had no intention of giving up on any of them.

EPILOGUE

TWO MONTHS LATER

EMAIL TO CLAY FROM REGINA FREDERICKS, OSH

Hello Clay,

First, I am so glad that we were able to help you and your niece connect. I hope you and Rosemary will be a blessing in each other's lives. Family is so important.

I am also glad we were able to find Rosemary's mother, your sister, although I wish it could have been sooner. Your sister's true name, Margaret Adeline Nilsen, will be included in the memorial service at OSH in the spring, along with others we have identified as former patients who have not been previously recognized. If you would like me to add either 'Meg' the nickname you knew her by, or 'Loretta' the name she used for the last few years of her life, let me know.

I'll send you an exact date so you and Rosemary may attend if you wish. And there will be an opportunity for you to say a few words, too. I will keep you posted on all that.

In the meantime, I also wanted to let you know that in preparing for the memorial service I went through some old admittance files and containers that were discovered recently in the back of a storage area during renovations at OSH. Among those files were a few items belonging to your sister. Sealed in a large, plastic bag with your sister's patient number and name—the one they gave her on admittance, Loretta—were a waitress uniform and a purse. Inside the purse was a comb, one key—probably an apartment key—and a wallet. There was no money or ID in the wallet, but in the bill compartment, there was a letter. It was yellowed a bit with age and there was no envelope, but it was surprisingly well-preserved.

Since the letter is addressed to you, Clay, I will be sending it and the rest of her things to your address by registered mail. I took the liberty of photocopying the letter first and attaching the image here so you won't have to wait to read it. I knew you would want to have it as soon as possible.

Your sister obviously loved you very much,
Regina Fredericks

1968

Dear Clay,

I've tried to write to you several times but just can't find the right words. I am determined to finish this letter this time because I don't want you to worry about me or think I forgot about you. I just haven't had news I wanted to share.

Where do I start?

The day I left, everything was good. Jimmy had a van, so we had wheels, a little money, and a tank full of gas. We were going to San Francisco to find a commune! Escape the stranglehold of our parents' lives. Jimmy was running from the draft. I was running from—well, everything. We heard it was always sunny in California, just like the song. We were going to live off the land, grow our own food, have some goats. It sounded so easy.

STONE COLD

We got as far as Eureka before we ran out of bread, songs, and gas. I don't know if you've ever been to Northern California, but the weather was definitely not sunny there. We did find some other people to hang with. They let us crash at their pad until we could get enough money to continue our trip. I made bracelets and sold them on the street there and Jimmy did some gardening work. But he started spending a lot of it on drugs. There was a Grateful Dead concert, some things happened, I don't want to get into all that, but I left that night.

I'm not proud of it, but I took the little money we had saved and caught a Greyhound bus back to Oregon. I can't tell you where I am, but don't worry about me. I'm okay.

I got a job! You wouldn't recognize me, Clay! I'm part of the 'establishment,' now. At least on the outside. And I'm engaged! How square is that? His name is Jack, but he goes by SB. We're getting married when he gets back from 'Nam. He joined up, just like you. He's nothing like Jimmy.

I miss you something awful, Clay. And Mom and Dad, but I don't think I'm ready to come home yet and have them say, "I told you so!" And I want to say I'm sorry. I'm sorry for all the things I said back then. What's crazy is that SB is over there, too. Have you met anyone named SB? I don't know if you're still over there or if you're home now. You'll like him, Clay, I know you will!

I don't know how to reach you over there, and if you're home, I've got to figure out how to get this letter to you without Mom and Dad reading it first, but when I do find a way to get this to you, here's a phone number at the diner where you can reach me. (503) 555-9306. Just leave a message if I'm not there when you call.

One more thing. When SB gets back and we're married, I'll feel solid enough to come home. And when I do, I'll have a grandchild for Mom and Dad to fuss over. You're going to be an uncle! If it's a girl, I don't know what her first name will be, but mom will be happy. Her middle name will be Adeline, just like mine and Mom's. In fact, that's the name I go by now.

Love you bunches,
Your sis,
Addie/Meg

ACKNOWLEDGMENTS

My life would be so much easier if I were a more formulaic writer! That's not to say there isn't room for much creativity even when using the same general structure for each book, which many well-known authors do, but for some reason, I can't seem to color within the lines. Or even see the lines! Whatever the reason, each book in the Logan series winds up being unique and this book is perhaps more unique than usual.

In *Stone Cold* I decided to strike out in an entirely new direction—putting Logan more directly into the world of law enforcement by having her volunteer with the Lincoln County Cold Case Unit. I loved the idea of there being several missing women over time, with some of the gossamer threads connecting and some being lost in the wind.

This story required an entirely different structure, so I am forever grateful to my husband and brave alpha reader, John, for plowing through the first drafts and helping in the initial shaping of the book. Another huge thank you goes to my beta readers, Kevin, Kelly, Jan, and John, for helping smooth out the rough spots and making sure the story flowed and stayed true to the rest of the series.

Crafting this story required a better understanding of how cold cases are handled and specifically, how the Lincoln County Cold Case Unit works. For this I relied on Linda Snow, the Lincoln County Cold Case team lead. She generously answered questions and shared with me how cold cases are investigated, always respecting and keeping private information about real cases secure. She also provided fun details that I used in the book, including the fact that their office is nicknamed 'the dungeon' and their official skeletal greeter's name is Murdoch. Newport PD Chief of Police (retired), Mike J. Miranda, is also on speed dial. His expertise is always appreciated. And lucky me, a retired Deputy District Attorney moved into my neighborhood. Thank you, John Turner, for explaining varying points of Oregon law.

A note about setting the novels in a county with real businesses, street names, and law enforcement organizations. In any one book and over the course of the series, organizations, titles, procedures, job descriptions, geographic or other details may change and sometimes I need to adjust reality for the purposes of the story, but I make every effort to depict each accurately and with respect. In this story, for example, a rookie volunteer like Logan would never be allowed to interview a potential homicide suspect by herself. She would receive a lot more training first.

I would also like to give a shout out to Oletta Lane and her amazing dobies, Kraken and Hawk. Kraken passed away this spring, but Hawk is still going strong at ten years old. You may remember Oletta from *Look Again: A Logan McKenna Mystery Book 10*, which features her Adventurous K9 training center out in Eddyville. In *Stone Cold*, Oletta informs the chapter where a new search and rescue cadaver dog she is training discovers small traces of human remains submerged deep in a reservoir.

Last, but not least, I would like to thank readers who take the time to let me know how much they enjoy my books. Of course, I always appreciate reviews, and those are very important to authors, but it really makes my day when someone stops me on the trail when I'm out walking Finn or taps me on the shoulder in the grocery store to tell me how much they are enjoying Logan's adventures. Just makes me feel warm all over!

Enjoyed the Book?

If you enjoyed *Stone Cold*, please consider leaving a review on Amazon, Goodreads, or BookBub. And be sure to check out the rest of the Logan McKenna series.

Novels

Shattered (Book 1)
Forest Park (Book 2)
Devil's Claw (Book 3)
Vanishing Day (Book 4)
Safe Harbor (Book 5)

Lies That Bind (Book 6)
Whisper Creek (Book 7)
In Plain Sight (Book 8)
Lost and Found (Book 9)
Look Again (Book 10)

Logan McKenna Prequel Novellas
Bella: An Appalachian Love Story
Jagged Dawn: Logan's Beginning

Want to know more about Valerie Davisson or her next book? Make sure to visit valeriedavisson.com and sign up for her newsletter.

ABOUT THE AUTHOR

A self-admitted book addict, Valerie Davisson was the kid with the flashlight under her pillow, reading long after lights out. After a life of travel, she now lives on the Oregon coast with her husband, John, and their English Cream Golden Retriever, Finn. When not working on her latest book, she's probably in the kitchen, cooking up a storm for family and friends.